T0130914

THE MAN FEARED BY DARKNESS

THE MAN FEARED BY DARKNESS

A ROOKER LINDSTRÖM THRILLER

PETE ZACHARIAS

THOMAS & MERCER

This is a work of fiction. Names, characters, organizations, places, events, and incidents are either products of the author's imagination or are used fictitiously. Otherwise, any resemblance to actual persons, living or dead, is purely coincidental.

Text copyright © 2024 by Peter Zacharias Jr.
All rights reserved.

No part of this book may be reproduced, or stored in a retrieval system, or transmitted in any form or by any means, electronic, mechanical, photocopying, recording, or otherwise, without express written permission of the publisher.

Published by Thomas & Mercer, Seattle

www.apub.com

Amazon, the Amazon logo, and Thomas & Mercer are trademarks of Amazon.com, Inc., or its affiliates.

ISBN-13: 9781662518478 (paperback)
ISBN-13: 9781662518461 (digital)

Cover design by Zoe Norvell
Cover images: © Chemival / Shutterstock; © LPETTET / Getty;
© Stephen Carroll / Plainpicture

Printed in the United States of America

A man who is of "sound mind" is one who keeps his inner madman under lock and key.

—*Paul Valéry*

Prologue

When he was just a boy, his sister told him that he could do anything, no matter how scary, after he'd counted to five.

At thirty-six, he still found himself counting and fabricating patterns around that number. He'd click the end of a pen or tap his finger or tick lightly over laptop keys until he reached the number five.

Today he'd shut his eyes and counted to five before sauntering into the boss's office and requesting two weeks off. The large, plump bastard in a dark suit smoothed back his wax-shined hair and approved. On his exit he'd nodded pleasantly at Lindsay Morris—the plain-Jane blonde who had asked him out for drinks once—when she wished him a good trip.

But he wasn't going on vacation—and he didn't intend to come back. Anything of meaning to him—which was only a photograph of him and his sister playing in their front yard—he'd taken with him.

He had two apartments, one of which no one knew about.

His gaudy fifth-floor apartment in Downtown LA cost $5,500 a month. The building had a rooftop pool and hot tub lit by string lights, a game room and a spa, and a bunch of other amenities he'd never once used.

It wasn't a place he'd ever afford on his salary. He shared this two-bedroom extravagance with Todd Evans, a lanky twenty-six-year-old with a frizzy black Afro who worked for a cryptocurrency start-up.

He often wondered why Todd hadn't gotten his own place with the money he was raking in. But they didn't communicate much. His roommate spent most days working and most nights eating takeout and yelling over *Call of Duty*.

When he unlocked the door and walked inside, Todd was sitting on the sofa in a gray long-sleeved shirt and boxers, engrossed in his laptop screen, his earbuds blasting EDM. He walked past the kitchen, a space with marble counters and lights that glowed behind the cupboards and beneath the island, unlocked his bedroom door, opened it, and shut it behind him.

The bed was already pristinely made. Everything had a place, and everything was in order. He opened the closet door, pulled out a black suitcase, and placed it on the bed. He folded every article of clothing he owned and set it all inside the case, along with his toiletries from his bathroom.

He wiped everything down with a towel. He extended the handle of the suitcase and wheeled it behind him to the front door.

In the kitchen, he pulled the largest knife from the wood block on the counter and hid it behind his back. He walked over to the couch and stood over Todd's shoulder. The hand with the knife shook, but he wasn't afraid of blood (a lie he often told people). He could see the red pouring out of Todd's skinny neck. Even so, he wasn't sure he could actually kill someone. He'd often wondered how the act of taking another life might change him. He shut his eyes and started counting, as if his sister were standing beside him with her maternal arm around his shoulder.

One. Two. Three. Four.

He squeezed the handle too tight and his knuckle popped. Then his pocket buzzed and dinged. He forced his eyes open, freed the phone from his pants, and read the message.

It's time.

Todd turned and stared up at him. The dark circles under his eyes made them appear sunk into his skull, and his face was covered in white-pink acne scars and long, scraggly stubble. "What's up, man? You're freaking me out. I didn't even hear you come in."

He smiled. "Sorry. Work trip. I'll be back in a few days."

He shifted the knife forward as he turned his back to Todd. He slid the blade back into the wood block on his way to the front door, and then he left the apartment for good.

PART I

Chapter 1

November 20, 2021

I'm a man marked by death.

That's what Rooker Lindström wanted to say to the question he knew was incoming. An inopportune time for such a morbid thought, on what would be his last night in Minnesota for a while, as the moon bled through the eastern windows and lit the shimmer of sweat glistening her goose-pimpled skin.

Caroline Lind squeezed his shoulder where the scar was—what remained of a tattoo of his dead son's birthday, which he'd carved out with a knife. Another three-inch white line cratered his palm, where she interlaced her fingers in his, this one from a stab wound during his fight to the death with Gregory Sadler.

"What's wrong?" she panted. She stopped moving and stared down at him. Questioning was as much an occupational what-comes-with-the-territory for her as a newscaster as it was in his line of investigative journalism. Though he rarely minded being the one launching the hard-hitting inquiries, he always hated answering.

"Nothing," he lied.

Rooker still found her presence at Lindström Manor surreal. Caroline Lind, the beautiful news anchor who had once deceived him for a story, now shared with him a life that felt delicate, fragile even. Ever since her stay at the manor, the place had taken on a look of sprucing, one that Rooker only ever imagined would resemble applying lipstick to a pig.

Despite a global pandemic, over the past two years Rooker had enjoyed some semblance of a normal life for the first time since his son's murder. He and Caroline sat at the kitchen counter to chat over breakfast. They cooked dinner and had date nights. And with the gruesome events of two years ago loosening their hold on him, he'd been able to enjoy thrillers again. He'd nearly cleaned out the local bookstore of every Murder Mystery title they had.

Red, the old chocolate-and-white border collie Rooker had adopted after the deaths of Charles and Eva Berglund, was still kicking. So was Geralt, the snow-white cat with the probing yellow eyes, who was probably stalking some poor critter out in the dark.

Of course, there were the occasional threatening letters from a Gregory Sadler or Tate Meachum or Hartley Caldwell obsessive, as well as phony leads on new bodies from wannabes. But thanks to the lead detective of the Itasca County Sheriff's Office, Martin Keene, each note had been checked out and confirmed as pranks, and eventually those petered out too.

Life had been approaching, dare he say, "stable," until the news of a dead girl in a drainpipe brought everything back.

And now Rooker heard the broadcast play on a loop in his mind: *"A gruesome scene tonight in Hemet, California, where a woman's body has been discovered . . ."*

As well as another voice: Hartley Caldwell's icy tone when he'd told Rooker, *You are merely a man trapped by shadows.* Even the Peekaboo Killer knew that Rooker was cursed.

Caroline was still peering at him, her breath slowing. Rooker gripped both sides of her waist and watched a drop of sweat glisten down her stomach to the perfectly smooth skin where her pubic hair had been waxed. "Sorry, my mind is just somewhere else."

"Well, you're about to leave me for who knows how long . . . ," she said. "Can you keep your mind here for a few more minutes?" She smiled and pushed her hips down onto him. But all he could see was the black bag on the gurney, the yellow police tape that surrounded the drainpipe.

When it was over, she stroked her finger along his stubbled cheek and said softly, "What are you afraid of?"

He hesitated. "That I caught the wrong man. That I lost part of me in that place, and for this to all be over, I have to go back. What if I lose more?"

"Meachum isn't innocent. You're more of a man than anyone I've ever met. Make it back in however many pieces you can, and I'll put the rest back together."

Unable to sleep, he watched the sky turn from slate black to gray, to a midnight-blue haze and marmalade, to a faded denim blue. With each color change, a wave of guilt hit him harder and harder for having to leave her. After all, Caroline was the one who'd saved him after Millie's death. The night of the funeral, he'd crumpled into her chest and wept convulsively at the memory of his closest friend sleeping kitten-like in a ball on his couch.

His throat tightened at the thought of it and of carrying Millie's casket. *The man trapped by shadows who traps everyone he loves with him.* He fended off tears as he listened to Caroline's peaceful breaths.

The next morning, beyond baggage check, he forced down half of a semiwarm breakfast sandwich on a soggy biscuit while he sat staring out through the terminal glass. A white-gray sky reminded him that winter was nearly here. As he watched the long, narrow body of the white airliner dock at the gate, he remembered how Britton would stand at the glass, pointing excitedly at the massive jet engines. He'd be fifteen years old now, probably hitting a growth spurt just as Rooker had done at that age. Crazy, really. Rooker tried to imagine Britton standing eye to eye with him—and then eventually sitting where he was, looking at this view with his own kid. Then he saw the bloody gash in the boy's chest, the bedding beneath him stained dark red, and he shut his eyes until the final boarding call came over the loudspeaker.

He always preferred a seat overlooking the wing. It made him feel as if he could walk out into the sky. Flying made him restless. Not because everything was out of his hands hundreds of miles per hour, tens of thousands of feet in the clouds. He never had anywhere to put his legs. And he rarely could sleep due to the drone of the plane, the clicking of laptop keys, and "pretzels or cookies" playing on an endless loop.

When the flight attendants came around with their carts, he said in his most charming voice, "Ma'am, any chance I can get a couple of those?" He pointed to the vodka bottles on her cart. "I have a terrible fear of flying," he lied and smiled.

She handed him two bottles and a cup of ice. "Thank you," he said, staring into her eyes and smiling again. He surveyed the little shooters of vodka but didn't pour them into his cup. For right now, it was enough to know they were in close proximity. He closed his eyes and pictured the dead girl waiting for him, his mind going over and over everything that'd happened yesterday . . .

It had been an ordinary Saturday night—boring even—until Caroline had gotten that call from one of her colleagues and they'd turned on the TV news to see Gruesome Homicide in Hemet trailing below crime scene tape.

As soon as the newscast had ended, Rooker sat on the couch stiffly, feeling a migraine come on. He closed his eyes and saw Tate Meachum's victims one by one: the large incision to the chest and the ball-peen hammer strikes to the face. The time of death carved into the blackened fingernail. This new murder was so close to the MO. And then there was the drainpipe, the scene teasing Rooker with an image from his favorite novel, *The Black Echo*. The story that begins with a body found in a drainpipe at Mulholland Dam.

He'd be damned if leaving the female victim in a drainpipe in Hemet—where Rooker had spent most of his life—and using the same MO as the Madman murders weren't some kind of message. Though who besides his ex would ever know how prominently that book had been displayed in his library? Rooker wondered if the signed first-edition copy was still in his old house or if it had been boxed up or tossed out along with the rest of his belongings. He dreaded the conversation he'd need to have if he wanted to find out.

But he knew in his gut that this new murder was somehow *for him*. Whoever had killed the victim in the drainpipe had either spoken to Meachum or they'd once been in Rooker's old home.

Rooker was running through a mental list of everyone he'd ever opened his door to when something started to flicker in his field of vision. And then he saw her. Her dead hands pulling the white sheet off. Sitting up jaggedly as if her spine had broken. Clumps of blackened blood tangled in her hair.

No. Not again.

He squeezed his eyes shut, and when they snapped open again, she was gone. He went to the medicine cabinet and shook a ziprasidone capsule into his palm and took it with faucet water cupped in his hands. Rooker had a unique subset of psychotic symptoms rare in PTSD. After his son's death, he started seeing things—*terrifying things*—that weren't there. When they caught Hartley Caldwell, the visions had become less and less frequent. He stood, gripping the sides of the sink, until his breathing slowed.

But then his phone had rung. He normally wouldn't answer an unknown number, but the timing seemed ominous enough to be important. As soon as he heard FBI Special Agent Scott Eckhart introduce himself, Rooker wished it had been another prankster.

The FBI had noticed the similarities to the Madman's MO too. Eckhart was leading the investigation, and he wanted an audience with

Meachum. Problem was, no one had gotten a word out of Tate since he'd last spoken to Rooker. Eckhart asked Rooker if he'd come out to California and see if his presence could draw something out of the maniac—anything that would help the FBI understand if they were dealing with a copycat or something new. Rooker wanted to say no, that bringing him back into Meachum's orbit would only bring more death—Eckhart could find another piece of bait. But then he heard Millie's voice when he had tried to stop her from chasing after Caldwell: *"I'm going. With or without you."* Rooker could hide here at Lindström Manor, but the world wouldn't stop turning. No one would be safe until he found out the truth—all of it. So he mumbled his acceptance and started to pack.

The descent was rocky. His knees plowed into the seat in front of him, and he could feel the same in the back of his. But after the plane touched down, he left the bottles unopened in the seatback pocket, got up, and squeezed his way off the plane.

As he walked toward the taxi stand, he sent a text message to Caroline to let her know he landed and that he'd check in later.

He made his way down the crammed escalators and was nearly out into the hazy skies and warmth and palm trees when the sight of four federal agents in blue stopped him in his tracks.

A man with messy light-brown hair and a stubbled square jaw stepped forward. "Rooker Lindström, I'm Scott Eckhart. I'm heading the investigation."

You poor bastard, he thought. "I'm sorry to hear that," he said.

The man smiled. "I'm good at what I do, don't you worry."

"I wasn't."

"This is my team: Isabel Esparza, Deion Quincy, and Jack Hall. Barry Lewis is at the crime scene. We're going to escort you to Hemet. If you've gotta hit the head, do it now."

Rooker shook his head no, and Eckhart continued. "Just to be clear, you're a consultant in the investigation. You listen to every command me and my team give. You don't interfere in any way, shape, or form. Otherwise, you can turn tail and head back to Minnesota. Those are my orders."

Rooker nodded again and bit back a retort about how much it must bother the Feds to need a "consultant." He was too tired to get into it with Eckhart.

They walked down a long corridor, away from baggage claim. Rooker let his mind wander until they rounded a corner, and leaning against a wall was a person he had never in a million years expected to see.

Her hair had grown back, long enough for an elastic to hold it in a ponytail at the crook of her neck.

Rooker stared into the blank expression of Tess Harlow. The former lead detective of the Itasca County Sheriff's Office.

Chapter 2

Twelve hours ago, Tess Harlow had been prone on a cold hotel balcony, breathing in the stale air of city traffic and shuddering at the gusts that slipped beneath her baggy black hoodie.

The room behind her was dark aside from one dimly lit sconce casting the bedside in a faint white.

She took a long gulp from a beer bottle, peered up at the dull silver stars, and set it back down beside her with a clink.

She peered through the Sony camera. Though the superzoom lens could pick up even the tiniest blemishes on her subjects' skin, waves obscured her vision. Her gold-flecked eyes ached from a lack of sleep; her dreams the last two years had mostly been nightmares. Memories, really. She preferred to stay awake.

For a moment she closed her eyes, rubbed her temple to take some of the pain away, and opened them.

Getting his room number had been as simple as flashing him a bright smile to "hold the elevator" when she'd seen him walk through the lobby and then fumbling with her purse while she tailed him down the hall. Just another ditzy woman who can't find her key. He didn't suspect a thing.

She'd already gotten a few candid photographs of the two. But now it was time for the action shots. The fat slob clasped an attractive young woman's hair in place while she performed oral sex on him. His dress shirt was fully unbuttoned and grotesquely open. Dark slacks a tangled web around his feet. Her forehead had pressed a small dent in the roundness of his hairy belly.

Snap.

That was the job. Hours on hours of surveillance, and a lot of clients trying to catch a cheating lover in the act. *Double if you get a picture of him sleeping with her,* the client, Mrs. Marcus, said. *I'll take that son of a bitch for everything he's got.* She peered down at the LCD screen of her camera.

Guess I'm making double.

She'd confirmed at least thirty cases of infidelity. Imagine that. Two serial killers and thirty dirtbag cheaters. The former were the reason she could charge a lofty price; the latter were as easy as sitting in a car posted outside a motel or tailing a suspect to a meetup. Stay-at-home wives run out for errands or groceries but end up at a fancy hotel. In this case, the husband would go on what he told his wife were work trips. Really, they were weekend getaways to Minneapolis. Tonight her work took her to an elegant building called Hotel Ivy. Out front, flags rippled like sails in a breeze. It made her think of a US embassy on foreign soil.

She didn't care to know whom she was watching. Though she'd learned that fifty-three-year-old Aaron Marcus was the six-figure-a-year owner of a storage company and the out-of-his-league blonde—Lindsay Austin—was the twenty-two-year-old secretary he'd hired, clearly not for her work experience. Marcus's record was clean aside from a few traffic violations and parking tickets. Other than that, he was guilty, as many men were, of breaking his marriage vows. Adultery in the first degree. Tess sighed. Even after two years, her detective mind hadn't shut off. Some habits die hard.

If there was anything she'd learned from Rooker Lindström, it was that seeing the worst in people worked wonders in the job of a private investigator and that drinking did temporarily numb the pain. On quiet nights like this, when she craved a cold beer after a night of stalking, she wondered if that's who she was becoming.

Lately she'd been doing most of her soul-searching at the bottom of a bottle. And more often than not, alcohol turned her emotions into a cocktail of resentment, sadness, remorse, and relief. There were nights when she felt at ease for ridding the world of two of the bad guys. And there were nights when she regretted what she'd done, or wondered what life would be like had her father not jumped out in front of that car. Sometimes she wished it had been Joe Harlow who'd shot and killed Jan Cullen and Clyde Miller so she wouldn't have the blood on her hands.

With Cullen and Miller dead, her mother would know it was her. She could never see Janice Harlow face-to-face again.

Her cell buzzed, and the screen lit up a call from an unknown number. She sent the first call to voicemail. The second one, she answered.

"Hello," she said skeptically.

"Tess Harlow?"

Her brow furrowed. "I'm a little busy at the moment. Who's asking?"

"Special Agent Scott Eckhart, FBI. I'm working a case that I'd like your expertise on."

Tess worried her index finger where her scar was. It originally started as a letter *X* with a line down the center. Since then, she'd carved little points that branched off and made it more lifelike. *Snowflake.* She heard that voice again and fought the urge to dig her nail into the scar to draw blood. "Sorry, I'm not a detective anymore."

"So I've heard. Harlow, I won't waste your time. I'm asking you to get on a plane to California tomorrow. The flight and your hotel room will be paid for. I'll get you compensation as a consultant. Double whatever you're making as a PI."

He'd done his due diligence. "What's in it for me?"

He scoffed. "Other than the money? How about working a case again. A *real* one."

"Is this about—"

"You're smart, Harlow. I can't talk about it over the phone. But if you watch the news, I'm sure you know what it's about. You can text this number with the flight details. I'll arrange for my team and I to get you when you land."

The call ended. It was only a few minutes. She thought that would be enough time for Aaron Marcus to come, but to her surprise he lasted slightly longer. Once he removed his penis and tilted the girl's head back, Tess turned away.

Not the face, girl. You're better than that.

She went back into her room, took one last look at the bright skyline, and closed the sliding door. Then she transferred the images to her laptop and sent them to her client via email. Not even three minutes later did the reply come through.

The room and dinner are on me.

She thought, *Hell hath no fury like a woman scorned.*

Tess envisioned her client in a courtroom full of pricey lawyers taking legal-jargon digs at her soon-to-be ex-husband, along with half his assets.

She closed the laptop, lifted the black phone from the cradle on the desk, and ordered a cheeseburger and french fries with a cocktail from the hotel restaurant. While she waited for room service to come, she packed up her camera gear. She was back.

Chapter 3

Rooker froze. He looked from Tess to Scott Eckhart. "What is this?"

"You don't know me, and I don't know you. I thought I'd bring someone in that you've worked with before and we can trust."

Trust? He wanted to laugh. *If they only knew the former lead detective was an executioner.*

Eckhart said, "But make no mistake: the FBI is running this. You aren't going off and playing cowboy the way you did in Minnesota. Everything you do, you run by me. Both of you. Understood?"

Rooker held Tess's gaze as they nodded in unison.

"First things first," Eckhart said to him. "You've got a date planned with the Madman himself."

"No," Rooker said, still holding Tess's gaze. He saw a flicker of a smile on her face before he turned to Eckhart.

His cheek twitched. "Excuse me?"

"I want to see the crime scene first," Rooker said. He told himself it had nothing to do with the sick feeling that sitting in front of Meachum gave him. "If I go and see him first, I have to take his word for everything. My guess is he'll be feeling chatty; he hasn't spoken to anyone—save for himself—in years. There's this thing between us—" He stopped himself at how strange it sounded to say aloud. "I want the upper hand when I walk in to see him."

"Forensics will already be finished with the scene. You'll be staring at a storm drain and not much else. Sorry, that's not part of the plan—"

"You want me to see Meachum? This is how you get it done. I want to see the crime scene and the body. Take it or leave it."

"All right, Lindström." Eckhart shook his head. "Let's go, then."

Doing his best to ignore Tess, Rooker followed behind the four bodies in blue. Eckhart told them what the FBI had so far, which wasn't much, even though they had a witness of sorts, a transient who had been abducted by the killer and had called in the body to the local police. This last part surprised Rooker, and he instinctively looked over at Tess, whose brow furrowed deeper. The FBI had managed to keep all news of a witness under wraps. *I guess even Caroline's contacts can't dig up everything,* he thought.

So according to the witness statement and the sparse evidence at the scene, they were looking for a male killer. Powerfully built. The tire-tread patterns at the scene were from a Firestone Transforce HT2 tire, LT215/85R16/E. That meant the killer was driving a pickup truck with a bed or a commercial vehicle with a trunk, probably the latter since the witness claimed he'd been thrown in a trunk. If the killer had ever gotten out of the vehicle, he'd swept his shoe prints.

Rooker listened to boots thump and squeak out of sync as he mulled all this over. When they rounded a corner, Eckhart flashed his badge at one of the gate agents dressed in a blue dress shirt beneath a dark vest.

Rooker walked down the ramp behind them, then out another door and down a metal staircase. At the bottom, he noticed their ride wasn't an SUV as he'd expected.

It was a Black Hawk helicopter. Jet black with "FBI" in white lettering beneath the side window.

Rooker stopped.

Eckhart turned around and smirked. "Not afraid of flying in one, are you?"

He lied. "No."

"Good. We don't have time to take a road trip. Let's go."

Rooker had read about the Sikorsky UH-60 Black Hawk. They were originally designed for the army. One cost somewhere in the ballpark of $6 million.

The dark twisting rotors let out a hellish scream. He ducked his head the way they did in the movies. There were two rows of three seats that went back-to-back. Quincy, Hall, and Esparza sat together. After Eckhart took the end of the other row, Tess took the middle. Rooker tossed his bag beneath the end seat, sat down, and stared straight forward. He tried to ignore Tess's shoulder against his, and the pleasantness of a fragrance he remembered.

A minute later, the doors shut, and they were airborne.

He endured the flight staring out the window or at the dials and buttons up front between the pilot seats. He took the headset he was offered but said nothing—and hoped Tess would keep up her surly-and-silent act too. He was not ready to talk to her.

He and Tess hadn't spoken since Millie's funeral. It was only a few days later that Jan Cullen and Clyde Miller had been executed at point-blank range. Rooker was sure of two things: Millie's death had driven Tess to kill the men who had raped her mother, and with her knowledge of forensics, there was no chance she'd left behind any evidence that would bring the police to her door. He couldn't say he cared one bit about what had happened to Cullen and Miller; it was Tess's hypocrisy that he couldn't shake. During the Gregory Sadler case, she had treated him as a murder suspect even before the fire at Lindström Manor had unearthed female remains beneath the cottage. She'd wanted him to take the fall so much that she destroyed her relationship with Millie in the process. And now she would have to live with being a murderer.

The helicopter touched down in a vortex. A cloud of sandy dust flew up around them. Rooker imagined it must've taken the whole roll of yellow tape to cordon off the area. A couple of police cruisers sat idle at the curb.

Tess asked the agents, "Aren't you worried about contaminating evidence?"

"This spot's already been searched with a fine-tooth comb," replied Eckhart. "Believe me. Come on."

The doors opened and the slicing rotors powered down. Eckhart escorted the single-file procession carefully through the dry dirt and wild grass that'd already been worked. He stopped not far from the opening of the drainage tunnel. Rooker could see no more than ten feet inside it; beyond that, there was complete darkness.

Graffiti tags and an overgrown thicket with dead leaves flanked the entrance. There was a busted chain-link fence above the tunnel. A broken shopping cart sat by the entrance and a dark-blue cross to the right of the hole. Rooker stared down at a brown blotch on the concrete.

"Told you," Eckhart said behind his shoulder. "Just a drainpipe and blood."

"Who found the body?"

"Asim Bell. Goes by the name Boots. Homeless junkie who hears voices, imagine that. Guy's a ghoul, skinny enough to fall through a crack in the sidewalk. Know why the local boys call him Boots? Anytime the police come round, he takes off running. Even if he's done nothing wrong. Wears a pair of worn-out Timberlands, and he's fast as hell. We found him all cut up—he ran through some prickers to get away—and sweating like a pig."

Rooker already had a good feeling where the story was going.

"Says some guy—*powerful*—was waiting for him in the parking lot. Caught him off guard and put him in the trunk of his car. It was lined with plastic. They 'drove for a long-ass time,' according to him. After a while, the car stopped and the trunk released. The guy stayed in the car, told him to walk to the drainpipe and dial the number on a burner phone that he'd left in the trunk. He told Boots to tell the guy on the phone what he saw in the drainpipe or he'd shoot him in the face. When Boots climbed out of the car and walked toward the body, the guy sped off."

"Christ," Rooker said. "Whose number was programmed in the phone?"

"Just one number. Former cop. Eduardo Arroyave. You know him?"

Breathe, he told himself. Suddenly he felt like someone was holding a bag over his head, with the tiniest pinprick of air allowed through it. *Just breathe.*

"Yeah," Rooker said. "I knew him."

Eduardo Arroyave was the only other person—beside himself—that Rooker could blame for Britton's death. Eddie had become one of his closest friends, up until he used Rooker as bait to get a killer to react, and his son's murder was the reaction. Rooker had throttled Eddie, and it'd taken a swarm of officers to pull him off. He hadn't seen him since.

"Arroyave called it in. Said he didn't know who Boots was—there doesn't seem to be any connection between them. Boots typically camps out around the beach in Oceanside. Does his drugs at night with some people under the pier."

Rooker didn't answer.

"I know what you're thinking," Eckhart said. "Why does someone throw a homeless tweaker in the back of the car and drive them over an hour—nearly sixty miles—to a storm drain in Hemet. Well, your guess is as good as mine. He could've grabbed someone a whole lot closer, saved himself the gas and trouble, that's for sure."

"No one saw Boots thrown into the back of a trunk?"

"Nuh-uh."

Tess added, "He never saw the guy's face?"

"Nope."

Rooker thought about that. "What about his voice? Anything there?"

"Voice changer, if I had to guess. Boots said it was low and robotic."

"Didn't see the car?"

"Nope. Something medium-size or large. Says he's good with cars, but he never got a good look at it."

Rooker thought for a moment. In *The Black Echo*, the kid who found the body was named Edward "Sharkey" Niese. A petty criminal and graffiti tagger. He conned and robbed gay men. Asim "Boots" Bell didn't exactly fit the bill.

Tess cleared her throat. "Where is Boots now?"

"After he gave his story, we cleaned up his cuts and sent him on his merry way."

"Heroic of you," Rooker said.

Eckhart snickered. "I don't stick the needle in his vein. You wanna pay for his rehab bills, go ahead. He'll be back to a spoon and syringe the night he's released. Begging for food and money by the freeway entrance."

Rooker said nothing. He was painting his own picture of Scott Eckhart. So far, it was of a pretentious, privileged white boy.

"All right," Eckhart said. "We set up temporary shop with the local boys. Hemet PD. They know the area better than we do, so we have to play nice. But make no mistake, the case is ours. Harlow, Esparza asked for your help with something back at headquarters, so you'll go with her. Take one of the vans." He cocked his head toward the vehicles parked at the curb.

"Coroner came once we called, drove in from Los Angeles last night. Joel Hunter. He performed the autopsies on Meachum's victims. If anyone can tell us whether or not it's an exact match to the MO, it's Hunter. He'll be working out of the Hemet Valley Mortuary. Hopefully not for long." He was in a staring match now with Rooker. "We'll take a van to the mortuary, you can take a look at the body yourself, and then we're off to Pelican Bay. Good?"

Rooker lied once more. "Good."

Chapter 4

Tess had always wanted one of those jackets—midnight blue with the three metallic-yellow letters glowing on the back—but things had changed. The visions had become unrelenting, the world soaked in blood: her father's blood on the pavement at a traffic stop, Rooker's blood in the snow outside Lindström Manor, Millie's on the floor of the hospital mixing with Hartley Caldwell's, and Jan Cullen's and Clyde Miller's blood.

And when she looked in the mirror, she saw a fraud. She made an oath that she'd gone back on. She was the same—if not worse—as most of the people she'd locked away. Her stint as lead detective felt like a lifetime ago, if not a different lifetime entirely.

Now, as she assessed Special Agent Isabel Esparza from the passenger seat of a nondescript black van, she wondered if she still had it, if she had anything to offer in an investigation. Esparza looked as though she had all the control that had slipped out of Tess's life: her shiny long black hair was secured in a tight ponytail, and she had the lean and powerful build of a mixed martial artist.

But when Esparza spoke, there was a warmth in her voice Tess hadn't expected.

"So, what happened? You were well on your way to local legend. Why'd you leave it all behind for the PI biz?"

Tess scoffed. "Another local legend is a serial murderer of thirteen women. Not the greatest company to be in."

Esparza was quiet a minute and then asked, "Why did you want to be a detective in the first place?"

If that isn't the all-important question to anyone who wore a badge. Her head felt heavy and thick, as though tight straps had been tied around her brain. She hadn't slept a minute on the plane, and she hid her exhaustion now behind a scratched pair of Ray-Bans. She sighed. "My dad was a cop. He killed himself after my mother was attacked. How about you?"

"Grew up in a rough area. Robberies. Gang shootouts. We were eating dinner one night and we heard the shots. My mom got us all under the table. But my older brother was walking home . . . he was killed by a stray bullet."

"I'm sorry," Tess said.

"Me too," Esparza replied. There was another pause before she chuckled lightly and said, "So, what's the deal with him?" She tilted her head as if Rooker were sitting in the back seat.

"If I'm being honest, I'm not sure. It's been a while. We haven't spoken in . . . two years. Right after the funeral . . ." Immediately she felt guilt for referring only to the one, as if John Riggs's life wasn't as important as Millie Langston's.

"Word is, he was a loose cannon. Drunk half the time. Interfering with the investigation. Made your life a living hell. That right?"

She smiled. "Not wrong."

"If I may, why is he here?"

"Didn't your boss tell you?"

Tess caught Esparza's smile, then turned to peer out her window at the palm trees whizzing by. "He's here because as much as I hate to say it, who knows if we would've caught Gregory Sadler or Hartley Caldwell without him. If we did, it would've taken longer. A lot longer, that's for sure. *His mind . . .* He was raised by the same kind of monster that you're chasing. He's spent years studying his father and others just like him. He caught Meachum all on his own—"

"Meachum may not have even killed *anyone*. For all we know, he caught some guy who carved some names into his wall—victims' names that were public knowledge. Maybe just some psycho who wanted to take the fall for the attention."

"Believe what you want," Tess said. "Meachum isn't innocent, whether he had an accomplice or was one. He talks to the walls of his cell and no one else. But he's obsessed with Rooker. If anyone can get him to talk . . . Rooker may be your best chance."

Esparza smirked. "You love him or something?"

Tess faced her. "Are we friends now?"

Esparza laughed softly but dropped the questions. When they arrived at the station, they went deep into a parking garage, and Tess replayed the memory of crouching behind a vehicle waiting to die while Gregory Sadler shot at her.

"You okay?" Esparza asked.

"Yep. Where are we going?"

Esparza led Tess into the building. Everyone inside was dressed as though they were attending a funeral or a wedding, aside from the handguns holstered at their hips. Tess nearly smiled when she thought of Vic Sterling, Xander Whitlock, and Martin Keene hunkered down behind the ancient desks in the old station and the small-town chaos that ensued. Esparza led her to a small room with a couple of computers and a whiteboard on the wall.

"Eckhart called your old boss. Jim Larsson, was it?"

Tess could picture the old bastard now. A wrinkled look of anything but wakefulness, with wisps of hair in every direction.

"He seems hell-bent on you taking the fall for these two." Taped up on the board were each of their photos side by side. Jan Cullen and Clyde Miller. Her heart sank. "Someone found a pistol at the edge of a riverbed. Larsson had it tested against your prints, but of course, there was nothing to find. We both knew there wouldn't be. Still, it seems that an FN 509 handgun had disappeared from the evidence room at the Itasca County Sheriff's Office. Around the same time you got canned. Care to explain that?"

Tess shrugged. "Coincidence."

Esparza smiled. "My point being: this isn't your country bumpkin sheriff's office. This is the FBI. That vigilante *ex-cop* shit doesn't fly here. I could get the best and brightest on the deaths of Mr. Cullen and Mr. Miller, but that's not what I want."

Esparza walked over to a desk, unlocked the drawer, and pulled out a file.

She handed it over to Tess, who opened it and stared at the wreckage from the fire at Lindström Manor. She flipped through the photographs of the bones, but she'd already seen them enough times to know each image by heart.

"You've always thought he killed her, right?" Esparza's voice snapped her out of a daze. "I want you to help me prove it."

Chapter 5

Hemet Valley Mortuary was an odd-shaped yellow stucco building with large stained-glass windows on the corner of North San Jacinto Street. A big white sign with funky red letters advertising burials and cremation was posted into perfectly cut grass.

Rooker knew it well: it's where his son's body had been taken.

In the basement, they found Joel Hunter standing over a steel table, where the victim's body was covered in a white sheet. Rooker's body went cold. It wasn't the drop in temperature that beaded his skin with freezing sweat or burned spots of his forehead with sharp pinpricks. It was knowing that Britton's body once lay on one of the ice-cold trays hidden behind the silver wall of refrigerator doors.

Rooker also knew Hunter from when he'd conducted his own unofficial, alcohol-fueled investigation into his son's murder. The coroner was just shy of six feet tall, sitting around two hundred pounds, with eggshell skin, a trimmed gray beard, and a grave expression. His head was the perfect model of male-pattern baldness, with the sheen of a polished bowling ball on top and silver hair poking out on the sides.

"Dr. Hunter," Eckhart said. "I'm Special Agent Eckhart. We spoke over the phone. This is Special Agent Quincy. And I believe you already know Mr. Lindström—he's consulting on this case."

"Nice to see you again." The man spoke in a low-enough tone to narrate action movie trailers. "This is my assistant ME, Lucian Hurst."

Hurst stood around Rooker's height and build with dark side-parted hair and a complexion far less ghoulish than Hunter's. He had an Ivy League look. *He must be popular at conventions,* Rooker thought, finding Hurst's normalcy almost offensive. Poring over murder victims should drain the sun and life from one's skin. Hurst nodded at Rooker and Eckhart and stood at the end of the table by the victim's feet.

"What do you have?" Eckhart asked.

Hunter shut his eyes and scratched his brow. "Victim is a white female, late thirties. Cause of death: fatal stabbing. The MO looks very similar, I'm afraid." He opened his eyes, pulled the sheet down to the victim's waist, and pointed a gloved hand at her wounds. "The lacerations were made by an eight-inch steel blade, possibly the same type of chef's knife Meachum used. And you can see the subungual hematoma—the trauma dealt to the finger." He held a small magnifying glass over the blackened fingernail so they could see the numbers: 10:52, the time of death. "Everything appears to be the same. Except . . ." With Hurst's assistance, Hunter gently rolled the victim over and pulled the sheet down to just above her buttocks. "He skinned her."

Rooker stared in disbelief down at the fat and muscle. "Sixteen inches long by twelve inches wide," Hunter said. He ran his gloved finger along the edge. "Done with surgical precision. This cut was made antemortem, meaning the victim was still alive when her killer skinned her. Judging by the ligature marks at her wrists, the victim was restrained. She was very likely awake in the beginning, but her body would have gone into shock, and she'd have gone unconscious. Either way, the signs of bleeding indicate that her blood was still circulating, and her killer took their time."

Killers evolve. Rooker knew that. Was this the real Madman he'd been hunting, or someone looking to "improve" on Meachum's methods?

"Why skin her?" Quincy said. "If I wanted people to think I was the same killer, why not just copy the MO of the other murders to the letter?"

"That I couldn't tell you," Hunter said. "But skinning a victim isn't entirely uncommon. It's like skinning a kill—wild game. Jeffrey Dahmer did it. Ed Gein was notorious for it; he may be the closest thing we have to a real-life Buffalo Bill."

Buffalo Bill. He remembered Millie confessing she wanted to catch someone like him. She wanted to be like Clarice Starling. To Rooker, she was more than that. Then he'd thought about Gein—denoted the Butcher of Plainfield and the Plainfield Ghoul—digging up bodies from the graveyard and making utensils and trophies out of their skin and bones.

He wondered how the killer would make use of the victim's skin.

"Is there anything else?" Eckhart asked.

"Afraid not," Hunter answered. "No DNA or prints anywhere on her body. No fibers. Just dirt from the drainpipe."

"Personal effects?"

"The victim was nude. All she was wearing were twenty-two-carat gold earrings," Hurst said. "No other jewelry on her."

Rooker asked, "How can you tell the carat?"

Hurst said, "It has a little hallmark with a '22.' Believe me, I'm no expert. I lost my ring once." He freed the chain where a ring dangled over his chest. "Had to get it replaced without my wife knowing."

Hurst and Hunter rolled the victim over again and pulled the sheet over her. Rooker fought off a shiver at the haunting thought of his son's body, cold, against the silver steel autopsy table. The large wound in his chest that Joel Hunter must have sewn shut.

Back in the SUV, Rooker spoke. "I just have one more stop to make. I'll be quick."

Eckhart snickered. "We aren't your chauffeurs, Lindström."

Rooker hesitated, but he knew he couldn't see Meachum without knowing if he was right about *The Black Echo.* "I have something in the old house, if my ex-wife didn't throw all my shit out. It's a hunch, but I think there might be something in it that will help us with the Madman."

"Like what?"

"I don't know. It could be a long shot. But the drainpipe, Boots—" He stopped to take a breath. "I think the staging of this crime is based on a book in my collection. I think it might confirm that Meachum has an accomplice."

"Why?"

"Because whoever did this has not only been in my house but spent enough time there to know what's in my library. My ex and I were never big on entertaining, so that leaves a handful of people we know well—and the person who stalked us and killed my son."

"All right, Lindström. Where to?"

Rooker peered up at the structure he'd once called home.

It had changed. The stucco was a creamy beige now, and the trim and garage were a matching chocolatey brown. It looked nice. Just . . . different.

While he peered up at the balcony he'd added on to the second-story bedroom, all he could think of was the countless mornings he'd brought Laura her coffee in a Cal Poly mug.

But once he blinked and snapped open his eyes, he saw it all over again. The night he got the call. He could remember how hard he'd slammed his foot down against the gas pedal. He could remember blowing through a red light or two. The screech of his brakes as he pulled up outside the yellow police tape. Flickering blue and red. Everything around him had gone silent. The moving mouths no longer making a sound. His legs no longer beneath him. Numb.

And then it all turned black. The stucco blackened. The trim a putrid sludge, oozing down. And the home twisted into a sinister grin. His throat tightened.

Stop, he pleaded. *Please stop.* He listened to his own words echo in his skull. Begged like someone was controlling what he was seeing.

He cradled his face between his hands. Trembling. And then he opened his eyes to the rap of knuckles knocking on the glass, and it was all gone.

"I'm good." He pressed a finger into the tear before it could fall. His eyes stung. He opened his door to Tess's judgmental stare. *The hell is she doing here?* But then he saw the black van she and Esparza had taken, parked a few houses down across the street. He ignored her. There would be plenty of time for a conversation soon.

Rooker hurried down the driveway to the front door. His heart thrashed in uneven beats. He rapped gently against the door, hoping it was too soft to be heard. Maybe Laura wouldn't be home. He wanted to cower in the tiniest space while the FBI broke into an empty home and did his dirty work.

He wasn't so lucky.

The door opened to a woman with straight hair that flowed like a silky brown river, with rippling curls at the ends. Even now, staring at him behind the glass storm door, she had the softest features and the calmest emerald eyes. Laura had an ethereal way about her that sometimes made him feel as though he were floating. The woman he'd chosen as his forever and hadn't seen in over five years.

She pushed open the door and softly said, "Hi, Rooker." Her lips quivered into a sad smile, but as the two tears fell from her beautiful eyes, he gritted his teeth. The hard slap landed across his cheek.

He peered through a half-open eye, waiting for the next shot. But it didn't come.

"I deserve a lot more than that."

"It's been *five years.* You're damn right."

He didn't bother to rub the pain away. "Hi, Laura."

She stared past him at the vehicle and the group of people. Locked her arms across her chest as if it weren't a sunny 70-degree day. "What are you doing here?" She paused. "They look like a serious bunch."

He nodded. "FBI."

"What is it now?"

"That body they found out in the drainpipe." He let out an uncomfortable snicker.

"*The Black Echo?*"

He smiled. "*The Black Echo.*" That was how he'd known he was in love with Laura. She read the same books as he did; they shared a fascination with serial killers and Nordic noir and true crime. She read every one of his news stories about gruesome homicides and gang turf wars and petty-cash armed robberies and often thought like a crime reporter herself. "I think it was a message. Someone else trying to torment me." He closed his eyes and shook his head. Inhaled a deep breath. With his next words, he tried to drop the bomb as softly and gracefully as he could. "It could mean that Tate Meachum didn't kill Britton. Whoever killed that girl did it to get my attention. They even called Eddie."

She shook her head. "Eddie's been retired for years. And Meachum confessed. He killed our son. You said he was the one calling your phone every night. You said—"

"*I know.* I know what I said. But everything the FBI told me . . . I've got this feeling in my gut that's making me sick. Do you still have my books?"

"I boxed them up. They're in the upstairs closet."

"May I come in and look?"

"Boots off."

He turned to the group of agents, all eavesdropping conspicuously. "Harlow," he called out and waved her toward him.

"Laura, this is Tess Harlow. Tess, Laura."

"I read about you. Nice to meet you," Laura said.

"Likewise," Tess answered.

Rooker spoke again. "She was the lead detective in Minnesota. Saved my life, more than once. We've had our ups and downs, but I trust her more than any of those people out there."

"He's not the easiest person to deal with, is he," Laura said wryly.

"No, he isn't."

"Still, thank you for saving him. Maybe one day he'll learn to save himself."

Tess didn't respond.

Neither did Rooker.

After he kicked each boot off, he walked inside and tried his best not to comment on everything that had changed. The paint colors. The art on the walls. The plants. They had never owned plants. A beautiful bouquet of roses sat in a crystal vase on a small table by the door. In all the time he'd known Laura, she'd never been one to buy herself flowers. A pain he shouldn't have felt suddenly struck harder than her slap to the face.

While Laura ushered the two of them upstairs, Rooker told Tess about the book and his suspicions.

At the closet door, Laura pulled it open and yanked the cord for the light. The box was massive, books pressing against the sides like rolls of fat in a skintight shirt.

"Wait," Tess said as Rooker reached for the box. "Everything has to be by the book this time. The FBI doesn't mess around." She snapped on a pair of gloves from her back pocket. After unfolding the top, she began to take books out one by one, setting them down on the floor beside her like they were rigged to explode. It was about halfway down into the depths of the musty box that she pulled out the one he was hoping would be there.

"That's it," he told her. It was black, with a clear sleeve over the hardcover jacket. The binding was still in great shape. He knelt down beside her and brushed her arm with his own.

She pulled back the cover. A scribbled signature that to many people might mean nothing. It didn't have the resale value of something signed by Princess Diana or Jimi Hendrix or John Lennon or Babe Ruth. But to Rooker, as a wannabe crime writer, Michael Connelly was his Michael Jordan.

With a careful touch, she flipped the pages, and they both saw something. "Wait," he said. "Go back."

There it was. A page marked with red. The time drawn there by a finger . . .

The first thought invading his mind was whether Meachum knew about the book. If he hadn't, whoever left the body in the drainpipe must've gotten into the house recently and planted it. Rooker imagined the killer did it while wearing gloves or using the victim's finger as a pen. But the color was unmistakable. Dark as red brick. Blood.

11:37

"I'll get them to bag all of it," Tess said. "I doubt there's a print to find, but they'll go through every book in here." She lifted the box in her hands and carried it down the staircase.

Rooker turned to his ex-wife, her gaze unblinking and empty, her leg jackhammering the way it tended to when she was afraid. "The FBI is going to keep tabs on you. Just to be safe. I'm sorry."

"Someone . . ." Her voice rattled. "How did someone get into the house?"

"I don't know. But it won't happen again."

"Let me guess: you asked the FBI to watch me."

For a long, uncomfortable moment, he waited. He wanted to give her a kiss on the cheek before he was gone. Instead, Rooker smiled sadly and left her standing there without a goodbye. If she were lucky, she'd never see his face again.

Chapter 6

Inside a makeshift room at the bottom level of the abandoned mall, the Madman switched on the portable light, shut the door behind him, and pushed the caged man back from the steel bars. The man in the box had gone missing five years ago. While the light droned and pale white glowed within the room, he ignored the man as he fell half onto a sunken mattress and half onto the bare concrete. The man shielded his eyes, and his naked body convulsed. Pleas came out in spittle-flecked screams, coughs, and wheezes, but the Madman did not move.

Instead, he stared at one of the few remaining fingernails, purple-black. The rest had been broken so long ago that the nail separated from the nail bed, and all that was left was broken bone beneath web-cracked skin.

There had been several redevelopment plans over the last decade—outlet mall, power center, housing units, office units, commercial units, dining—but the mall was as ruined as the man inside the box. A few homeless encampments had sprouted up inside, and the police came around occasionally to kick them out. Still, no one ever ventured down this far.

He'd built the little room himself. It was as small as a jail cell—a place he'd never see. Made of plywood and screws, with two-inch-thick acoustic foam panels that trapped every scream that came out of the man's mouth. His throat was as dry as his cracked lips. Years of light deprivation had turned the man's eyes milky. Every day, he sat in total darkness.

Putrid air spilled out from the steel cage and was trapped within these four walls.

His other victims had experienced mercy. They were met with a quick death. But none of his other victims had ever wronged him. None except for this man, and the man who wrote lies about him, now come home to find him, Rooker Lindström.

"Why are you doing this to me?"

The Madman started pulling off his gloves, and the man inside the cage knew.

Chapter 7

The Black Hawk touched down outside Pelican Bay. Beyond the fence that wrapped around 275 acres of prison, an ominous sky and the threat of rain loomed over a forest of redwood and spruce trees. A sky fit for a meeting with a monster. The blades cut through the air in two tones: a high-pitched whizz, and the deafening judder of a jackhammer overhead. The force of it made Rooker feel as though holes were being drilled into his skull. He climbed down and fought the powerful wind at his back.

When they'd managed to get far enough from the noise, Eckhart said, "The guards will insist they be inside when you speak to him."

He shook his head. "He'll never talk with them—"

"I know. It'll have to be the two of you. Just you and him. Which is why I need you to promise me something. You don't touch him. Understand?"

Rooker didn't answer.

"Believe me, I get it. You've probably dreamt of this moment . . . where you can reach out and kill him with your bare hands. Hell, I know I would. But . . . if you try anything, I can't help you. You'll have guards on you in seconds. You'll be escorted out. And you'll have no part in my investigation unless it's from a holding cell. Are we clear?"

This time, Rooker nodded.

Entering the fortress that was Pelican Bay made Rooker's skin itch. The simple act of turning out his pockets here made him feel like they were going to lock him up and throw away the key.

Boots clopping and the ringing in his ears were the only two sounds now as he advanced the length of concrete corridor that stretched at least five hundred feet. The smell of cleaning supplies clung to the air. It was dark. Harsh fluorescent lights left eerie shadows. Gray walls were stained as if they wept or bled. For a moment, Rooker imagined the dark shapes were inmates trapped inside the walls. Then again, he wasn't far off.

Doors clanged. Locks bolted shut.

The only color was rust, the dull metallic shade of the cell doors and the catwalk level above them. As he passed each perforated steel door, Rooker did his best to avoid looking through the holes. In his peripheral, he'd caught a straggly mustached man with a bald white head and a swastika tattoo on his massive sternum. The Aryan Brotherhood, if he had to guess. He knew being a neo-Nazi wasn't enough to be in solitary. To end up here, you had to do something wrong in general population. Violence toward the guards, stab another inmate, run contraband into the facility, possession of weapons, order murder for hire or trafficking on the outside. Or in Tate Meachum's case, you rape and kill a child. Kid killers don't make it long in prison.

Ten minutes crawled by in the time Rooker removed everything on him and was patted down before sitting at a table in an empty room. Eckhart sent him in with a manila folder and a report on the victim, which he set down on the table. The write-up wasn't necessary. All Rooker needed were the photographs. He didn't know what to do with his hands, so he steepled them over the folder and sat with a straight, powerful posture. In reality he was a mess. He hadn't been face-to-face with Tate Meachum, ever. Not once. He'd seen him in the rear seat of a squad car and from the back corner of a courtroom proceeding. He'd seen his face on television many times. But never had he been close enough to reach out and touch him, or feel his breath pollute the air around him.

In all honesty, he didn't know what to expect. After a lengthy trial and a unanimous jury verdict, Meachum had been in solitary confinement for five years. For half a decade, he had spent his time alone in a box. There was rumor that he'd been getting visits from an attorney recently to appeal his sentence, but Rooker knew that Tate Meachum was never seeing the outside of a cell again.

Still, Rooker was better than a death rower's last meal, and he knew that too. Tate Meachum didn't care about food or what books he could read in his cell. He didn't care to have a nice view overlooking the trees. But a chance to talk face-to-face with Rooker . . . that was better than any present.

The thought made his stomach wrench. His leg jittered nervously to a rhythm he heard buzzing in his head. Minutes later, two armed guards flanked him and stood silently in powerful stances slightly behind him. He stared at the empty chair across from him. A hum whispered from the lights and the multiple video cameras aimed down at the table.

A loud, quick buzz and a door opened. Rooker watched as the man who killed his son hobbled into view followed by another set of burly prison guards. He wore a blue prison jumpsuit with silver restraints around his wrists and ankles. Meachum was thinner than he remembered. The guards hooked his restraints to the bolt on the table and took a step back but made no motion to leave.

Warden Hastings would have given Rooker the space he needed, but he was long gone. He couldn't blame Hastings for leaving. Rooker knew all too well what happens when you don't take a serial killer's warnings seriously.

He steeled himself, screwed up his eyes, and met the cold smile of the Madman. The two sat there, still and silent, frozen in time.

That was, until Rooker spoke. Without diverting his stare, he said to the guards, "He won't talk with you guys here."

"Orders are—" Rooker heard from behind him before cutting the voice off.

"You can't be here. FBI Agent Scott Eckhart and his team are waiting outside. I need you to do the same."

"With all due respect, Mr. Lindström, I know who you are. And I know who he is. I can't have you do anything in here or it's my ass."

Just as Rooker was about to respond, there was a loud bang on the door. He didn't need to look to know that it was probably Eckhart, summoning the guards from the room. There were hushed voices and the clang of the door; then the room was empty. Just the two of them.

They stayed silent for another minute. Rooker's gaze fell over the dark-maroon blotches, like pinpricks where Meachum had torn the hair from his scalp before they shaved his head. He looked down at his chalk-white hands, the mangled remains of his fingertips and nails. Rooker did his best to keep his stare vacant. Mostly, he fought the urge to strike or dive across the table and dig his fingers into Tate's windpipe. *Stay calm.*

Meachum was the one to break the silence. "Do my eyes deceive me . . . The infamous Rooker Lindström!"

"Tate . . . not looking so good. Solitary not treating you well?"

"Maybe not my complexion, but my mind . . ." He leaned forward, and his manacled wrists clattered. It was just enough room for him to jab the blackened fingernail at his temple. "Sharp as ever." He smirked. "Inmates used to call this place Skeleton Bay." He sounded reminiscent. His head turned slowly, as if he were speaking to the atoms floating in the room. "Funny, huh? Probably more *bones* beneath Lindström Manor."

Meachum's eyes, cold and menacing, fell back on Rooker. His voice came out harsh, like he hadn't used it in a while. Rooker remembered Hastings saying that he mostly whispered in his cell. Now he wondered if—*how*—Meachum knew about the body that the firefighters had found beneath the cottage.

He didn't want to answer. But he knew the faster he got Meachum talking, the faster he could be out of here and never look back. "You may be right."

"They say this place drives people *crazy*. I'm not sure I buy it."

Rooker didn't budge.

"I hear you're quite famous now . . . I still see them, y'know."

Rooker ignored him and changed the topic. "The FBI asked me to speak to you."

He smiled and batted his sunken eyes. "And here I was thinking this was a social call . . . just you stopping by to see an old friend."

"'Probably more bones beneath Lindström Manor.' Why did you say that?"

Wearing a facetious grin, he answered, "Whatever are you talking about?"

Someone was feeding Meachum information. Somehow Meachum found out about the girl. The one beneath the floor. He decided to let it go. Better to hold on tight to the upper hand.

"You may be a lot of things, Tate, but you aren't stupid. I presume you know why I'm here."

"Of course I do. I know you better than you know yourself."

"Why don't you tell me, then?"

"And risk this lovely visit coming to an end too soon?" He shook his head hard. "That would be a shame, Rooker. Downright rude of me. You're my guest here. Tell me, do you miss our calls?"

"Not particularly."

"I do. Sitting in the dark. Thinking about how determined you were, like a lost little boy. The phone pressed to your ear for the smallest clue. Trying to keep me on the line for the wiretap to work." He laughed and the chains rattled. "How I wish we could go back to those days."

Rooker was sick—sick to his stomach, sick of the games. Sick and tired of the filth that spewed from Tate Meachum's mouth. He went with a different approach.

"We found a body." He flipped open the manila folder and turned it around so Meachum could see the image. It was the victim on an autopsy table. He slid the next photograph out from under it and put it in Meachum's view. It was a close-up of the fingernail. Blackened. The time of death carved over it. "Same MO. Funny, huh?"

Now Rooker's face held the slightest hint of a smile. And suddenly, the mischief in Meachum's face was gone. He leaned back in his seat. Disbelief, Rooker thought he could read.

"How's Laura? Have you seen her since you got back?"

Rooker laughed. "That's the best you've got? I just told you that we have a new victim with the exact same MO as the victims you claimed to have killed. And you ask me about my ex-wife? I expected better, Tate."

Meachum leaned forward again, and while the manacles rattled, he pressed his fingers to his lip as though he was deep in thought. His face fell slightly, but he stared up at Rooker with a devious expression. "So it went that bad, did it? She must despise you for getting her son killed . . . You're right, Rooker. I would never let you down. I know all about your whore in the drainpipe."

Rooker's veins chilled. He said nothing.

"Too close to home, huh? That's why you came running back, like the wounded dog you are. Did you suspect it was Laura lying there?"

It was actually the first thought he'd had when he got the news. "So the rumor was true."

"What rumor might that be?"

"You had an accomplice. Someone helping you. Or . . ." Rooker slid the photograph back in the folder and closed it. He sat up like he was ready to leave. "You never killed any of them."

"Oh, Rooker. We both know that's not true."

"Enlighten me. Why did you kill . . . *him*? Why not Laura?"

"Still can't say his name, huh? Pity. I did what you never expected. I took the one that would hurt more. You spread lies about me. You would grieve Laura, maybe one day find a new wife. But a new son . . . *never.*"

"Tell me: Why was this body found in a drainpipe? The victims you confessed to the murders of were all killed inside their homes."

Meachum shrugged. "Beats me. I don't get out much anymore." He raised the cuffs until they ran out of room. "Maybe someone out there is a fan of my work."

"Like Gregory Sadler was a fan of my father's?"

"That's right."

"Tell me about that night. The night you killed him."

"Get me a slot on your girlfriend's show. I'll give her the exclusive."

"Maybe I can have these guards kick the shit out of you a little bit. Put a kid killer back in general population and see how long you last. Would that work better?"

"You still drinking, Rooker? Usually I get the faint taste of gin or vodka that tickles my throat when I look at you. But not today. You look sober to me."

Rooker smiled. "I'll tell you what: if you can't tell me why the body is in the drainpipe, I think you've got a pretty good alibi for the death of my son."

Tate's expression darkened. His face went blank, a stare from two curiously vacant eyes. Rooker had more or less expected to get nothing out of Meachum and leave with a feeling of nausea and a thirst for alcohol. He'd felt both since he'd entered the prison. But now he felt like he had Meachum right where he never expected to get him.

Meachum didn't answer.

"You know what I think? I think someone was helping you. Or you were helping them. And I'm going to find them and end all of this."

"You won't find them," Meachum said with a straight face. Then he turned to the cameras and the door. "Neither will the FBI."

"I found you. I found Sadler. I found Caldw—"

"Yesss," he hissed. "How *did* you catch me, Rooker? I mean . . . how did you *really* do it? Oh, never mind. You can tell me next time we speak."

Meachum craned forward and started digging at his skull. When he couldn't break skin, his head started to convulse. The door clanged. In came three of the prison guards. "That's enough!" one of them screamed.

"Is this what you traveled all this way to see, Rooker?" Tate asked. "You want to watch the Madman go *mad?*"

Rooker watched Tate's head shake and his mouth bite down on the end of his finger. He gnawed it off so fast that Rooker wasn't sure what he'd just seen.

They started to restrain Meachum. Blood gushing down his hand. Splattering against the table.

"No—we aren't finished," Rooker pleaded. He looked to the door but didn't see any sign of Eckhart or the members of his team.

"He just bit the tip of his finger off. You're done—"

"I don't have time for this, or for him to *calm down.*" Rooker shot to his feet. "Tate . . . Who is it? Tate!"

Meachum smiled over his shoulder, red dribbling from the corner of his lip. "Come back soon, Rooker."

Just like that, he watched the wide backs of the prison guards exit the room. The Madman was gone.

Chapter 8

Sundays used to be her favorite day of the week.

Tess would drive down to Crossbones Firing Range, the maple trees flickering past, sometimes as red or yellow as fire during the fall. In the heart of winter, the icy limbs shivered against the cold wind.

Martin Keene would be waiting for her there. And the two would bet some money on who would be the better shot. She always won, but Martin would pony up every time as if he was surprised. When she inhaled now, she could taste the metal and gunpowder of the firing range on her tongue. Feel the snapping jolt of the gun as the gases within expanded. Hear the soft pops surrounding her like distant fireworks beneath the earmuffs.

She hadn't had much in Minnesota—a father in the ground, a mother in a state worse than death, sour memories, and work. But she'd had Martin and his wife, Sheila, who would have dinner waiting when they were done at the shooting range. The three of them would talk over wine for hours.

This Sunday had pushed her past exhaustion.

After Rooker had been whisked away for his date with the Madman, Tess had stayed behind at the house with Esparza and Hall to help process Rooker's book collection and look for other hidden "messages," as well as any sign of how the killer had managed to remove and return

The Black Echo. While Hall questioned Laura about who had access to the house, Tess and Esparza started their search in the most obvious place: Britton's old room.

In the dimly lit space, Tess was opening and shutting the small dresser drawers while Esparza sprayed an ultraviolet light over the room, when suddenly she heard Esparza's judgmental tone. "You think he's got any bones beneath *this* house?"

Tess's brow furrowed. "Excuse me?"

"You heard me. You don't think the girl in Minnesota is the only one he killed, do you?"

"This isn't the time," Tess said. "His ex-wife is out there having to relive her worst nightmare and you want to discuss taking Rooker down for murder while we're standing in his dead son's bedroom. Give me a break."

"Give you a break? Or do you want me to give him a pass?"

"*Look*, I don't care what happens to him. You want to crucify him, go right ahead. But is that why you want him to be a killer so badly? You want to be the celebrity?"

The corner of Esparza's smile flickered in the dark. "I want him arrested because he murdered a woman and let his daddy take the blame." She clicked off the light, which had picked up nothing. Tess had come up with the same: no fibers, blood, hair, fingerprints, footprints. Whoever had broken into the house hadn't left anything for them to find in here. There were no signs of Laura having been in the room recently either. "We both know damn well that if Gunner did it, her head would've been in that freezer box. But like you said: there's zero proof. So find me some."

◆ ◆ ◆

The rest of their search yielded nothing. And Laura had been working so many shifts at the hospital, no one had been by in weeks. There was a doorbell camera, and another with a limited view of the backyard, but Tess knew there was no way a person calculated enough to select that book would be sloppy enough to get caught on video. She was not looking forward to telling Rooker they had no leads.

On their way back to the hotel where the FBI had put up Tess and Rooker, Esparza had gotten a call from Quincy, which she'd put on speakerphone for Tess to hear. Quincy sounded alternately sarcastic and shaken as he recounted Rooker's bloody meeting with the Madman. The only thing Tess found surprising was that Rooker had been able to keep his cool.

Now, looking at the sad microwave burrito she'd picked up in the lobby kiosk and thinking of Sheila's home cooking, she felt intensely homesick. Through blurry eyes, she stared down at the contact in her phone, at the little photo of Martin Keene in the circle. How badly she wanted to call him. But she couldn't. If even that idiot Larsson suspected she'd been behind Cullen's and Miller's deaths, there's no way Martin Keene hadn't figured it out. She wondered if she had confessed to him what she'd done, if she told him how sorry she was, if he'd take her back or turn her in. She pressed the lock button, and her tears splashed onto the phone screen as it faded to black.

She launched the phone into the wall. It fell to the rug. A dark scuff marked the paint above it. Two cracks webbed through the display now. She downed the rest of the beer on her nightstand and dug her fingers into her throbbing temples.

She couldn't breathe. She needed to get some air.

She shrugged on a dark zip-up jacket and tucked the SIG Sauer into her pants. Luckily for her, she was considered honorably retired law enforcement—despite quitting when she was demoted, calling the chief a "worthless old prick" to his face—and could legally carry a concealed firearm. She made her way out of her room. Once she was outside, she pulled the hood down and kept her head low.

Despite the bitterness of the beer that coated her tongue, the night air sobered her. She walked for a while. A pleasant breeze pried a few hair strands loose from the hood of her jacket. This was better than Minnesota in late November—a constant cold draft and threat of snow.

She decided then that she'd throw fuel on the fire and confront Rooker once she got the chance.

When a loud group of three men were walking in her direction—dressed dark as shadows in backward hats and hoods, sweatpants, and jeans—she moved aside from the curb to let them pass. She kept her eyes trained on the lines and cracks in the sidewalk and the bubbles of blackened gum now one with the concrete. Two of them wore Jordans—one in red-and-black mid-top retro sneakers and the other in purple-and-gold basketball shoes—and the last one was in dark Timberlands. When they did go past, she was hit by the strong smell of alcohol and weed. She caught one of them staring. Trying to peer up beneath her hood.

Her body tightened. She turned away.

Then one of them said, "Yo. Wait up, girl."

She kept walking. But then she heard the scuff of sneakers. *"Ahrrooooo,"* one of them howled. She turned around fast, pulled the pistol, and aimed it between a set of glossy brown eyes.

"Can I help you?" she said.

"Shit. Whoa." The pupils grew. Two of the men put their hands up and backed away slowly.

The third stayed still and half-heartedly said, "Crazy-ass bitch," which made Tess laugh. *You have no idea,* she thought. She lowered the pistol a few inches, and the group took the cue and quickly turned the corner away from her.

Tess stood there until they were out of sight. Sweat trickled down her back. She felt as though someone was watching her. She would have fired had they moved any closer.

Chapter 9

Rooker was dreaming of the morning he had left Caroline. His bag was packed. She lay on the bed watching him get ready to leave before her own busy day of work. He told her she'd be under police watch. She didn't approve of that, but too bad. Alive and angry with him was better than dead. She'd understand.

He remembered her last words were a phrase he used to despise. "Have a safe flight." As if anything he did on the airplane had any impact on whether the plane floated above the clouds or crashed in a fiery ball to the ground. Nosedive or tailspin, safe or not, that was up to the pilot. Yet still, when Caroline said the phrase, he smiled and didn't mind it as much.

Red was doing what he did every day: sleeping by the front door. Before he was out the door, Rooker gave him a pat on the head, just as Caroline kissed Rooker goodbye.

But when he saw Geralt in the yard, he turned back to get something he'd forgotten. As he opened the door, he saw Red still fast asleep, beside Caroline's sprawled body. Her face stark white. Eyes empty. Dead. The fingernail black.

He jumped up.

The hem of his shirt was wet with sweat. His chest heaved like a wave, rising and falling. He pressed his palm to the cold, empty space beside him. Rooker sat over the edge of the bed and changed out of his T-shirt. In the darkness, his fingers brushed over the scar on his shoulder. He checked the time. Ringing in his ears was Tate Meachum's voice: *Probably more bones beneath Lindström Manor.*

The hotel alarm clock read 2:06 a.m.

The FBI put him and Tess up in the Best Western Plus on West Florida Avenue. From a room high enough on the south end, he would've had a view of Diamond Valley Lake. Boaters from around the world traveled to Diamond Valley to fish for black bass and whatever else swam around in the reservoir. Rooker had taken Laura there once on a date, what now seemed a lifetime ago, well before they had Britton.

But his east-facing room was on the second level and barely overlooked a piece of the street and the hotel pool.

The room was dark. Through the blinds he caught the flicker of a streetlamp and the rare strobe of headlights at this hour, but otherwise the sky was distant and black. He opened his phone and dialed Caroline.

After three rings, she answered.

"Hmm," she muttered sleepily. "Hi."

"I'm sorry," he whispered. "I didn't want to wake you. I just wanted to hear your voice on your voicemail."

"That's sweet. What's wrong?"

"Bad dream," he said dismissively. "That's all."

"Want to talk about it?"

He shook his head in the darkness, as though she could see him. "No . . . the nightmares are how I know I'm still alive. Oh, I had a chat with my ex-wife. On the same day I had a conversation with Tate Meachum."

He thought better than to tell Caroline how Meachum referred to her as his girlfriend.

"*Jesus.* Are you okay?"

"Yeah." He nearly laughed. "The first one slapped me. The second one felt like it killed me."

"A weaker person, maybe."

It wasn't that he was strong. It was that he'd seen so much in his life, that however much in vain or however stupid he seemed for it, he just kept going.

"How's the investigation going?" she asked.

"Off the record?"

She laughed. "Yes."

"It's early. Too early. There isn't much. Not yet, at least. They brought in Tess hoping that it would make me a little more cooperative."

"Tess *Harlow*?"

Rooker smiled at the shock in her voice. He'd never told Caroline about his alcohol-induced night of intimacy with Tess and now wondered what she would think of Tess sleeping a few doors down. *Nothing* is what he told himself. Caroline had a confidence about her that warded off jealous feelings. "The one and only."

"She hasn't been a cop in two years."

"I know."

"When you have something . . . will I get the exclusive?"

"If you play your cards right."

"I'll make up for it."

"I know."

Rooker told her to get back to sleep and said he'd do the same. By now he knew that she knew better.

He got up and reheated a cup of coffee from the pot, then sat down at the desk and opened his laptop. Eckhart had provided him copies of the files on the victim. Crime scene images along with the postmortem examination written up by Dr. Joel Hunter.

He clicked the arrow key slowly, going one by one through the crime scene images as well as the photos and report from the coroner. What terrified him was the fact that the victim could have passed for his ex-wife. He pictured Laura's face ruined and dead, her hair in wet tangles and knots. The thought that it was intentional made him shiver. The thought that she could be next froze him with fear.

Eckhart had also given Rooker the FBI's files on Meachum, as there was likely stuff in those Rooker hadn't been privy to as a reporter. As he looked through them, one thing plagued his mind: Tate Meachum had an alibi for one of the victim's deaths. Julieta Rollins. Everyone called her Julie. Rollins was a thirty-two-year-old single mother of two (a boy, seven, and girl, four) who had been living in a one-story house in Temecula. Her son was the one who found her when she never came out of her room to make them breakfast. Rollins was naked on her bed and had been mutilated by a chef's knife incision to the chest and strikes inflicted by a ball-peen hammer.

Her time of death was between the hours of one and three in the morning. Rollins's daughter, Martina, remembered hearing whispers coming from her mother's bedroom but thought it was just the television.

The problem was that Meachum had been in Palm Springs at the time, staying in a Motel 6 on a work trip. There were bank records and receipts and an eyewitness—Joey Miggs—who confirmed it. Miggs worked with Meachum all the time. On that trip, the two were staying in rooms next to each other. Miggs said that the work van squealed like a pig in shit. If Meachum left in the night and returned by morning, he would have known. Unfortunately, there were no working surveillance cameras in the motel lot. And no street cameras ever picked up the white Ford van.

Still, it didn't mean that Meachum couldn't have taken a different vehicle there and back. But it also could mean that there was someone else helping him.

It was a large inconsistency that had eaten at Rooker ever since his own investigation into the Madman, but he never found anything. He decided then that he'd take a hard look at each of the victims. The relatives and friends of the victims.

At four in the morning, he opted for a run. It wasn't his favorite thing in the world, but he'd already been up for more than two hours staring at the computer screen. Images of dead people had embedded in his brain far too early in the day. At 3:00 a.m. he'd tried to distract himself with his latest article for the *Los Angeles Times*, but that only reminded him of the killer that was still out there and did little to evict the victims' faces from his skull.

He threw on a dark pair of joggers and a T-shirt and running sneakers before heading down to the lobby. The main level was quiet. There were a few employees stirring about and a hotel concierge standing behind a desk the size of a small boat, enduring a long and, by the looks of it, painful yawn. The man's neck snapped to the side, and he smiled when he noticed Rooker.

Rooker made his way out the automatic doors and was off. He started slow. But after a couple of minutes, he ran like he was running from something. Someone. Hell, it seemed to be a recurring theme in his life. In his mind, he'd never stopped running. Away from his father, or the perpetual tether that connected to him. Away from the agony, the memories of his mother's mind decaying before his eyes. Away from his dead son, and the wife he selfishly couldn't bear to look at. Away from this place. Away from the murders of Evelyn Holmberg and who he considered his greatest friend and colleague, Millie Langston. Everything served as a reminder of pain.

And so, he ran. Hard footfalls slapped the concrete. At a pace not much slower than his all-out sprint, he breathed hard. Sweat ran down his face and the back of his collar. In his mind, he saw Tate Meachum's buzzed scalp and his mocking face and tone turn serious.

You won't find them.

Rooker's face ran hot. He ran harder.

Who won't I find, Tate?

Them. There was something there in the way Tate had said that one word. Maybe Tate didn't know exactly who it was. If he didn't, then they still had to be communicating in some fashion. The mail? Meachum had all sorts of deranged fans—maybe the killer was posing as one of them to send messages. He'd have to ask Eckhart about that.

He finally stopped when his lungs seemed ready to pop and his airway felt as if it were being squeezed in a vise. He bent over, hands on his knees, wheezing. And then he dropped to the grass and fell over onto his back, staring up at what remained of the stars before the earth's ceiling would turn blue.

He bawled. He saw his son's face behind the lens of the telescope in his bedroom. He smiled and cried. And then he heard a door creak open, and her voice.

"Rooker?"

He sat up and wiped his face with his shirt. Then he turned halfway toward her. "Hi, Laura."

"What are you doing here?"

"I couldn't sleep." He wiped his nose with the back of his hand. His legs ached. "I decided to go for a run. To be honest, I didn't know where I was running to. And then I ended up here. Why are you up?"

In regard to her sleep, Laura was a creature of habit. She was always up and about around 6:00 a.m. This was too early for her.

"The doorbell camera went off. Do you want to come in? I can make some coffee."

Rooker envisioned his son's bedroom door closed, and in his mind he slowly backed away from it. He shook his head so hard that it hurt. "Maybe next time. I'll let you get back to bed."

He pushed off the cold ground to his feet and noticed the unmarked Ford Interceptor a few houses down. *What a fool you must look like,* he thought.

"Rooker," she called out to him while he began to walk away. He stopped. "It'll kill you if you let it."

He cleared the rasp from his throat and for a moment imagined his thoughts suffocating him with a plastic bag and his fears stabbing him all over with knives. He offered her a half smile.

"I know," he said.

Sometimes, he still wished it would.

When he got back to the hotel, he showered and changed his clothes. He made a fresh cup of black coffee and switched between sipping from that and a bottled water.

He wanted another crack at Tate Meachum, but Eckhart assured him that wasn't happening. Not yet. There would have to be stricter protocols set in place for him to return, since his last visit ended in the Madman biting off the tip of his own finger.

Funny how that works. He'd rather take another bullet than be locked in a room with Meachum, but he needed whatever it was he had.

Just as he'd sat down behind his computer screen at the little desk in his room, a knock came at the door. He got up to answer it and put his eye up to the peephole. It was Tess.

The latch clanged against the door, and he pulled it open.

"Hey," she said.

"Hey."

"I want to be transparent with you."

"Okay," he said as he stepped aside so she could walk into the room.

"I spoke to Peter Sundgren two years ago. After Caldwell . . ."

"And?"

"And he told me about the girl."

Rooker shrugged dismissively. "What girl might that be?"

"The one who disappeared when your father was active. Olivia Campbell. She's the one from the story you wrote. The girl you killed."

He shook his head. "You have no idea—"

"Save it. She even lived on Deer Lake. Sundgren is positive all these years later that Gunner killed her. But your father didn't kill her. We both know her head would be gone. *You did.* She's the girl under the floor, Rooker. Well, congratulations. Her body was in such bad shape, she could never be identified."

"I will say that hurts coming from you. I respected you once. But this is your problem. You can cast all the judgment you want. After two years, you have the balls to come here and accuse me of murder when you executed two men in cold blood. Jan Cullen and Clyde Miller. Tell me it wasn't you. They raped your mother. They're the reason your father killed himself. I'm assuming Martin figured it out, which is why you two haven't spoken since."

"Yeah?" She crossed her arms. "Prove it."

He laughed. "You walked right up and shot Miller in the face. Then you went upstairs and knocked, probably let Cullen think that it was Miller at the door. Then when he opened it, *bang*, you killed him too. That's why you didn't fight Larsson when he got rid of you. Isn't that right? And you've come all this way at the FBI's call, knowing that it's only because of *me* that you're here, because it's the last chance you'll get to work an investigation."

She said nothing.

"Get over yourself," he continued. "You keep trying to hold on to this idea that you're a better person than I am—high and mighty, righteous—but you're *worse*. Anything I've done, I was forced to do. I'd be dead if I didn't. You had a choice. Now if that's it—"

"*I trusted you.*"

"Yeah. I trusted you too, *once*."

"Eckhart wants us outside in five." She turned away and left him standing there.

◆ ◆ ◆

Tess steadied herself against the wall as soon as she was out of Rooker's view. Had he just confessed? She had been right all this time? The nights obsessing over the bones discovered beneath Lindström Manor . . . Rooker really killed her. She tried to tell Martin and Millie, and they hadn't believed her. But she was right. Olivia Campbell was the dead girl beneath the cottage.

◆ ◆ ◆

Rooker forced himself to breathe. He and Tess hadn't spoken since Millie's funeral. Tess had been one of the few people he had trusted, but whether she was still angry with him or with herself, it seemed that her guilt and rage had set its sights on Rooker. As he grabbed the last of his things before heading downstairs, he told himself it didn't matter. The two of them would work together one last time, and then they'd likely never speak again. He thought of Laura standing at the door watching him cry on the ground, wondered if he was ruining whatever life she'd managed to build since he'd left.

Eckhart and his team were milling around in the lobby. As he approached, Tess looked away from him with her arms locked across her chest.

The air was warmer now than during his morning run, and he started to sweat as the group crossed the parking lot to a pair of SUVs. Quincy and Hall climbed into one, while Eckhart gestured for him to get into the car Esparza was driving. Rooker was relieved to see Tess had taken the passenger seat next to her, leaving the back seat to him and Eckhart.

"We found something," Eckhart said as Esparza pulled out to follow Quincy and Hall. "This was discovered late last night, about a half mile west of the drainpipe. When we didn't find anything aside from the body and our junkie friend Boots, I widened our search grid. The four corners were tacked into the ground."

Rooker took the evidence bag out of Eckhart's hands. In it was a physical copy of the *Los Angeles Times*. Four thumbtacks had been removed from its corner margins.

'THE MADMAN' KILLER APPREHENDED IN SOUTH PASADENA POLICE RAID

Scribbled all over the paper, large across the words, squeezed in between lines and around the margins, were red letters that said: WRONG.

Chapter 10

November 22, 2021

How could he have been so stupid?

It had been six years to the day. How could he forget? The date Meachum was arrested. Six years later, they found the woman in the drainpipe.

But why now? Why would the killer let Meachum take the fall—or the credit—entirely for six years?

"We got a print," Eckhart said, breaking Rooker from his daze like the snap of a finger. "Before anyone gets excited, it's too perfect and it's the victim's. We've identified her as thirty-eight-year-old Natalie Carlisle. She was a research fellow at UC Irvine."

UC Irvine was an hour and a half away. Where Asim Bell would've been picked up in Oceanside was more than an hour away too. Someone went through the trouble of choosing them, picking them up, and escorting them quite a ways before dumping them in Hemet. What the hell was going on?

"Research assistant for what?" Tess asked.

"The Department of Neurobiology and Behavior," Esparza said. "She works with a professor of psychiatry and human behavior. Name's James Bardot. Get this: Ms. Carlisle was doing a study on psychopaths."

One thing Rooker felt in his bones: Natalie Carlisle was carefully selected, as was Asim Bell, as was the drainpipe for a dumping ground.

Not only had the killer murdered a woman studying psychopaths, but they'd picked an addict to find her body, in a remote place far away from any main road. What he wondered now was where Natalie was taken and murdered.

"Did the family have anything to say about Natalie's last few days?" Tess asked.

"They haven't been notified yet," said Eckhart. "Quincy and Hall are going to talk to the family now. In the meantime, we're taking a little day trip to UC Irvine. We need to find out exactly what Natalie Carlisle was working on."

◆ ◆ ◆

On the way to the campus, Rooker searched for information on Natalie. There were hits. More than he'd expected.

She had her name attached to papers published in several prestigious journals, including *Journal of Neuroscience*, *Human Brain Mapping*, and *Brain and Behavior*. The studies cited mostly centered around genes and gray matter in the brain, with some focused on schizophrenia and personality disorders.

The home of the Department of Neurobiology and Behavior was a five-story building with large beige towers and a seafoam-green exterior. It reminded Rooker of a New Age version of the Colosseum in Rome if it had been dropped into a massive futuristic greenhouse. Beneath a hazy blue sky, greenery wrapped all around the building, except for an unsightly large, flat patch of rock and dusty ground that resembled desert.

They found Dr. James Bardot in his office. He was a heavyset man with peculiar features. He resembled a hobbit, with curly taupe hair and a beard that appeared frostbitten and rodent-like eyes adorned with crow's-feet and dark bags.

When he saw the four of them, he pulled his glasses down from the top of his head to cover his eyes and adjusted the stretched collar of a loose-fitting brown floral polo shirt. Rooker thought he resembled a recent divorcé headed for Hawaii.

"Dr. Bardot?" Eckhart extended a hand. "I'm Special Agent Scott Eckhart, FBI. I apologize for showing up unannounced, but unfortunately, we don't have time to be delicate. I'm sorry to tell you that your colleague, Natalie Carlisle, was murdered."

"What? Natalie . . ."

"The body found in the drainpipe in Hemet? It's been on the news. You're aware of this?" Eckhart asked crisply. Bardot winced and shook his head yes. Eckhart continued. "It was Ms. Carlisle. We're investigating her murder and whether it was connected to her work here."

"I . . . I don't know what to say. How tragic." Bardot's lips narrowed, and he shook his head again in disbelief.

While Eckhart answered Bardot's questions, Rooker glanced around the lab: glass equipment with various labels and colored caps, vials, droppers, blue vial trays, clear bottles filled with clear liquids, gloves, boxes, trays, and all sorts of machines throughout.

James Bardot's office was clean and clutter-free. There was a small collection of magazines on a bookcase along with a few awards. A newer Apple desktop monitor sat atop a dark-brown desk. But the room was also full of color—on one wall, there was a row of brain scans, some with splotches of red, orange, green, and yellow. Rooker stepped closer to inspect them.

"Gray matter," Bardot said. "The one on the left, the orbital cortex is firing. This is the center for an individual's ethical behavior and moral decision-making. It controls the amygdala, which is vital in our memory and regulates our emotional response, but it also is in control of our reactions, our perceptions, to fear and aggression."

In the brain scan on the right, the orbital cortex was barely lit up. Rooker already knew what that meant. He was looking at the brain of a potential psychopath, if not a confirmed killer.

"This one, if you haven't guessed, is consistent with a psychopath. Now, psychopathy really is far more complex than the average person believes. This isn't a lecture, sorry. But if you look here, the limbic system is shut off. The amygdala is firing, but the orbital cortex is not. They share all the genetic markings. But believe it or not, this isn't a serial killer. They've never killed anyone."

"Not that you know of," Esparza said.

Dr. Bardot smiled. "I believe I would know if I'd killed anyone."

A pin drop in the room could have been heard. It took a lot for Rooker to be stunned, but even he could hear only his own heart thumping behind the walls of his chest.

James Bardot must have an airtight alibi, Rooker thought. Because otherwise he just shot himself up to the top of the suspect list.

"That's *your* brain, Dr. Bardot?" Eckhart said.

"It is. Ironically, I have killers in my lineage that date back to the late 1800s. The only reason I believe I'm not one of them is that I never sustained any physical or emotional trauma. Nature versus nurture. I believe Mr. Lindström here has written about that."

So Bardot knows who I am. Bet he would love to get a look at my brain. Rooker imagined that after his argument with Tess, she'd like nothing more than to use the doctor's expertise to paint him as a killer.

"When was the last time you saw Ms. Carlisle?" Eckhart asked.

"Thursday," he said. "Thursday evening."

"Did she seem different to you at all lately, or that day?"

"Yes. Very, actually. She was excited. More than usual. She'd been working on identifying psychopaths through the study of their monoamine neurotransmitters. Serotonin, dopamine, adrenaline, noradrenaline. She was researching MAOA and CDH13 among violent offenders. The monoamine oxidase A genotype, or MAOA, has to do with a low dopamine turnover rate. And CDH13, or cadherin-13, is an important gene seen in ADHD, which is common in violent criminals. They're now known as the serial killer genes.

"Natalie wanted to find a way to identify potential violent offenders who weren't already in any criminal database. She thought that maybe you could identify them early enough . . . *before* they became violent criminals."

"So, she wanted to find a criminal who wasn't already convicted," Tess said, and Rooker couldn't help but feel that remark was pointed at him.

"Precisely. But then something changed. Later in the day when I was getting ready to go home, Natalie was frantic, stowing all her things in her bag."

"Is that strange, to take your work home with you?"

"No. I oftentimes back up my files on my personal laptop so that I can get some work done from home. But she was taking *all* her files. Her data. Her samples. *Everything.* I thought that maybe it was just a breakthrough she'd made somewhere, and she didn't want anyone else to see it. But this was . . . compulsive behavior. She kept checking her phone. I asked her if everything was all right, and she smiled. It was unlike anything I'd witnessed from her. Anyway, now that she's gone and you're here in my office . . . I think it's safe to say she did it."

"Did what, exactly?" Eckhart said.

"She was looking at DNA samples from an old study for genetic predisposition to Alzheimer's, the candidates of which had either a parent or grandparent with the disease. When they contributed their DNA to this study, there would have been no way to foresee that someday a research assistant would go poking through those tests for evidence of other disorders . . . So to answer your question, Mr. Eckhart, I think somewhere in the bunch, Natalie found someone with all the serial killer genes."

Chapter 11

Ten miles outside Downtown LA, parked over the lines in a secluded space of a pet store in Culver City, the Madman drummed his gloved fingers slowly on the steering column. The gloves were black, more importantly cotton, which didn't leave prints. The steady muted sound reminded him of a muffled scream.

One by one, he plucked the material from his fingers and tossed the gloves on the dash beside a teeny-tiny bright-yellow collar.

The Madman pulled his cap low, stepped out of the black van, and marched through the automatic doors. This was the third pet store he'd hit. Behind the cash register, an auburn-haired girl with a scrunchy ponytail and moss-green T-shirt looked up at him and smiled before returning her eyes and fingers to the cell phone hidden behind the desk. Walking past aisles of colorful squeak toys and a wide selection of kibble and wet food and treats and various sizes of aquarium tanks and cages and beds, he followed the sound of yapping and cawing and caterwauling until he locked eyes with the caged beasts at the back of the store. He paced slowly with his arms behind his back. The options were scarce.

There was a dark Labrador named Duke, two Yorkshire terriers named Cosmo and Wanda, and a couple of terrier mixed breeds. Gray cats and calicos and all-black cats. But there was one tuxedo that looked just about right: short black hair with white fur on the chest and feet and a leaf-shaped blotch of it on the face and a black-spotted nose. Her name was Lucky. If anyone was lucky, it was him and not the cat.

The last cat he owned caught him in the dark hours of the night carrying a large piece of a woman's skin into the garage. Natalie Carlisle had managed to track him down. But he'd taken care of it. Now, the cat was the only living, breathing witness to what he'd done. And each meow that left its mouth was a voiceless accusation of what he'd done.

"Shuuuut. Uuup," he'd hiss back. *"Shuuut up! Shuut up! Shut up!"*

Each time he heard that damn *meooww*, the thought of his secret coming to light angered him. *Meowww. It's him, he's the killer. The Madman.* He couldn't bear that cat any longer. He'd driven until he found a young girl walking alone, dumped the cat in her arms, and drove off.

The Madman smiled.

At the cash register, he beamed at the young woman and frowned when she returned one with crooked teeth. "I'd like to take Lucky home. Today, if possible."

Thirty minutes later he'd made his way back to the van with a blue-and-gray carrier in one hand and tossed it to the floor beside him.

His head began to hurt again. The front of his skull throbbed anytime he looked down. His eyes filled with painful waves. He knew it was the gene. Damn Nana and her ugly disease. His thoughts were escaping him, and that was his worst fear: forgetting everything he'd done.

He didn't want to forget.

When the van eased into the driveway, the Madman killed the engine. The nondescript vehicle was a business expense, a simple 225-horsepower, 4.6-liter V-8 that could carry up to fifteen people, though it had never transported more than one person at a time. He unlatched the door and pulled Lucky out of the carrier. Then he put the yellow collar around her neck, thinking how easy it would be to snap it.

"You're Miss Freckles now, got it?"

The Madman carried the cat under his arm and inside the front door.

"Honey, is that you?" a voice called out from the other room. Vivian.

"Yeah, dear." He tossed his keys into the tray beside the door. "Look who I found."

Moments later, Vivian turned the corner and smiled. She folded a dish towel in her hands. "Where did you find her?"

"She was a few blocks down. She's hungry."

Vivian kissed him on the cheek and patted the stranger on the head. She didn't notice the purrs that sounded foreign and nothing like their daughter's previous pet. "She's going to be *so* happy. Kaity!" she called. "I'll get some food for her."

Miss Freckles slept at the foot of Kaity's bed every night. Somehow, he'd have to get this damn cat to fall asleep in her room this evening.

Just then, a small figure with braces and hints of her mother's features came into the space and sprinted at him with the scrawny gallop of a young deer. "Is that—"

"You bet, sweetie. Miss Freckles."

He handed the stranger off to his daughter and kissed her on the forehead. She beamed and cried. Then he went to the door that led into the garage, unlocked it, and shut it quietly behind him. The garage was where he *really* worked. It had the musty smell of a basement, laced with chemicals. This was where he'd treated Natalie Carlisle's skin and made his own homemade glue. His smile left. He had work to do.

Chapter 12

Natalie Carlisle's ranch home in the West Floral Park area of Santa Ana was modest but tidy. The exterior was white with a new roof, round rocks bordered the dark-green front door, and a tall white fence surrounded the home. At the back of the house was a small pool and a large white stucco garage with a black door.

Quincy and Hall hadn't gleaned much from their talk with Natalie's parents—just that she was highly intelligent, but she never had much of a life outside her work in the lab—and so they had started processing the scene. The forensics team was still gathering gear from their van when the four arrived. As he stared at the front of the house, Rooker felt his heart start to pound, and he saw flashes of yellow police tape outside his old home, his son sitting up slowly in the twin-size bed, glaring at him from dead black eyes. *No. Stop. It isn't real.* He snapped out of it when Tess touched his arm. She handed him a pair of booties and gloves. She didn't look so steady herself.

As Rooker made his way into the home, the first thing he noticed was nothing. There was no furniture. As he walked down the hall off the living room, in every room he passed, it was the same. Nothing. The house reeked of bleach.

What in the world . . .

"Here." Hall poked his head out from a bedroom at the end of the hallway and gestured to Rooker. Esparza, Quincy, and Tess were already inside. He heard Eckhart's impatient footsteps come up behind him.

This room was empty too, except for a small corkboard on the wall that reminded Rooker of the one in Tess's old office. It looked like a police investigation, only instead of victims and suspects there were photographs of Scott Eckhart and his team pinned up by thumbtacks, with a reel of string running all around them.

Somehow, the killer had already been watching them. How was that possible?

And then there was a newspaper of sorts. Same masthead and font as the *Los Angeles Times* print edition, though it was clearly handmade.

TATE MEACHUM INNOCENT: 'MADMAN' KILLER STILL AT LARGE

"Cute," Eckhart said.

But that's when Rooker realized there was something very wrong with the texture of it. The little bumps and grooves, and that awful color . . .

Eckhart moved closer to it.

"Wait," Rooker said. "I wouldn't touch that . . ."

"What?" Eckhart said.

The size of it looked awfully familiar. His mind did its best to recall the dimensions. *Sixteen by twelve, was it?* "Remember he skinned part of her back?"

Eckhart looked at Rooker and then at the corkboard again.

"Christ."

And then there was a note at the bottom that looked like a redacted file, with words crossed out with black marker. It was a piece of one of Rooker's articles for the *Times*. He read his byline and the scattered letters that weren't crossed out.

ROOKER LINDSTRÖM

Welcome home.

In the garage was where they found everything. Every piece of furniture that was inside Natalie Carlisle's home. Sofas, nightstands, coffee tables, even kitchen appliances. All of it had been cut open or disassembled and searched meticulously, based on the white clouds of stuffing tossed in the corner and the pieces of furniture unscrewed and smashed to pieces.

It would take a crime scene unit some time to go through every piece, but Rooker was confident they wouldn't find a single strand of hair or any piece of DNA that didn't belong to Natalie. Worse, there seemed to be no sign of any files or a computer.

Chapter 13

November 22, 2021

She wrote their names on the page again. Heard them in her own mind's hollow whisper.

Millie Langston. John Riggs. Joe Harlow.

A sharp pain lodged itself in her fingers. It was from writing over and over again, pressing too hard, hard enough to puncture through the paper with their names, squeezing the pen too tight.

Tess and Rooker were now staying at a Best Western on South Sepulveda Boulevard, under two miles from the FBI's LA field office. You'd think the FBI could spring for the Beverly Hilton or maybe something a little nicer, but it would do.

She tossed the hotel brochure into an empty drawer. She was living out of her unpacked carry-on bag.

She had replaced the brochure with the black notebook that now sat in her lap. It reminded her why she was here. This case would be how she'd repent for their deaths and maybe move on. Maybe. What it was she'd move on to next, hell if she knew. Being a detective was the only thing she was good at. Despite Rooker rightfully calling her a killer, being back at a crime scene and a person-of-interest interview felt strangely comforting. It was the only thing she knew.

But now, she regretted following in her father's footsteps and not taking Joe Harlow's advice as a little girl. *Anything but a cop.*

On bad nights she'd write the name of every murder victim in her cases, even a girl they never found but she knew to be dead. She wrote it now. *Amy Berglund.*

Amy was the reason Millie became a detective. The fact that Millie died at Hartley Caldwell's hands—the same as Amy Berglund—made Tess want to cry and scream. She'd done plenty of that the last two years.

Tess sat up in bed. She closed the notebook and tucked it away in a narrow space between the mattress and nightstand. When her eyes shut, she saw them again: Clyde Miller sparking up in that loud, rusty Pontiac, and Jan Cullen when the door swung open. Then she saw Miller with a bullet in his head and brain matter in his lap and Cullen with a bloody opening in his chest.

She'd driven past the apartment that night when the police arrived, the street flickering blue and red while officers she knew canvassed the neighborhood, put down evidence markers, and barricaded the street with yellow tape and sawhorses.

The thought of it all left her skull pounding. She went to the mini-bar and pulled out two Heinekens, downing half of the first one before she ran out of breath.

She tilted her head to peek at the nips of straight alcohol. No one actually enjoyed liquor neat. That was her philosophy. It was a machismo thing. Hold a straight face while liquid burns as it goes down. She pictured herself back in a cop bar surrounded by men who tried to drink just like that, especially in her presence. She swung the door shut and listened to the glass bottles clink.

When her phone began to buzz and rattle on top of the nightstand, she read his name on the display, sighed, and cursed in a low hiss. "Fuck."

She scratched her head and winced before answering. "Hello, Lead Detective," she said and took another long gulp.

"How's the weather?" She heard a smile in Martin Keene's hushed voice.

"Oh, great. Sunny and seventy. *During the day*," she added. She checked the time: 9:55 p.m. It was 11:55 p.m. in Minnesota. *I've got one killer on the loose and one in the next room,* she wanted to add. But Rooker was right—she was just as bad as he was, if not worse. "Why are you up?"

"You hear that?" Suddenly she heard a floor-rumbling snore. "You try to sleep next to that. Sunny and seventy, sheesh. Freezing my ass off here. Anyway, I figured you'd be awake."

"How's Sheila?"

"She's good. We miss you . . . Vic and Xander are good too."

Vic Sterling and Xander Whitlock . . . her old team. The team that *she* was in charge of. *Was.*

She did her best not to spite Martin for taking her old position, but it wasn't easy. He was more than capable of the job. She was the one who told the old prick Larsson to give it to Keene when he canned her—but when she pictured Martin sitting behind her desk, it bothered her.

"Yeah? Tell them hi for me."

"I will. How's the case going?"

"It's too early to tell. No real leads that'll take us anywhere . . ." She gulped another mouthful. "On one hand, I feel like I'm back where I belong." Though she was haunted by the most gruesome cases, the ones that had pried away pieces of her, she missed leading the team. She stared at a spot on her hand, where a scar the shape of a snowflake dug deeper into her fingertip than ever. "On the other, I know I'm only here to keep *him* in line."

"That's not true. You're damn good at what you do. You know that, and they know that. Plus, you know better than anyone that Rooker doesn't play well with others. But he knows you. He'll play ball with you by his side."

"*Please*, Martin. I'm not here to work an investiga—"

She stopped herself. She knew that telling Martin about Esparza's secret agenda would benefit no one. He couldn't do anything to help her.

She'd come to know Rooker better than most. Though she had an unrelenting anger for him, and at herself for sleeping with him in a moment of weakness, he was much more than the son of Gunner Lindström, one of the most famous serial killers in Minnesota history.

"Well maybe if you work well with them, they'll bring you in. FBI Agent Tess Harlow. Has a nice ring to it."

She drank again. "Yeah, we'll see about that."

"I'll check in again soon. Be safe."

"Okay," she answered.

The line went dead, dead as she felt, and suddenly she missed Martin Keene more now than ever.

But when the tracker on her phone pinged, she thought about the stolen FN 509 handgun floating somewhere down the Mississippi River, two dead faces, and their executioner.

Chapter 14

Rooker couldn't sleep. Not that there was anything wrong with the room or the bed. Both were fine. But his mind was a game of tug-of-war, tethered too far in the direction of consciousness.

He was rereading his personal copy of *The Black Echo*, which Eckhart had given back after forensics came up with nothing. No fingerprints on any of the pages, aside from his and his ex-wife's. When his brain was too busy to focus on the story, he set the book on the nightstand and flipped off the small lamp switch.

He called a cab and walked into the hotel lobby. Ten minutes later, a yellow Crown Victoria pulled up to the front doors. Rooker zipped his jacket and stepped out into the night.

The cab took him from LA back to Hemet: Soboba Street. Holy Spirit Catholic Church had five small archways on either side and two larger arches at the entrance. A light at the top of the building illuminated the gold cross. Four trees were planted out front, where two lampposts did little to light his way.

Inside, there were only a few people scattered on the pews. The liver-spotted bald head of an older gentleman sat stiffly, and a woman with curly brown hair sat with her head drooped to the floor. Rooker snuck into the end of the pew at the far back.

For a long while, he stared up at the stained glass above a large cross where Jesus hung. Now that he thought about it, the few times he was in a church, he always stared off at the paintings and the sculptures. The saints. The architecture.

His phone lit up with an email from Dezzy King, his contact at the *LA Times*. Desmond King was a large, trim Black man with stubble hair plugs as fake as his teeth. Rooker had never met him, but he'd seen photos—always in a tailored suit and brown-tinted glasses—of the *Times* senior editor.

Dezzy wanted him to write an op-ed piece on what it felt like to be back in California covering the Madman again. Rooker closed out of it.

When the door opened twenty minutes after he'd sat down, he didn't turn to see who it was. Instead, he waited until he heard the creak of the pew beneath their weight, got up, and walked out.

He stood there with his back to the cool stucco. Standing still in the shadows. Waiting. It was only a few minutes before they walked out, looking left and right.

From his pocket, Rooker tossed the device, the size and shape of a quarter, at her feet. "Why are you following me?"

He watched her body tense. In a black long-sleeved shirt and a pair of blue jeans, she snickered, and her head dropped the slightest bit, a few hair strands falling in front of her face.

"Did Eckhart send you?"

"No," she said. "He didn't send me."

Tess Harlow stood there, unable to look at him, if he had to guess.

"After all we've been through, you still have the nerve to treat me like a suspect." He shook his head, and before she could object, he continued. "This is where my son was baptized. Kid cried like a banshee." He laughed. "Me . . . I've never been a church person. I can't say I've ever believed in any of this. I don't believe that a sin can be cleansed. All of mine—my father's, even—seem to follow me everywhere I go.

"Anyway, Laura wanted him to be baptized Catholic. Her parents were heavy on the faith." He sighed. "*Dawn and Richard . . .* Never had much use for me. What good parents would? I had a father who severed heads and a mother whose mind crumbled and died. How's that for your daughter's in-laws?

"The only one who ever embraced me was Laura's sister, Cora. But I haven't heard a word from her since . . . I couldn't say.

"Still . . . part of me hopes that all of this is real . . . I'd like to think my son is in a better place than this one."

Tess sighed. "The only thought that comes to mind in this place is chasing Henry Hult through the church. Gunshots. Xander on the ground, bleeding."

"That was a long time ago."

"Then why does it still feel like it happened yesterday?"

"Because nightmares are the strongest when they come from real memories. When you jump up and see the monster's face or feel yourself falling or whoever's chasing you finally stops, you can tell yourself it was just a dream. But for you and me, we aren't so lucky. We've lived our nightmares."

"They never stop, do they."

Rooker didn't answer. Because he knew better than anyone, tragedy is lifelong and timeless. And in his case, repeating.

"Your ex—Laura—she seems great."

He smiled. "She is."

"After you caught Meachum, why did you run? Why not go back to her?"

"The same reason you come to a church and see Xander bleeding on the ground and Elias Cole standing over Hult's dead body, knowing now that he was Sadler all along. Every time I look at her, I see my dead son and know it's my fault."

Chapter 15

In the dark hours of morning, Rooker's eyelids flickered violently. He was fast asleep, having driven back to LA with Tess. It had been years since he'd dreamt of that day. February 19, 1997. The day the police came to the door to finally take Gunner away. You would think it would have been one of the best days of his life. Only it wasn't.

He's lying on his stomach reading a tattered hardcover book on the living room floor. *The Client* by John Grisham. A legal thriller about young brothers who stumble upon a man in the woods about to kill himself. It made him wish he had a brother. His mother sat in a spindle-backed wooden chair behind the kitchen table. The crossword in the *New York Times* is folded over and stained with tea, and she dices golden potatoes. His father is in the kitchen washing a cut on his hand. A small gash between his thumb and wrist. There's an old wooden calendar that hangs from the wallpapered wall beyond it. The months and days interchangeable pieces. Sirens chirp outside. Through the window, blue and red lights flicker. That's when he stands up to look and wanders into the kitchen. The door blasts open. Fast, snap-of-the-finger quick. They move inside. Boots stomping. Large, faceless men in tactical gear. Helmets hiding whoever they are. A few with their assault rifle sights trained on Gunner.

"Get on the ground!"

Gunner doesn't move. He doesn't so much as look at them. He doesn't glance over at his wife or Rooker. His head is down. The edge of his face blank.

They slam Gunner up against the wall. The wooden pieces of the calendar fall to the floor in slow motion. They snatch his arms behind his back and snap the cuffs in place around his wrists.

When he still doesn't move, they tug his shoulder and shove him. And then he walks out the front door as though it were an ordinary day and he's leaving for work.

A few more people enter the house then, wearing bulletproof vests. One of them holsters a sidearm. Rooker can't actually remember who it is, but now his mind fills in the blank face with Peter Sundgren's.

His eyes snapped open. Heart thrashing, he put a hand to his sweat-soaked chest. The shirt was drenched. He listened to the racing of his pulse. The snap and click of the refrigerator in his room. The ringing in his ears.

He twisted his knuckles into the crusted corners of his eyes and strutted over to the desk with a fire in his belly. Seeing the *Los Angeles Times* logo in bold, black letters above his name was always satisfying, but it had been a long time since a story made his hands jitter above the keys or his heart thump in his chest. In fact, the last time that happened was when he was writing about the Madman murders, and that fire within him quickly went out, shrunk into a black pit of fear.

Several hours passed. He wrote about how he felt to be back in California, the dream of the day his father was arrested, and his days covering the Madman murders. He wrote about viewing Natalie Carlisle at the same mortuary where his son had been examined. He wrote about his encounter with Tate Meachum at Pelican Bay, which he knew Dezzy King would eat up.

By the time he was finished, his story was one thousand words. Most *LA Times* articles were tapped off at the 750 mark, but Rooker had a feeling Dezzy would cut very little of it.

Rooker opened his email, attached the file, and hit send.

Chapter 16

November 23, 2021

At two in the morning, the Madman sat bolt upright. His eyes went wide. *Miss Freckles?* The last Miss Freckles would caterwaul just the same as the one that woke him.

Had he dreamt it?

His wife snored sporadically beside him, like the critters in the dewed grass who chirp and then fall silent for a moment that feels long only because of the absence of the beat. He liked peace and quiet when he slept. Now, as he listened to the grotesque sound, his eyes rolled back and shut. He took a long breath and opened them.

Slipping out from beneath the sheets, his feet gripped the cold wood floor. He tried his best to skulk out of the room—the floorboards creaking hauntingly beneath his weight—and down the hall to Kaity's bedroom. He pushed the door open. Sleeping on the blanket beside his daughter—not at her feet like the former Miss Freckles—the cat purred, its belly climbing and falling.

Stupid fucking cat. The Madman walked into the room silently, staring daggers into the ball of fluff. He picked up the new Miss Freckles and put her on the blanket beside his daughter's feet. Then he returned to the hallway.

When he sauntered into the garage, he didn't flip the switch on the wall. He didn't want the hum of the fluorescent light above him. He wanted to be bathed in silent black.

Once the room swallowed him whole, the stench of death hit him like a jaw-shattering kick to the teeth. The scraps of Natalie Carlisle left over from his special edition were getting ripe.

The Madman pulled a metal shovel with a wooden handle down from the wall. Then he grabbed the plastic bag—formerly clear, now darkened and rotting—and strolled out the door and into the darkness of the backyard.

The night air should have felt refreshing. There was a cool wind that gently rippled his clothes. But instead, he felt like he was on the receiving end, a victim of himself. The darkness lurked menacingly. Watching his every move.

The earth was cold. Hard, as though it were compacted with a bulldozer.

The Madman jabbed the blade spear-like into the ground. *Crunch.* Then, with a death grip on the handle and his knees bent, he pried the soil loose. There was a metallic whisk as he flung brittle chunks of ground from the blade. He dug. And dug. A mound of dirt clumps and rock grew beside the fattening hole. His back began to scream.

He kept going. Three, maybe four feet deep. Too shallow and you risk animals digging up the remains.

So he dug blind, quietly in the night.

Sweat had begun to tick down his face when just then, behind him, the porch light burned bright. The bolt unlatched. Out stepped his wife onto the back porch in pajama bottoms and a white top. Two little peaks in the cotton where the cold hardened her nipples.

She crossed her arms across her chest, shivering. She whispered, "What are you doing out here?"

He knew he must look crazy. Blank-faced and sweaty, digging suspiciously in the dark hours of morning. The Madman jammed the shovel into the hole. The crunch of soil and gravel clashing with metal.

He did his best impression of a man who'd seen something awful. "Go back to bed. It's late."

"Yeah, I know. I woke up in an empty bed. Why do you have a shov—"

"I heard a noise out here. An animal screaming. A possum got caught in the trap."

She walked forward. "What trap—"

"No, hon. You don't want to see it. The head is gone."

His wife stopped. "Are you all right?"

"Yeah."

"Come back to bed."

"I will. Once I'm finished. Promise."

His wife turned on her heel. The Madman looked up at his daughter's room. The night-light was on. Staring at him from behind the fogged window, his daughter watched him. *Damn it.* But the bag was closed. Double knotted. There was no way she'd know what was inside. In the morning he'd spin her the same story he'd told his wife: that a possum got caught in a trap. A trap that he never had. And that Daddy did the humane thing and buried the possum, because that's what you're supposed to do when something dies. When he waved, she waved back. And then she disappeared. He imagined she'd gotten back into bed.

He dropped the remains of Natalie Carlisle into the hole and dumped shovelfuls of the piled soil back over it. Once the hole was filled even with the yard, he patted it down and returned the shovel to its place on the wall in the garage.

In the bathroom he shut the door silently behind him, flipped the dimmer switch, and changed out of his T-shirt, which stuck to him in the areas damp with sweat. Kicked off his shoes and removed his pants and underwear. He fought the rigidness of his muscles and craned over his shoulder to peer into his reflection. The muscles in his back were flexed. Painfully so. And there at the low base of his neck, between his trap muscles, was the black ink needled into his skin. The Madman stood naked. Staring at the word FEAR.

Chapter 17

Rooker followed Scott Eckhart into a large conference room in the FBI's LA field office.

Esparza, Quincy, and Hall were absorbed in their laptops. Barry Lewis from CS was slowly flipping through crime scene photos. Tess was sipping vacantly from a cup of coffee. She looked tired but more relaxed than usual. He could relate. Though he hadn't gotten much sleep after sending his op-ed off to Dezzy, he felt lighter and clearer than he had in months.

"Esparza, what do we have for a profile?" Eckhart said as he dropped his coat onto a chair.

Confused, her eyes narrowed, and her head swiveled to give Eckhart the side-eye. "*Profile?* We don't have anything to go off."

"Pull Boots out of his trash bin, see if we get something new."

"He said they used a voice modulator. We can't—"

"Maybe he'll be able to remember something. Someone that looked out of place by the docks. A detail of the car, even the trunk he was in. We need to get something out of him. Suspects—"

Esparza implored, "He was told he'd be killed. I don't think he was trying to kick at the taillights to signal help or break through the back seat to escape. He was scared."

Eckhart crossed his arms. "Yeah, well, if I'm scared and think I'm going to die, I'll die fighting."

Hall changed the subject. "Well, we've gotta put the doc on the list, right? Bardot?"

"James Bardot," Eckhart said. "Hall and Quincy, check out his alibi. If there's a hole—*one pinprick-size hole*—we put him on the board. Hell, maybe we still do. Lewis, look into the old victims, see if there's any connection to Ms. Carlisle. And let's get forensics on the lovely newspaper he made for us. See what they can find. Esparza, we've gotta get a profile going. Bring Boots in."

The old victims . . . That didn't sit right with Rooker. His son was one of them.

"Lindström, Harlow, thoughts?"

"It couldn't hurt to bring in Joey Miggs," Rooker suggested. "He worked with Meachum, was his alibi—a pretty weak alibi—for Julieta Rollins's murder. Miggs and Meachum were staying in adjacent rooms at a Motel 6 the night she was killed."

"You think it could be him?"

"No," Rooker said. "But your colleagues dropped the ball on Miggs the first time around. I thought maybe I'd save you from following in their footsteps."

Scott Eckhart was unraveling. His smug face turned flush. The arrogant smile had faded. Usually, his hair was held flawlessly in place, but today the few out-of-place threads gave him a disheveled look. He was doing now what Rooker had watched Tess do. Despite his bravado, he was no better than her. If anything, he was less experienced.

"Funny," Eckhart said. "I remember Warrel Haney writing that *you* were Meachum's accomplice. At least you're already here."

Rooker let out a hot breath and squeezed a fist so tight that his knuckle popped. A fury singed with the force of a purpling sunburn beneath his skin, where every piece of him wanted a crack at FBI Agent Scott Eckhart.

"I wouldn't go there if I were you," Tess said to Eckhart.

"You wouldn't be threatening an FBI agent—"

"How about everyone settles down," Esparza tried.

"At one point, *she* thought it was him too. Ain't that right, Harlow?"

"Enough!" Esparza shouted. "We all want the same thing, right?"

No one said a thing. Quincy and Hall exchanged glances. Eckhart fixed a loose hair that fell over his brow.

"Speaking of accomplices," Tess said, "we never did figure out how Caldwell and Meachum were communicating." She turned to Rooker. "Any chance you could get Meachum to talk about that more?"

"That's a nonstarter," Eckhart said. "Meachum's not having any visitors—something about his safety."

"Then I need to see his mail," Rooker said.

"Why?" Eckhart sounded genuinely curious this time.

"He knew about the bones found beneath my cottage. Meachum has always been in the loop. He's communicating with someone."

"That's all public," Quincy said. "He could've gotten his hands on a newspaper."

"Yeah, and his appeals lawyer could be keeping him up to date on anything publicized," said Hall.

"Besides, the prison confiscates or censors most of his mail—whatever fan mail he gets from his crazy supporters," said Eckhart. "And correspondence from his appeals team would be considered confidential."

"He's talking to someone," Rooker said. "I know it. Everything that makes it into his cell, and any mail that he sends out, I want to see it."

"I'll see what I can do," Lewis volunteered. Rooker gave him a small nod of appreciation. Eckhart might be a prick, but at least he'd built a competent team.

When the congregation broke off to their assignments, Esparza said, "Don't worry about Eckhart. He's all right."

"I wasn't," Rooker replied, before Esparza's eyebrows raised and she too was gone.

"You good?" Tess asked him.

Rooker spat out, "Fine."

Chapter 18

Rooker set the dusty box down at the foot of Tess's bed and poured himself a glass of water from the pitcher. He closed his eyes and imagined a stiff drink—neat—but to his senses it was all too wrong. He sipped the bland liquid. It was after one o'clock, and he'd eaten only from the vending machine at the end of the corridor. A pack of Peanut M&M'S and a pair of protein bars. He tapped the edge of the box. "This is everything. Why is your room nicer than mine?"

She ignored him. "I want every victim on the wall." She had tacked up a map of California where a framed photo previously was. "Old victims with yellow pins, then Natalie Carlisle's home and the drainpipe with red pins. Let's throw the dock where Boots was taken up there as well."

Rooker lifted the lid off the box and pulled out a manila folder on each of the six victims. He spread them out on the bed in order. Then he had a thought. "The seventh victim."

She sighed. "Carlisle *is* the seventh victim."

"You know what I mean. Meachum drew seven tallies in his cell. If there's one that we don't know about, maybe they're the missing piece in all this. Maybe if we find them, it leads us to the killer."

"But we don't *have* a victim." She scratched her head. "Come on, Rooker. Six confirmed victims and he draws seven tallies. Don't you think it's just another way for Meachum to terrorize you from his cell?"

"You're right," he agreed. "This is all a game to him. Meachum's a lot of things, but he's not a liar."

"Okay. Let's say you're right." Tess uncapped a pen and swirled her hand over a blank sheet of paper. She tacked the question mark on the wall with #7. Then she moved Natalie Carlisle's photograph to the right of it. "We look at all the victims and treat one as unsolved. Either way, it helps narrow down the grid. If there is a victim to find, maybe it even leads to her—" She stopped.

"It's fine," he said. "All of his victims were female until I . . . wrote what I wrote."

"You gave the name Joey Miggs to Eckhart. Why?"

"Because it's the first case where Tate had an alibi for one of the murders, whether he wanted one or not—Julieta Rollins. Joey Miggs said they were staying in rooms next door to one another at Motel 6. Meachum doesn't strike me as someone who has a friend loyal enough to lie for him. And when Miggs was interviewed, he didn't make it sound like Meachum was one of his drinking buddies."

"For Miggs to provide an alibi, the police must've looked at him as a suspect too. An accomplice."

"Right. But Miggs . . . there's no way. He has an alibi for all of them. And the guy had a boating accident. He has a thirty-eight-foot lobster boat docked down in San Diego Bay. Traumatic finger amputation; got two of his fingers caught in a gill-net reel. He wears a prosthetic now. Miggs isn't the biggest guy—maybe five foot nine—and I can't see him dragging people around with one arm. Based on Boots's description, we're looking for someone much bigger and strong."

Rooker knew that eyewitnesses got things wrong all the time, but Tess didn't say another word.

◆ ◆ ◆

Half an hour later, the two of them had finished taking turns tacking photographs on the wall and jabbing pins in the map. The only photo that wasn't on the wall was his son's.

"It's like old times, huh?" she said.

Rooker shook his head. "I'm not sure we ever worked 'together.' You were too busy treating me like a suspect. Millie was the one—" He stopped himself.

"I miss her," Tess said.

You miss her? He responded angrily in his head. *What about me?* He pictured his closest friend curled up in a ball on that awful sofa that he'd decidedly kept. And then he saw her lying dead in his arms. *Damn you, Millie. Why did you have to leave me too? You would have loved to be a part of this one, Mill.* "Yeah, I miss her too."

Chapter 19

She was dying and she knew it. She'd be lucky to make it till daybreak.

She'd grown up in a rough area of Bed-Stuy, Brooklyn. She remembered what her father told her after a double shift at the factory: *You get out of this place, hear me? You stay here, you livin' on borrowed time, sweetie.*

They had rats and roaches. Sometimes you got one—nasty lumps of reddish gray—that looked as big or small as the other.

Now all she wondered was what critters and animals would pick at her meat.

The knot over her eye ballooned to baseball-size proportions. She couldn't see it or see out of it. But she could feel the lump pulsing, leaking blood or pus or some warm liquid. If she survived this nightmare, she might not ever get vision back. Her memory flashed to the ball-peen hammer down at his waist . . . coming over the top and swinging with a one-handed grip, hurling down with the force of a sledgehammer or an ax.

The vague memory of pitch-black and crinkling plastic sprung into her mind. She imagined she was thrown into the trunk and driven somewhere far, just like Boots had been.

"Fuck you," she heard in her own tired voice before her skull cracked. Wherever they were, the sound echoed more than once. It was as if there were three of her in the same room, her voice coming from different angles. Then she screamed. Whimpered. She'd breathed hard to get the fight back in her, until the next strike broke the little bones in her finger.

"Funny things, guns," he spoke. She lifted one eyelid and stared angrily as the man in the dark ski mask turned over her service weapon in his hand. In the other hand, a device that changed his voice. "Glock 19M, Gen 5. Fifteen-round nine-millimeter mag. Marksman barrel, night sights. FBI issue."

"You read the manual," she said.

She watched a new line form in the ribs of the mask and knew he was smiling. Then, faster than her only working eye could process, he aimed between her legs and fired. She flinched. The round sparked off the cold cement ground. Her ears rang.

"Now why would I do that . . ." He took his finger off the trigger and scratched his head with the pistol barrel. "Because I want you to know that you can scream all you want, but no one is coming.

"Soon, your body will go into shock, and that's when I'll cut open the back of your shirt and skin you. Don't worry, it won't go to waste. I have a message for your friends."

Chapter 20

The Madman stood powerfully at six feet two inches and just over two hundred pounds, baking in the warm sunlight. He looked up past a silver shimmer cast over the power lines, where a white jet hissed through a denim-blue sky and would be landing shortly at LAX. Spaced-out palm trees as high as skyscrapers. In the distance were the dirt and shrubs that made up the Hollywood Hills, where the famous white letters stood out like a sore thumb, calling and waving to all the tourists.

Studio City was to the west of Cahuenga Pass, in the southeast San Fernando Valley.

Laurel Canyon News was an independent newsstand on Ventura Boulevard. Despite it being a small setup beside the massive white exterior of a CVS, there was a lot of foot traffic this afternoon.

He stood across the street. At his back was a bank and a strip mall—with outdoor escalators and underground parking—filled with shops and salons and restaurants and bars.

Behind dark sunglasses and a surgical mask that trapped his hot breath, and beneath the bill of a cap, he stared at the newsstand under a blue awning with white letters printed across the front of it that read Los Angeles Times. A few parking meters sat empty. Sprawled out on one of the two graffiti-tagged park benches there was a bronze-skinned man with blond hair in tattered navy shorts and a grungy white T-shirt attached to a shopping cart with a sleeping bag in the top rack.

In a gap of traffic, the Madman weaved between cars with the leather messenger bag slung over his shoulder bouncing against his side. He moved laboriously in public, as if he'd had some form of sports injury when he was younger. In reality, the Madman was in peak physical condition, with the grip of a strong grappler, and he could consistently sprint a 5:30 mile.

People picked at stacks of tabloids and newspapers and sports and health and fashion magazines. He scanned the celebrity faces that he knew nothing about, some of them probably living nearby, a close commute to the CBS Studio Center and everything in LA.

He waited there. Looking at the newspapers, a shudder of joy coursed through him when he saw the headline: The Real 'Madman' Killer at Large by Rooker Lindström.

When no one was looking his way, he slipped a black glove over his hand, grabbed a copy of the *LA Times* off a rack, and replaced it with his own rolled-up newspaper from his bag. It was handmade, the text carefully cut out, pieced together, and glued to a thick sheet of human skin.

No fingerprints to be found.

The Madman used the gloved hand to pay in cash and took one last look at the newspaper he'd left. The yellow Post-it note on the front had three numbers and a name cut out and glued to it.

9-1-1

Special Agent Scott Eckhart

Chapter 21

"I guess you're his favorite now," Rooker said, gesturing to Tess's cell phone, which was lighting up with a call from Scott Eckhart.

Favorite informant, Tess thought, and she put the call on speakerphone.

"Is Esparza with you?"

"Yeah, we're drinking cosmos and complaining about you," Tess shot back and saw Rooker smile.

"I'm serious, Harlow. We've got something—"

"What is it?" Rooker said.

"It's another newspaper. Laurel Canyon News . . . The guy working the register said that someone replaced an *LA Times* with it. It had a message on it. '9-1-1 Special Agent Scott Eckhart.'"

The killer's getting antsy, Tess thought. *He wants attention.* "Does he remember what the person looked like?"

"He said there was a guy—big guy, white, maybe six three—who had a hat and sunglasses on with an N95 mask. He bought an *LA Times* and was wearing black gloves. But not latex ones like some germaphobe—cotton gloves."

"Yeah, it's a little warm for heavy gloves . . . ," Rooker said.

"Quincy and Hall are here, but I can't get ahold of Esparza. Her cell's off."

Tess felt a chill shoot down her spine to the pit of her stomach.

Rooker rubbed his eyes and stared blearily at the Thanksgiving decorations flashing past the SUV's windows. He'd almost forgotten about the holiday—though now he thought of Caroline. Last year, when they'd been riding out the worst of the pandemic at Lindström Manor, they'd gone all in on tradition, turkey and all. It had been a joke at first, and then it had just been . . . nice. Things were decidedly less festive now. Tess had tried Esparza's phone a dozen times while they'd waited for Hall to pick them up, but it kept going to voicemail.

On the way to the field office, Rooker heard Tess asking follow-up questions and Hall giving one-word replies, but he tuned them out. He felt sick—and sure that Esparza was dead.

Not another one, he thought. *And I barely knew her.*

"Where was her phone last on?" Quincy asked.

"Cherry Canyon Park," Hall said.

"Pull it up," Eckhart said.

Hall pulled up a GPS location and a map that Rooker knew would mostly be dusty trails and greenery.

Rooker nodded his head at Tess, then appraised Eckhart's worried face. "She isn't there."

"Yeah, probably just her phone broken and tossed in a bush."

"I think I might know where she is."

Tess turned to him. "What?"

"There's a place beneath the 210 Freeway. It's called Devil's Gate."

"Why—"

"There's a shape in the rocks that resembles a demon. Some people say it's a portal to hell. Some say it's haunted. Really it's just a dam that was built in the early 1900s. Flood control for the reservoir. Twenty years later, some wackjob cult types tried to open a portal and summon the Antichrist. Some kids disappeared there in the fifties. Two of them were later confirmed murder victims of Mack Ray Edwards."

"Jesus." Tess sighed. "Why would Esparza be there?"

"Because in *The Black Echo*, the character is a detective in the LAPD. Formerly a Tunnel Rat in the Vietnam War. There are tunnels all over the dam."

"Seems like a stretch."

"I didn't say it wasn't. But our killer left Natalie Carlisle in a drainpipe, just like in the book. My gut tells me Esparza's phone being shut off so close to the dam is no coincidence."

Chapter 22

November 23, 2021

A cold breeze hit her back like a thousand needles, doling out a pain unlike anything she'd ever endured. She opened the eye that worked.

A crack of sunlight was coming in from somewhere. In it, she saw the concrete walls that were headstone gray, and she prayed that this wouldn't be her grave.

Graffiti tags and stains on the walls. Debris littered the ground. She looked down at a narrow puddle that trailed beneath her feet.

The man in the mask was gone. For how long, she didn't know.

Suddenly, she heard her father's voice again. *You stay here, you livin' on borrowed time, sweetie.*

She did her best to look up. The stress on her muscles and the burning in her back . . . She swallowed a scream. Tears welled up in her angry eye. She blinked them away. She thought she could feel blood or tears building up in the one that was shut.

She was shackled to the ceiling. Her arms hung limp above her. Restraints clawed into her wrists. They were too tight. There was no slipping out of them.

Isabel Esparza kicked her legs up and let all of her weight fall hard. But nothing happened. Nothing except for the loud clink of steel chains and a scream with her face pressed into her arm.

She closed her eye and tried again. And again. She breathed hard.

When she opened her eye again to a strange flutter, her body froze. Her pulse, her heart thumping, her head like it was squeezed in a vise.

She heard it again. And that's when her eye found them. Small and black. Twitching. Huddled together like tarantulas in the corner of the ceiling. The shine of dark eyes.

Bats.

Maybe twenty of them.

She fought the tears and started throwing all of her body weight in erratic leaps up and down and side to side.

She tried and tried, until something above her snapped. And she screamed in pain while she fell to the ground. The bats took off above her. She stayed low. She felt the wind in the force of their flight over-head. What she couldn't tell was if she'd just felt a bite in her back. She jumped up and moved, while the swarm of darkness went somewhere in the tunnels.

Move.

Her legs ran on autopilot. Swaying toward a tiny sliver of light. Her feet shuffled through a puddle.

He might come back, she told herself. *Hurry.*

She moved faster. She turned into a larger tunnel. It was the way out.

The opening was at least twenty feet high. Two massive steel doors had been swung closed. Thin steel rods created bars maybe three inches apart. But when she pressed her hands against the cold steel, they didn't budge. Instead, she heard the rattle of a chain. And there on the oppo-site side of the bars, she saw the black chain wrapped around the doors and a heavy-duty lock that secured it shut.

She fell to her knees and cried.

Chapter 23

November 23, 2021

Tess pulled the car over and shut off the engine. She and Rooker got out and started walking.

"This way," Rooker said. "There're stairs that go down that way"—he pointed past the chain-link fence where a gate topped with barbed wire was latched shut—"but it's not as direct."

They walked toward the freeway and across a bridge overlooking the valleys all around them. Under a hot sun, a hazy shimmer hung above the tree line, where the sky was a mixture of cloudy blues and whites. Reflected in the murky brown water below were the trees and brush growing out of a hillside. Rooker turned at the end of the bridge and led her into a damp tunnel that opened into an overgrown path.

"There something you're not telling me?"

Rooker smiled. "Is there ever a day you aren't suspicious of me?"

"Not really. How do you know this place so well?"

"When I was trying to find my son's killer, my search led me here. Ana Sofia Acosta lived on Fairview Avenue. If you head west on the 210 that's above us, or take Orange Grove Boulevard, it's only ten minutes from here."

"But you said that all of Meachum's victims were killed and staged in their homes."

"They were. But in the forensics report, there was a small mixture of concrete, rock, and sand found in the carpet at the Acosta home. There was sodium silicate present in it. The techs got a partial boot print that was too large. She was a single mother, not dating anyone at the time. Someone tracked it into the house."

"Still, concrete, rock, and sand? That could be material for pavers. Hardware stores—it could be a lot of things. There are hundreds of beaches in California—"

Rooker shook his head. "Not that kind of sand. It was gray. The write-up said there were pebbles in it, but the mixture was mostly concrete debris. At first, I thought of structures, something like an old bridge or building. But sodium silicate is used as a setting accelerator. It makes concrete denser. Durable. And in our case, *waterproof*. So still, maybe a bridge or a tunnel. But when I found out about this place, and that it was so close to the victim's home, right on the reservoir, it seemed obvious. Only I never found a thing."

Tess didn't say anything.

"From where Esparza's phone pinged, it's a twelve-, maybe fifteen-minute drive. They could've tossed the phone, hopped on Highland Drive, and brought her here."

"I'm impressed."

"Don't be. We haven't found her yet."

The two of them kept moving. The earth was dry where they stepped. A staggered path of crumpled water bottles and crushed beer cans and filthy cigarette ends. And suddenly he pictured Isabel Esparza's body sticking out from it, just as dry as the ground where the underbrush had bent outward at grotesque angles. He wondered if the same portion of her back would be missing.

Where the path ended and the concrete began, graffiti tags took over. Rooker looked up at the so-called demon in the rocks and pointed it out to Tess.

For a moment he imagined the portal opening and wondered if he would be granted entry into the fiery underworld.

The two of them made a turn, and that's when they saw the large steel gate pushing open.

Isabel Esparza hobbled out of the darkness, half-blind and bleeding, and clutching a large rock.

PART II

Three Weeks Later

Chapter 24

December 14, 2021

The lights were on at 1865 Webster Avenue. It was a retro two-bedroom, two-bath on a hill in Silver Lake, with a sign posted in the weeds at the end of a long, narrow drive that read: BEWARE OF DOG. At the side door, bushes had grown out of the concrete stairs, and a warped and dead tree pushed up from the ground. At the back was a detached garage and a cactus taller than he was.

Joey Miggs stepped over the weeds and flung open the screen door and pushed his way inside. He set his prosthetic down on the end table, plopped down into the La-Z-Boy with a greasy take-out bag and a cold beer, and stared at the dusty screen of the television. He turned it on. *The murder again . . .* He sighed. That woman in the drainpipe. FOX played a segment of *Late Night News with Caroline Lind*, where a table of idiots spoke on the case.

He scratched the patchy reddish-brown fuzz that lined his jaw before his fingers worked the bag open and he reached down inside.

"'ere ya go, buddy." He gave the spotted head a pat and put a french fry in the German shepherd's mouth. "Good boy, Duke."

Fuckin' Tate. Even locked up, that freak keeps sending police to my door.

Joey Miggs was a simple man; he liked meat and potatoes—a medium-rare kind of guy—and a cold Coors Light. That was all he needed.

What he didn't need was attention. And when Tate Meachum, a weirdo he barely knew and barely tolerated, got nabbed for killing all those women and that kid, Miggs's life was turned upside down. He was brought in and questioned for hours. News stations camped outside his home. Seeing Tate's photo on the television now dug it all back up.

He switched to the Westerns channel. *Butch Cassidy and the Sundance Kid* was on. The Hole-in-the-Wall Gang. A classic. He cracked the top of the beer and sank into the cushion. An ideal night after a hard day's work.

Really, all he'd done was schmooze a new client into having him—and by him he meant some undocumented Mexicans he'd hired for cheap—remodel a Spanish-style home in West Hollywood. Ever since his accident, his manual labor days were over. He'd shifted to contractor work. That's where the money was. The blueprints for the three-bedroom, two-bath house would land in his inbox soon, and he'd start picking out materials online to show the owner that he was the initiative-taking type. Then after the job he'd collect a nice profit, some asshole would park their Porsche or Mercedes-Benz in the new driveway, and Joey Miggs would search for the next project to make some quick cash.

Duke reared his head. His ears went stiff as the hairs on his back. Then he scrambled to his feet and hopped up on the sofa and snarled. Usually it was just the delivery trucks that got him riled up.

The shepherd growled and barked a low, scary tone. He bared his fangs.

"Quiet, Duke."

But Duke didn't stop. Miggs perked up on his elbows and checked the window. The sky had turned a dark gray, and a glossy black van was at the curb outside.

Strange. He hadn't even heard it pull up.

Joey Miggs slipped his prosthetic back over his hand—a nude strap over his wrist and two clearly fake fingers in place of the ones that were gone—and went to the front door. He told Duke, "Easy, boy."

He'd opened the door halfway when a man in a dark cap waved at him. "Sorry, man. I'll be outta here once I get the damn engine to start."

Miggs hesitated. "You have Triple A?"

"Wife says it's a waste of money."

Miggs sighed. "I've got cables. My work truck is a piece of shit, but it can give you a jump."

"I'd appreciate it."

Miggs walked to the detached garage and pulled the door up. On the tool bench beside the old Ford Ranger he found the set of black-and-red cables he was looking for and brought them around front.

"Hey . . ." He stopped himself when he didn't see the man. He was gone. Maybe he went back into the van to pop the hood. He walked slowly. Then he heard Duke again, barking his damned head off.

Goddammit, Duke.

"It was never Meachum" were the whispered words behind him before the hammer came swinging down.

The blood on his head was cold and dry. He was naked, shivering in a cold wooden chair, and he could feel a stream of urine dripping down his leg. He wrenched his sagging head upward. Then he felt the searing pain in his hand. As his eyes focused, he peered down at it and saw blood and bone.

"Fucker," he hissed. "My *fucking* finger."

The digit adjacent to it was still there, though he couldn't feel it. It had mangled beneath the heavy swing of a hammer. The nail had turned black.

Miggs shivered. A small desk was before him. In his periphery, he could see a large armor-gray steel door and white metal shelves along two walls. Between his feet was beige tile flooring. *Am I in a storage unit?*

Somewhere overhead a fluorescent light flickered, and he could hear the jagged hum of a heavy-duty fan blowing out icy air behind him.

A pungent odor like plastic and freezer burn clogged his nose.

"Joey Miggs," an eerie voice called from right beside him. "Give me your hand."

His head rattled back and forth.

"Last chance. Or I'll cut off another one."

Miggs grimaced and let his shaky hand fall against the table.

"Write this down," the voice told him. "Word for word and I'll let you live."

"Bullshit, fucker."

"No? *Another finger?* Why don't you choose—"

"Fine. I'll do it."

"I, Joey Miggs, killed Natalie Carlisle. I left FBI Agent Isabel Esparza for dead. I am a sick man. I am the Madman. Please forgive me."

Ink and blood swirled over the paper beneath Miggs's hand. When he lifted it, blood began to trickle down his wrist.

"That wasn't so hard, was it?"

Miggs didn't reply.

"Joey, don't be rude. I took your finger. Not your ears and lips."

Miggs sucked his teeth angrily. It wasn't in his nature to back down from anyone. But right now, his options were to listen or die. "No one will believe this. Why bother?"

Miggs watched the real Madman smile. The figure reached for the hammer at the other end of the table. Dragged it with a cruel slowness over the top of it, a violent scratching sound as it stripped the wood.

"Because history is important, Joey. Your experiences are the reason you are who you are. And mine—boy, history has a funny way of repeating itself, wouldn't you say?"

Miggs again was silent.

"How do you kill what's already dead? You bring it back to life. How do you kill what's ready for death? You give it a reason to live."

Joey Miggs closed his eyes and braced for what was coming.

◆ ◆ ◆

"Where did you see the dog?" Eckhart asked her.

"We know Duke, my husband and me. We go for a walk every night and feed him his treat. Joey never minds."

Eckhart repeated his question. "Ma'am . . . the dog?"

"He must've got out the side door. The front was closed. We saw him walking up our road."

Ernestina and Arturo Zepeda were Joey Miggs's neighbors. Despite the 70-degree night, Arturo wore a button-down shirt and a gray vest with pleated dress pants and boat shoes. The balding man fixed a few unruly hairs that strayed from his wife's smoky-gray bob. Ernestina wore trainers and purple sweatpants with a gray zip-up sweatshirt knotted around her waist. The couple had lived across the street for twenty-seven years and knew that Miggs would never let Duke wander around the neighborhood at night. When they walked Duke back to the house and found the lights and TV on and garage open but no sign of Miggs, Ernestina decided to call the police, who had been instructed to forward anything involving Miggs to the FBI.

Now Webster Ave was a stream of LAPD cruisers and Bureau vehicles.

The Zepedas said that although Miggs wasn't really a talker, he was always pleasant. And he never played any loud music, like the Prescotts two doors down from them did.

"How long after you saw Duke did you call the police?"

Ernestina looked briefly taken aback, as if Eckhart had accused her of wrongdoing. Then she thought. "I'd say thirty minutes . . . maybe forty-five. I sat with Duke while my husband walked the property. I thought maybe Joey had run out and was on his way back. But my husband saw his truck in the garage."

"When did you last see Mr. Miggs?"

"Last night. He's a homebody. Goes to work, comes home. He's home just about every night," she said.

"Has he had any visitors lately?"

Arturo and Ernestina exchanged glances. Then the wife spoke. "There was a van that we saw leaving."

"A van?"

"Yeah, it was black."

"Was there any writing on it?"

"I couldn't see."

"How long was it?"

"I don't really know."

Eckhart wrote it down. He'd have Jack Hall look into a large black van on nearby street cameras. Commercial vans weren't commonly black, though it could have been a work van that had been painted over or wrapped.

"Did you happen to see the driver? Or the license plate?"

"We never saw the driver. It didn't have a license plate."

"Mr. and Mrs. Zepeda, we believe Joey Miggs to be in danger. If you see anything or remember anything else, could you please give me a call?" Eckhart slipped a card out of his pocket and handed it to Ernestina.

Arturo nodded.

When Eckhart turned around, he heard Ernestina's voice. "What'll happen to Duke?"

"Usually the dog will stay with whoever else lived in the home, or a family member—"

"Joey didn't really have anyone. Would it be okay if we look after him for now?"

Eckhart smiled weakly. "Of course."

◆ ◆ ◆

In the garage was where they found it.

"Boss," Deion Quincy called out as Eckhart stepped through the open garage door. He'd just finished a quick sweep of the home. There didn't appear to be a struggle. The only thing that had caught his eye was a silverfish dashing through the shag rug of the downstairs bathroom. Quincy took a step back from the passenger side of the Ford Ranger.

"What is it?"

"The cooler."

Eckhart stood beside Quincy. On top of a small cooler—royal blue and dirty white—was a thin piece of paper folded over, with a name written there.

ROOKER.

With a gloved hand, Quincy lifted the paper and delicately opened the cooler. Inside was what was left of Joey Miggs's lunch—a piece of peanut butter and jelly sandwich crust, a PowerBar wrapper, and a Dr Pepper bottle—kept cold with a pair of blue refreezable ice blocks. Also there was what was left of Joey Miggs's head.

Chapter 25

He shut the headlights off and veered into the carport. Killed the engine. It was after two in the morning. The sky was dark. The back of the van had been lined with plastic to collect the remains of Joey Miggs.

The Madman opened the door and went around to the luggage compartment. With it open, he jammed a flashlight in his pocket and stuffed the Glock 19M in the back of his jeans.

When he was sure no one was watching, he slung the tarp-wrapped body of Joey Miggs over his shoulder. Instantly the deadweight felt like it pinched his neck, yet he carried him through a gap in the chain-link fence and up a flight of stairs, into the last door on the right.

The elegant building in Van Nuys had been abandoned for months. He imagined it as a bad apple, shiny and ripe on the outside, rotting and worm-ridden in the core. Graffiti painted the walls. He'd done a quick check of all the rooms on the second floor.

There was no one.

In the room on the end, Miggs's headless body flopped hard against the ground, and a layer of dust flew up. He made another trip back to the van to retrieve an incinerator that looked like a metal trash can dotted with dime-size holes. Really, though, it was galvanized steel. It would burn the body of Joey Miggs with relative ease, but it would take a little time.

But time was on his side.

He lit the starter and fed the climbing fire. A plume of smoke grew in the room, some of it escaping out through the broken windows. Still, in the dark, the smoke would be difficult to see.

While the flames crackled, he folded up Miggs's body—chest to knees—and dumped him inside. Slowly, the body melted away from the feet up. The stench was awful. Singed hair . . . burning leather and polyethylene. The Madman went to the window and inhaled.

Decades of planning . . . creating this false life . . . Not only was it all set in motion, but it was worth it. Leaving Rooker a souvenir of Joey Miggs, reminiscent of Gunner, would seem careless. It was far from it.

Now with Miggs dead, Rooker would know in his heart that the person he'd caught wasn't the true Madman. He would know that he had only put away a psychopath crazy enough to take on the name, and his place in prison. For Rooker, each dead victim was a price he'd pay, and the Madman didn't plan on cashing out anytime soon.

What he'd told Miggs was true. *How do you kill what's already dead? You bring it back to life.* Jesus brought Lazarus back from the dead. But the Madman had brought Rooker back from the grave that was Lindström Manor. He'd given him a brief period of normalcy, only to snatch the rug out from under him. What the Madman had in store for him next was truly incredible.

Chapter 26

December 15, 2021

Rooker sighed as Tess added a red pin to the map: Silver Lake. Joey Miggs. It wasn't much, but it was more than they had a few weeks ago.

The FBI's Evidence Response Team hadn't found a shred of new evidence in the tunnels at Devil's Gate where Isabel Esparza had been taken. Or in Joey Miggs's home. Miggs's phone was gone. On his desktop computer, he was still logged in to his email. But all they found were price indexes for construction costs and building materials and blueprints. Nothing linked them any further to a six-foot-three Caucasian male who wore black cotton gloves. What they did find was blood spatter on the concrete and grass out front of the Webster Avenue home, consistent with a strike to the head.

The blood was Miggs's.

Esparza had endured several surgeries on her eye and back, including a large skin graft. It had been rough, but she was at home and expected to make a full recovery. Why did the killer let Esparza live? Or had he simply left her for dead? And why go after Joey Miggs? Why have him write that obviously bogus confession? Maybe the killer hadn't counted on the police getting to Miggs so fast. Rooker was starting to think the new Madman was just as crazy and unpredictable as Meachum.

Esparza had never made it down to the pier in Oceanside to look for Boots, as Eckhart had ordered. In fact, she hadn't made it far from the field office when the killer managed to take her in broad daylight and travel in the opposite direction. And she'd only been able to confirm what the newsstand owner said: the assailant was a tall male, probably Caucasian, though much of his face was obscured by an N95 mask.

It was clear the killer was still surveilling the FBI team closely. He knew exactly when and where to attack Esparza. He'd also shown off his knowledge of Esparza's FBI-issued service weapon. Rooker wondered if that was all to throw the FBI for a loop—have them chasing their tails, looking into their own. Make them suspicious of each other. Then again, even when it seemed certain there was no way for Esparza to escape, the killer took precautions: he never took off his mask or stopped using the voice modulator. Why? Was Esparza's escape a surprise or part of the game?

Without Miggs's body, there wasn't much for Joel Hunter to autopsy. Miggs's left eye socket had burst. The frontal bone was broken. It left him looking like a Halloween toy, where if you squeezed hard enough, the eyeball popped out. The right side of the face looked as though it'd been bashed into a wasp nest. Dark bruising the shade of purple-black ink. He had been brutally and repeatedly assaulted.

None of the other victims had experienced this type of beating. The MO had been more methodical and precise until now. It's common for serial offenders to become increasingly violent, sure. But this felt different. It seemed personal.

The cluster of pins was mostly in and around Los Angeles County, with a couple in Hemet and one in Oceanside. Tess was focused on a photograph pinned to the wall of Joey Miggs's head in a cooler.

She looked at the map. "Why would he go after Miggs? The Feds cleared Miggs in their second round of questioning. If he's been watching our every move, he had to have known none of us would believe that confession."

Rooker was flat on the bed, fingers interlocked on his chest, staring up at the ceiling. He sighed. "Because he's a psychopath?"

"You could win every argument that way." She raised an eyebrow at Rooker. "But really, why bother with Miggs, other than to mess with you by leaving that note?"

"Maybe he's just tying up loose ends. Miggs was the only living proof that the case against Meachum isn't airtight. So far, he seems really pleased with himself that we—that *I*—got it wrong. Maybe like with Natalie he sees Miggs as something that could help me get it right and finally figure out who killed my son."

"He does really seem obsessed with proving you wrong. The redacted article from when Meachum was apprehended, the change in the MO, making the newspapers out of Natalie's and Esparza's skin . . . What is it about the newspaper coverage in particular that bothers him? Is it just because you're writing for the *Times* again?"

"I don't know," Rooker said. He pinched the bumpy bridge of his nose. "Maybe we had it right. Maybe this guy is Meachum's accomplice, and he's doing things his way now. It feels like he wants to be the author of his own story. Oddly enough, I think he's doing a pretty good job of it."

"What're you saying?"

"I don't know what to think right now. That's the problem." Rooker was beginning to feel lost, like he had before. Locked away in the darkness of his son's bedroom, drinking, with photos of the dead circled all around him like headstones. "I need to talk to Tate."

Chapter 27

December 15, 2021

Rooker sat behind the desk in the hotel room, his toes firmly in the carpet, as though the gravity in the room were about to change and send him flying like a balloon losing air. Despite not having to make the spine-chilling walk through the prison, he didn't feel any calmer. Patched into a video call, he waited anxiously while at any moment, several guards would escort Tate Meachum to a table and chain him like a rabid dog. Any minute now.

Standing out of camera view were Tess and Eckhart and his team, minus Esparza. Still, with everyone there, it felt as if he were having a private conversation that shouldn't be overheard.

Several moments passed before the clink of chains came closer. Three large bodies came into the room behind Meachum's shaved head. The pale man took a seat, while each body behind him secured some strap or chain somewhere.

For a long moment, they stared at each other. Meachum always made the first move, and today would be no different. Rooker would wait as long as he needed, ready to counterattack.

"I'm disappointed, Rooker. I thought you cared enough to at least come and visit face-to-face."

"I would've loved to," he lied. "Unfortunately, there were a lot of people who were worried about what you'd bite off your body next."

Meachum smiled. Then with his best effort, he raised a cuffed hand, where the tip of a finger was gone. "To what do I owe the pleasure?"

"I have some questions—"

"Surpriiise, surpriiise," Meachum said. "Always so predictable, aren't you. If *you're* the FBI consultant, what does that make *me*?"

He ignored the comment. "Whoever is killing these people now, he says he's the real deal. He says he's the real Madman. Says you're a fake."

"Does that mean I'm free to go?"

"Why don't we play a game."

"Oh, I'd *love* to play a game."

"I'm going to tell you what I have so far. Why don't you tell me where I'm wrong. Good? Six foot three, Caucasian, athletic build. Potential hypochondriac with genetic predisposition to Alzheimer's, possibly already suffering from the disease or dementia."

So far, Meachum hadn't said anything. He wondered if that meant everything he'd said was accurate and decided to push it a step further.

"Law enforcement."

Meachum smirked. "Cute, Rooker. You want me to tell you if the killer is standing in that room with you."

"Is he?"

Meachum bobbed his shoulders in an amused shrug.

"Or is he a writer?"

"Grasping at straws, Rooker. Come on."

"He drives for a rental agency."

Meachum's head shook side to side. "You don't—"

"So he owns it, then. The black van."

Meachum's head stopped.

It isn't stolen, then. "Okay, we're getting somewhere now. Have you heard about your old friend?"

"Mr. Miggs, I presume?"

"Did he own that beat-up truck when you worked with him? The Ford Ranger? Found his head inside a cooler in his truck. Now what kind of buddy kills a friend's pal."

"Miggs was never my friend, Rooker."

"Tell me something: Is he losing his memory?"

"How was Laura when you went to see her? You must have gone home by now, right?"

Now it was Rooker who smiled.

"Did you sit in Britton's room?" Meachum asked. "Remember how much blood—"

"Do you have anything else for me, Tate? Maybe his fascination with newspapers?"

"I'll tell you this. There are two victims you haven't found yet. One old and one new."

Rooker stopped. Again, with just a few words, Tate Meachum had the upper hand. For a moment he imagined himself as he was years ago with a bottle in his hand, waiting for the phone call when the clock struck 11:37 p.m. His head felt like it could explode. "Bullshit. You drew seven tally marks in that cell—"

"That's right. Six confirmed victims. One that never was."

"And that would be the 'new' victim?"

Again, Meachum smiled and shrugged.

"And what about the old one?"

"I wish we could chat all day, Rooker. But I must get back to my cozy room. Give Laura a kiss for me."

◆ ◆ ◆

"One old and one new," Eckhart said sarcastically. "Any thoughts on where to start with that?"

"I think it means the past is somehow connected," Tess said. Rooker turned his head to peer up at her fixing a stray lock of hair from the front to behind her ear. "That's how it was with Sadler. He had been taught . . . *things* . . . by Gunner Lindström. His motivation seemed driven by his hatred for Rooker—that he shared a bloodline with Gunner—and Sadler felt he was the 'rightful heir,' as he'd put it."

"And you think this killer knew Gunner too?"

"No. I'm saying that something in his past is the reason he's doing this. It has to be why he went after Miggs and is leaving messages for us. He hates law enforcement. He clearly wants to torment Rooker. And judging by the 'one old and one new' comment from Meachum, there's either a body that's never been found or a homicide case that's linked."

Eckhart wore a pained expression. He scratched at what appeared to be several days' growth of facial hair. "California is the state with the largest number of missing persons." He sighed. "Before anyone says it, I'm aware that the victims prior to Natalie Carlisle were all found inside their homes. Still, there are scenarios of why a body wouldn't be reported missing. Estranged. Illegal. Wanted for a crime. Let's look at when Meachum was active. Search ViCAP. Missing persons. Let's look for a female who vanished. Maybe someone that wasn't even officially reported missing. It may be someone who can't be reported missing."

Rooker pondered the conversation with Meachum. For the first time, there was a moment he began to crack. If Meachum were going to reach out to whomever he'd been communicating with, it would be soon.

"Boss," Quincy interrupted after getting off the phone. "Got something."

"What?"

"LAPD got an anonymous tip out in Van Nuys. Said the caller sounded strung out. Some junkies were staying in a condemned building, and they found what looks like human remains, pretty badly burned."

"How does that—"

"The head was missing. So were multiple fingers."

Chapter 28

December 16, 2021

Rooker was thinking about bones. Dirt-flecked, beetle-dwelling, pure-white bones. A skeleton could take hundreds of years to fully disintegrate. With his hands interlocked behind his head, he prodded at the tangled hair over his skull and stared vacantly at the hotel room ceiling, wondering if he'd never destroyed Olivia Campbell's bones because he wanted to be caught. He tried to picture the gruesome crime scene in Van Nuys. But he couldn't exterminate the thought of bones.

There was a knock at the door, and he opened it to find Tess shrugging on her jacket.

"It looks like your chat with Meachum made him feel like writing something," she said. "He tried to mail a few letters, and Eckhart wants us to look at them. Come on."

When Rooker and Tess had taken their seats in the conference room of the field office, Eckhart nodded at Lewis, who hit a few keys on his laptop. On the screen in the front of the room were images of two pieces of paper covered in ugly handwriting.

"Both letters are to his lawyer," said Eckhart. "One is asking about an update for his case reopening. The other is meant for his ex-fiancée."

Rooker's eyes fell over the apology letter first. Why on earth would Tate write to the woman he'd given an engagement ring to after it'd been taken off a dead victim? She wanted nothing to do with him after the FBI took him away.

Eckhart continued. "Meachum's lawyer is Gwendolyn Schaffer." A photograph of a dark-haired woman with high cheekbones and a stern expression was up on the screen. "They call her the Gavel. No place she'd rather be than inside a courtroom, and she's one of the highest-profile criminal defense attorneys in the world. I was able to put a temporary hold on Meachum's mail going out, but our window is only a couple of hours. I've got Cryptanalysis and Racketeering Records on it; they specialize in code breaking. If we take too long, we risk going against his First Amendment rights, and the Gavel will have a field day with us."

Quincy said, "There's gotta be something else we can do. Can't we follow the lawyer? Or the ex-fiancée?"

"I don't think that's it," Rooker said. "The mail is going to the lawyer, but it isn't meant for her."

"You think she shows it to someone?" Lewis asked.

"I think the killer intercepts it. Somehow."

"Okay," Quincy said. "So we follow the mail."

"Only if we can't crack the code in time," Eckhart said.

Jack Hall leaned back in his chair and crossed his arms. "Can't we reach out to Schaffer? Ask her to help us out?"

"Are you reading what I'm reading?" Lewis turned toward Hall. "You think someone like her is going to kill her chances of getting her client out of prison? There's someone else out there killing with the same MO. If there's ever been a time for a jury to believe Meachum is innocent, that he was framed, it's now. Schaffer will be foaming at the mouth once she reads this."

"There's no telling how long this'll take. We could be at this for days," Quincy said. "Maybe even years. It took fifty-one *years* for them to crack the 340 cipher. Even then, the FBI didn't crack it. Three private citizens did."

The 340 cipher, Rooker knew, was the 340-character message the Zodiac Killer mailed to the *San Francisco Chronicle*.

Quincy was right. Time wasn't on their side.

Rooker said, "Tate Meachum is no Zodiac Killer."

Eckhart passed out copies of the letters to the team. Rooker stared down at the one to the ex-fiancée, tapping each fourth letter, then each fifth letter, every second word, every third word, trying to make sense of the code.

But the pressure of time put a lock on his brain. The letters began to jumble and dance around the page before his eyes. He started tapping his pen seesaw-like, then thought of Elias Cole and dropped his pen.

Come on, he thought. *You know this guy—the real Tate Meachum—better than anyone.*

Hours passed. It hadn't been deciphered by any of them, or any one of the cryptanalysts.

Eckhart sighed. "We're out of time. Everyone pack up. We follow the mail."

Chapter 29

December 17, 2021

On the thirty-third level of a thirty-three-story high-rise, Gwendolyn Schaffer's office towered over downtown Los Angeles. On the roof, there was a helipad the size of a small house. Rooker imagined that from up there, everyone below looked like ants marching around a miniature model city.

The elegant building was encased in dark granite and glass. Inside the large main lobby, marble floors conquered the room. They even ran the length of the security desk, where a large, clean-cut man in a pristine white dress shirt and crisply ironed black tie sat imposingly.

Rooker electrified the second the SUV pulled to a stop across the street from the ground-floor lobby. Jack Hall killed the engine. He sighed. "Now we wait," he said and sank deep into the leather of the Suburban's driver seat. City traffic roared past them up and down West Seventh Street. A stream of shiny cars and the various tones of car horns. Commuters ambling beneath the warm ball of sun blazing in the sky.

A bank of polished mailboxes shimmered along the wall. From behind the window tint, Rooker made out the small black pinpricks in each, where they needed a key to be unlocked.

Unfortunately, all of the post going to and from Gwendolyn Schaffer's office would be sorted through a mail room. This was going to take some time. The hope was that it would be as simple as staking out the Gavel's PO box.

Barry Lewis—in the other unmarked vehicle along with Deion Quincy—had the idea to replace the receptionist with an undercover agent. Even someone who wasn't on Eckhart's team. But they couldn't risk it and the killer not even making a play at the letters. To be honest, they hadn't had enough time to formulate a solid plan. Rooker thought there really wasn't a plan at all, aside from waiting for someone suspicious to intercept the letters. Luck is what he would've called it. But they needed a win today.

Eckhart ticked the nail of his index finger against the glass in the passenger seat. Tess was in the back with Rooker.

The radio crackled. "Incoming, boss." It was Quincy. "Post van coming your way."

Eckhart shifted in his seat and spotted the white truck. He held his thumb down on the transmit button. "Got it. Stand by."

The van parked at the curb a few spots down from the main entrance. From where Hall had parked the car, they could just make out the driver. The door was on the right side, facing away from them. "Quincy, I don't have eyes on the door. Go on foot. Lewis, stay in the car in case we need to move."

Lewis interjected. "I got it, boss."

No more than ten seconds later, Rooker caught Barry Lewis strutting down the sidewalk in a beige T-shirt and black pants. But then he refocused on the front of the building. The mail truck door opened, and a Black man with a white mustache and dressed in a cap and postal blues—a light-colored short-sleeved button-up and dark pants— stepped laboriously down from the seat, headed into the lobby, and moved out of view. Rooker's gaze snagged on the small cluster of people walking by the front of the building.

A black-haired woman in a lavender sweater and dark jeans. An older man, sixties, wearing a gray cap with a dark brim and carrying a bright-yellow backpack. It wasn't much longer before the mailman came out of the building. And then they waited. And waited.

The minutes crawled by. This was a bust, and a complete waste of time. The sun had begun to fall behind the buildings, the sky still blue but hazy.

They were coming up on an hour. A new group of people walked in front of the building. A man in a gray hoodie with white shoes and a white bag slung over his shoulder, lighting up a cigarette. A woman in a purple tracksuit and matching basketball sneakers. A man with a neck bent to the side, a dark beard, and what Rooker thought was a San Diego Padres hat, a polo shirt, and jeans on a motorized scooter.

Rooker wanted to get out of the SUV and go back to the hotel. There were more useful ways he could be spending his time. But when a figure stood in front of the wall of mailboxes and began unlocking them, Rooker sat up straight.

Eckhart spoke into the walkie. "Got someone at the mailboxes, Quincy. Stand by."

Whoever it was, he looked young. He swung a few mailboxes open, sliding wads of envelopes inside, and locked them with a thick set of keys. Rooker had expected the kid to go back the way he came, past the desk and out of view. But when he pulled up a dark hood and scurried head down outside, he felt the blood pumping between his temples.

Rooker pointed. "Hey, hey."

Eckhart leaned forward. "Lewis. Black hood. Quincy, keep an eye on it."

"Got it."

Just as Eckhart had said it, the hooded figure cocked their head toward the Suburban. "No," Hall said. "No way, right?"

The person turned and sprinted hard away from them. "Fuck!" Eckhart yelled. "Everyone move!" The doors burst open.

Eckhart and Hall were after the figure. Rooker got out too. Bolted to the front of the building. Tess was right behind him.

Lewis was on the ground, bleeding badly from his left side. His hand was wrapped around the knife through his ribs, putting pressure on the wound. He breathed heavily.

The scooter was toppled over. The man Rooker saw in the cap with the crooked neck was gone. "Shit!" he said. He tried to remember fast. "He had a hat on, dark beard. Light jeans I think—"

Tess knelt and put pressure where Rooker thought the knife penetrated Lewis's spleen. She unlocked her cracked phone screen and dialed 911. "Who?"

"The guy on the scooter—it was him!"

Rooker took off running.

"Wait!"

That was the last time he heard her voice.

Rooker shot off like a rocket and peered up and down the street. He thought he could see someone in the distance, walking hurriedly. They could have had on the polo and jeans he remembered, but he wasn't sure. Rather than question himself, he ran harder. Footfalls slapping off the hard concrete. Adrenaline coursing like a shock wave through him.

Chapter 30

He was gone.

Rooker felt sweat dripping down his spine when he came back to find an ambulance speeding away and Eckhart and Hall standing a block from the building over the unhooded figure.

It was just a kid. Probably somewhere around eighteen, wearing a black *Five Nights at Freddy's* hoodie. Manacled at his skinny wrists. Grime coated his prominent cheekbones. Rooker imagined Eckhart or Hall had pressed his face into the ground when they'd caught him. He saw a thorned rose tattooed black and gray on his neck below his left ear.

Eckhart was pacing back and forth. With his right hand, he massaged his forehead, then down the edge of his tight jaw. "Lewis is gone . . . *They're* gone. The fucking letters . . ."

Rooker's gaze hitched on Tess Harlow's hands, where dark red puddled in her palm and spread out weblike to her fingers. Judging by the amount of it, Barry Lewis had bled out before the ambulance arrived.

"Man, I told you. I didn't do nothin' illegal."

"Then why'd you run?" Eckhart asked.

He didn't answer.

"Kid, you don't know what you're mixed up in."

"Why don't you tell me, then."

"The guy we're after killed a woman. They stabbed a federal agent—"

Rooker cut in. "What's your name, kid?"

"Robby."

"Who sent you here?"

The kid looked up at Rooker but said nothing.

"Come on. Someone told you to be outside after the mail was delivered, right? Told you to run. What did they give you?"

"Five thousand dollars."

"Cryptocurrency?"

"Yeah . . . but I wasn't sent here. I work in the mail room."

"You work in Gwendolyn Schaffer's office?"

"No. I just sort the mail and deliver it to the tenants."

"How were you contacted?"

"A DM on Instagram. They told me that if the lawyer gets anything from Tate Meachum, or from the prison, to take it. The first day of every month, they send me a different anonymous messenger app to download, and I let them know when anything from Meachum comes in."

Why not just send a photograph of Meachum's letters? Why risk picking up the mail in person? Maybe there's a secret message . . . something on the physical piece of paper he needs . . . "Show me."

Robby told them his cell phone was in his front right pocket. Eckhart pried it loose and faced the screen at the kid so it would unlock. When they went to pull up the message, the account had already been deleted.

Eckhart placed the kid under arrest. Then he made a phone call to issue all the traffic and surveillance cameras in the area to the FBI. He'd get a few guys from the Bureau to look through it all.

Chapter 31

December 18, 2021

The news report was playing in the living room, and the Madman popped a salty kernel from the warm, buttery bag into his mouth, sucked on it, and spit it back out. His leg juddered. He couldn't contain his excitement, or his wide smile.

He turned the volume several notches higher than normal.

The popcorn smell infected the room. As he reached his hand in for another, the bag crinkled, and residue collected on his knuckles.

They'd been *this* close to him. And they had no idea. No one looked at the man with the bent neck whose legs didn't work. Who would look the way of the man who wheeled himself around, compared to some punk in a dark hoodie?

No one.

The FBI would try to track the five grand, but the money was untraceable.

They'd fallen for such a simple misdirection. He wasn't in the habit of living as dangerously as he had outside Gwendolyn Schaffer's office. He'd usually planned everything out years ahead. Every possible scenario meticulously thought out. But now that he held the letters in his hand, he knew it was worth it.

He stared down at the coded message he'd circled. The message left to him by that imbecile who could only ever live in the shadow of the true Madman.

Still, Meachum had fulfilled his purpose.

Arranging the letters with the code was simple. Meachum's cipher would begin after the first use of the letter *r* or *l*. After that, he would use words with alphabetical characters from the Madman victims' names, along with select keywords from one of Rooker's old articles from the *Valley Chronicle* titled "The Battle of Angels and Demons," the satisfying irony that they communicated through something Rooker had written.

Then the Madman would find those letters and words, rearrange them, and decode the message. It revealed four words and an address.

Make the family watch. Thirty-three Marina Ln. Gleneden Beach.

Chapter 32

December 23, 2021

Rain was falling sideways over LA, blurry beneath the veil of night. It was after eight in the evening. The parking lot was nearly empty. There were only a handful of cars, many of which probably belonged to the people working the register or stocking shelves. He could've sworn there was a black van somewhere . . . with a logo on the side? A clock? But if it were ever there, it was long gone now.

His phone chirped. He slipped it out of his pocket and shielded it beneath his other hand. It was a message from Tracy, his wife, with a heart emoji at the end.

Don't forget we need milk.

Christ.

He'd given up his life as a detective. He used to do ten-hour shifts that oftentimes ran late. Now he was sent out to fetch groceries whenever his wife tugged on his leash. Water beaded down the screen's display. He wiped it away and pushed it back into his pocket. With his T-shirt getting soaked, he rushed in through the sliding doors of a Ralphs. The fluorescent lights hummed overhead. He wiped his feet quickly on a floor mat and headed to the back where the cold items were. He opened a condensation-misted door, took a quick glance at the date on the white jug, and grabbed it.

While he checked out, his phone buzzed again. "You've gotta be kidding," he hissed under his breath. His gaze fell over the tabloid magazine racks. Celebrities on the cover of *People* and *Us*. There was one magazine with a small blurb that read: Is He On the Loose? A photograph of Tate Meachum was positioned below it. He turned away. Every time he saw anything about Meachum, all he could picture was Rooker's son . . .

He punched in the four-digit code for his debit card, snatched his receipt, and pried the phone loose from his pocket once more. It was an unknown number. A video file had been sent.

"What the . . ." He pressed the play button as he walked slowly toward the sliding doors. In the video, he watched through the window of his home as his wife was in the kitchen and his son was sitting at the table doing schoolwork. Then whoever was filming moved to the side door beside the garage and opened it.

"Fuck!" He sprinted out the doors and into the parking lot. He was just about to dial 911 when a second text came through beneath the video.

If you call the police, they will die.

"Son of a bitch."

A pin suddenly dropped into the text message, with GPS coordinates not even five hundred feet away. Eddie ran to the car, tossed the milk into the passenger seat, and pulled a Smith & Wesson M&P from the glove box. It was there beside a leather ankle holster. He left that.

He looked up and down the street. Then back the way he came where he parked the car. No one.

He considered making a run for the driver's seat and slamming his foot down on the gas pedal the entire way home. If sirens flashed behind him, he wouldn't pull over. He'd let them chase him home. But that could put his family's lives in danger. He didn't know what would happen to them if he didn't follow the coordinates.

He moved toward the pin. Four hundred feet away. *Breathe, Eddie.* Bad decisions happen when people panic. He wouldn't. Then three hundred. He'd called in a favor to a couple of old pals on the force after he was phoned the night they found the woman in the drainpipe. He had people watching the house. They were there, weren't they? Two hundred feet. He'd shown his wife how to use the .45 he kept locked in the box by their bed. She could get to it. Plenty of time to enter the pin, swing the door open, and insert the magazine. *Come on, baby. Point and shoot.* One hundred feet.

Eduardo Arroyave looked around. Graffiti. Metal garage doors on the left. Pipes. Fire escapes. To the right, solid-blue fencing. Trash. Crushed cardboard boxes. Puddles. No footprints. Fifty feet away, a green dumpster spray-painted white and black. An apartment door—abandoned, by the looks of it—that had been busted open. With his back against the east-facing wall, he moved in a shooter's stance, hands gripping the pistol too tight. He peeked into the opening. Nothing. He checked the other side of the dumpster. Rain beat down over his head and down his clothing, pooling in his shoes. He blinked hard and swept the rain away from his face with a shoulder.

Then he had a thought. He clicked the circle on the caller and tried dialing it. He jumped at the sound of a ringtone playing somewhere upstairs. And then it stopped. He tried again. This time, nothing.

Eddie took the stairs silently. The way up was narrow. Water-rotted with black spots of mold. The dampness clogged his nose. But it was the least of his worries, so he kept moving. At the top of the staircase, he quickly jutted his head out into a room and pulled it back.

No gunfire. He cornered the door and stepped inside. Something crunched beneath his step. When he looked down, he saw little gray bones. Something in here had eaten a rodent, something small. He kept moving. He was in an apartment. The cabinet doors in the kitchen had all been left open. Nothing was inside them. He turned into the hall.

Walked past a bathroom, where the toilet had no seat. A plunger was stuck in it. Dirty blue tile crawled the length of floor. A stain left from where a small rug had been removed from in front of the mirror, which was broken to bits.

At the end were two bedrooms opposite each other. He dialed the number again and this time heard the ringtone sound in the one to the right. Eddie turned the corner into the room with the gun raised. Something . . . the phone! It glowed beneath the bed. He ducked low and aimed. Nothing. He started to stand. And that's when he heard the creak behind him, and everything turned black.

◆ ◆ ◆

His vision blurred. He was being dragged downstairs, the back of his skull clanging off each step.

Stars flashed behind his eyes. There was something dangling before him . . . Eddie's head felt like there was a bomb inside it, ticking at the disturbingly quick pulse of his heart. The agony . . . the warm blood that gummed beneath his hair . . . the searing burn in his abdomen. What had been done to him? He touched a fingertip to the pain beneath his shirt and felt . . . something crinkle? His legs fell hard to the ground. And whoever had hit him, whoever had done something to him, powered his phone back on, placed it on Eddie's chest, and left him there.

He strained. "Motherfucker."

He tasted metal. Blood, surely. For a while he stayed still, unable to move. Until he remembered that someone was at his home. His wife in the kitchen. His son at the table. They'd unlocked the door. Opened it. His family . . .

His phone chirped.

He reached for it. Pain shot through his body. Through narrow eyes, he saw his wife and son in the background. Eddie Jr. was younger then, in a baseball cap and Little League uniform. His wife was behind him, pushing him higher and higher on the swing set.

He saw the number of texts from his wife. Eleven of them. The most recent was only minutes ago. Unless someone had her phone, that meant she was okay.

He typed: Sorry baby. Ran into an old buddy, got caught up. Be home soon.

He stumbled to his feet and hobbled the excruciating half step down to the pavement. He searched for a set of footprints, but they'd already been washed away in the rain.

Then he read the message in the bubble that popped up. He began to cry.

Chapter 33

December 23, 2021

Tess Harlow undressed and stepped under the strong hiss of warm water. The room was dark. She'd kept the lights turned out and the P226 only feet away, set on the toilet lid. That was about as far as she liked to keep it these days. Just out of reach, but she was quick enough to snatch it and squeeze the trigger before anyone could get close.

The last two cases in Minnesota made her that way. Paranoid. She hated to say it, but they'd changed her. Altered her DNA.

She would check locks two, three times now. Study the darkness beneath the bed. Imagine the flashes of a muzzle, the violent clap of a semiautomatic. Walk with her hand on the grip of the pistol, glancing over her shoulder. On the bad nights, she'd even prop a chair beneath the door handle so no one could get in. If someone *did* knock or turn the handle, she'd press the muzzle up against the door and check the peephole.

Gregory Sadler and Hartley Caldwell would room with her for the rest of her life. Occupants enjoying cozy stays inside her nightmarish mind. Now there was one more to add to the list.

When she was finished, she turned the nozzle off and wrapped herself in a white towel.

Seeing Barry Lewis dead reminded her of both John Riggs and Millie Langston, two of her people that had died at the hands of a serial killer. She picked up the phone and dialed Martin.

After a few rings, he picked up. "Hey."

"Hey," she tried, her voice tired and fighting off tears.

"What's wrong?"

"I don't know if I can do this anymore."

"What happened?"

"One of the agents is dead. It's just like Riggs and Millie all over again. I'm tired. I'm angry all the time. I want to come home."

"You can't," he said. "Tess, you've gotta remind yourself why you're there. You've caught two of these bastards already. Unfortunately for you, you're too good at this to have the luxury to call it quits. Those FBI agents need you. So does Rooker. When it's all over, you can come home."

"Promise?"

"Promise. Your seat at the dinner table will be waiting when you get back. Get some sleep."

Chapter 34

He'd been typing up a piece on his recent conversation with Tate Meachum, along with the death of Joey Miggs, when a knock at the door made him jump.

He shut his laptop and opened the door to find a disheveled Eduardo Arroyave, pale-faced and red-eyed and damp with the rain. A faint scar blemished the edge of his jaw. Rooker recalled the night his knuckles cracked there and knew that it had taken a surgical procedure to mend the bone.

The man he once knew stood shaking in the doorway. He was in a pair of dirty jeans and a dark-gray shirt that clung to his skin; his shoes were coated in water. His hair was cowlicked, spiky with a wet sheen. Rooker saw what appeared to be darker stains on his upper abdomen; dark crimson smears and blotches that resembled blood. Only at first glance, he didn't appear to be bleeding. He was clutching a plastic bag from Ralphs.

"Hey, man." Eddie blew out a shaky breath, stepped inside, and leaned against the wall. The powerful aroma of rain—but more like wet pavement—and perspiration radiated off him.

"Eddie," Rooker said in disbelief. He did his best to put his feelings about the former cop behind him. "What're you doing here?"

Arroyave spoke in a grave voice. "I . . . man, it's been a while."

"Yeah, it has."

"You look good, Rook."

"You've seen better days." Rooker cracked a smile. Arroyave returned a weak one, and then his face snapped back into its former look of exhaustion, and what Rooker imagined was fear. He turned his hand over and stared into it. His right hand had been balled tight since he'd walked in the door, his knuckles white and raw. Rooker asked him again what he was doing here, followed by how he knew where to find him.

"Man, I didn't want anything to do with any of this shit. You know that, right?" Before Rooker could respond, Eddie spoke again. "When I got that phone call . . . *shooot, maann.* I was hoping it was a joke. The body . . . I should've known . . . I should've taken the kid and Tracy and gone . . ." His voice trailed off.

"Eddie. What happened?"

Eddie unlatched his hand and showed it to him from afar. His fingernail had turned black. Arroyave lifted his shirt. Rooker's eyes went wide with shock. Surrounding the wound was a fair bit of coagulated blood. Stitched into Eddie's abdomen was Rooker's latest article in the *Times.* On it, dark Sharpie letters read: 9-1-1 QUINCY.

"Fucker got me, man. Lured me into a trap. I think he's got Tracy and Eddie Jr."

"Jesus Christ." Rooker spoke low, appraising the black sutures and large silver staples that embedded deep—too deep, Rooker thought—into Eddie's skin. He sent a quick text to the team, then led Eddie over to the sofa, where he was able to recline and take some pressure off the mess of his stomach. Rooker couldn't think of a thing to say to his old friend. They sat in shaky silence until a few minutes later when there were more urgent knocks on the door.

As Eckhart, Hall, and Quincy filed into the room, Eddie pulled up his shirt again and showed them the message. Quincy crossed his arms and said, "Shit, guess it's my turn."

Rooker saw Eddie give Quincy a peculiar look as he slowly sat up and put his feet on the floor. "I'm supposed to give you this," he said to Eckhart and gestured to the Ralphs bag on the floor by his feet. Eckhart snapped on a pair of gloves and opened the bag. He pushed the sides of the bag down so the rest of them could see what was inside: a ball-peen hammer.

The face of it was smeared dark red. Eddie stood up and walked a few paces into the center of the room. "He said there's a print on it."

A fingerprint? Rooker appraised the look on Arroyave's face. It was the look of someone who had done something horrible—or was about to. *What the hell is going on?*

He turned to study the hammer more, but in the corner of his eye, he caught Arroyave bending forward, and Rooker swiveled back toward him. Eddie's face was cradled in his hands, and Rooker could now see a golf-ball-size welt on his head.

"Fuck, man. I'm sorry," Eddie mumbled. Fast, he reached down to his ankle and pulled a pistol out of a holster.

"Gun!"

As Rooker heard Tess's voice from the doorway, he yelled the only words that came to him. "No, no! Eddie! Wait!"

Just as Eddie brought the gun up to fire at Quincy, Rooker watched a bullet tear into him. As Eddie collapsed to the floor and the gun fell from his hand, Rooker saw the dark pit beneath the grip. There was no magazine in the weapon. Jack Hall was quick to kick it away anyhow.

In that moment, he'd realized how guilty he'd felt for blaming Eddie, and how sorry he was for throttling him and not stopping until he was pulled away. Because now he just wanted his old friend to live.

Chapter 35

December 23, 2021

Arroyave was alive. In police custody albeit, but alive. His family—Tracy and Eddie Jr.—were placed in protective custody, someplace unknown and guarded around the clock. Rooker told Eckhart to get him out and that any good person would've done what Eddie had done.

In Rooker's eyes, the death of Barry Lewis and the media shitstorm that followed the shooting at the hotel made Eckhart look like he was one more mistake away from getting pulled off the investigation.

All the big channels had been tipped off. The pavement was swarmed by pairs of cameramen and reporters.

The killer had chosen his messenger well. He knew that Eddie was the kind of man who would do anything to save his family, even if it meant dying. And whether Eddie killed Quincy or not, there'd be no keeping any of what happened under wraps: an ex-cop was shot after showing up to the FBI's door with a murder weapon and a pistol.

But the news outlets didn't get the full story. Forced to give them something, Eckhart filled them in on Arroyave's abductor and family in danger. But he didn't tell them that it was a civilian—former Itasca County Sheriff's Office lead detective Tess Harlow—who fired the bullet.

Rooker stood by Tess while she watched the muted news broadcast, white closed-captioned letters ticking across a solid black bar on the bottom of the screen. When Eckhart appeared on the screen being interviewed by a reporter, Rooker powered the television off. "Why would he do all this?"

She didn't answer.

When he turned to her, he noticed the pain in her face. The anger in her eyes. "This isn't on you. You thought you were saving everyone in that room—"

"I could've killed him. The killer sent him here to die. I pulled the trigger."

Rooker sighed. "Sending Arroyave here to die at the FBI's hands. Esparza left for dead. Messages for Eckhart and Quincy. I'd assume he's next, right?" Rooker nodded his head in the direction of Hall.

"Yeah," she said. "Or me."

That's right. He cursed himself. The killer left his name on the cooler where Miggs's head was found. If there was another message to be found, it would in some way be intended for either Jack Hall or Tess Harlow.

Rooker's phone buzzed with a call from Caroline. He walked out of earshot and answered it.

"Hey."

"Hey," she said.

"Calling for an inside scoop?"

"I was actually calling to see if you were okay."

Shit. He shut his eyes. "I'm sorry. Yeah, I'm okay. Everything's just getting crazy all over again. I just want to come home."

"You will soon. And then all of this will finally be over."

"Who says?" he shot back. "Every time, it's something new. Someone different. Someone who wants to torture me or see me dead. How do I know this is where it ends?"

"Because whoever's doing this, I think this is where it all began."

Rooker thought about that for a long moment. After Britton, there were no other victims found. And if it really wasn't Meachum, the killer hadn't murdered anyone else until Natalie Carlisle found him. Was Britton meant to be the grand finale all along until, by some miracle, a researcher found him in an old experiment and came to him all alone? He pulled a pen from his pocket and scribbled on the back of his hand. "Maybe after all this is over, we fake my death. I grow my hair out and dye it. We go somewhere far, where no one will ever come looking for me."

She laughed. "Quite the plan. I've gotta run. Be careful."

"I'll do my best."

The call ended, and Rooker peered down at the inked letters between the light hairs and veins of his hand.

WHO ELSE HATED GUNNER?

WHO HATES ME?

WHY?

"Lindström," Eckhart called out.

"Yeah."

"I've got good news and bad news. Which do you want first?"

"You call it."

"The print came back. The good news is that it isn't Tate Meachum's."

"So whose is it?"

"Well, that may be the bad news in your eyes. Whoever sent Arroyave in here, they went through the trouble of dusting the handle of the hammer with carbon black . . . maybe even a long time ago. The latent print is old. But in at least ten points of the print—keep in mind criminal courts usually accept eight to ten points of similarity—it's a match with Gunner Lindström."

Rooker shut his eyes and rattled his head side to side. He opened them, staring with disbelief into Eckhart's face. "How is that possible. You're sure?"

"Positive. I had his file pulled just to be sure. It's a match."

Rooker had been through Gunner's file front to back several times. There was never a hammer entered into evidence.

Why would a hammer have his father's prints on it?

Chapter 36

December 23, 2021

Rooker did the only thing he could think of doing. He pried open his laptop screen, navigated down his files, and double-clicked on one labeled GUNNER.

What it was he was looking for, though, he wasn't sure.

But an hour later, he was standing in the center of at least fifty photographs that covered the floor. Every crime scene photograph that was taken at Lindström Manor was on the left portion of the carpet, and every crime scene photograph taken of the Madman murders—except for his son's—was on the right.

In his underwear, he maneuvered his methodical steps in the gaps between the printouts, scrutinizing each photograph and comparing what he saw between the victims and the objects in the background.

The photos from Lindström Manor were mostly the same. The padlocked ice chest. Clusters of dead faces and individual shots of each. Incision marks at the base of the neck. The drops of blood that specked the large cubes of ice, and the shard-like crystals that glazed the cadaver-white skin and tangled shades of hair.

All the Madman murders had been the same. The killer had stalked his victims, learned their routines, and found a way of entry into the home. But that all changed with one victim.

He looked at Natalie Carlisle's image again: the bruising, the blackened fingernail and the time carved into it, the incision wound deep in her chest. The skin removed from her back was the clear difference in MO. Still, there was something different . . . something odd. A little redness and puffy skin at her earlobe. He bent down and snatched the photo up. It was too tough to see. He pulled up the photograph on the laptop and tapped the touch pad to enlarge it.

There was a tiny black pinprick there, with the faintest redness circling it.

Had she just gotten her ears pierced? Had the killer pierced them? Or had he removed her earrings by force, and that explained the redness?

Rooker looked at the rest of the Madman's female victims. Focusing on their ears. Each one had her ears pierced.

But does that mean something?

He did a quick search on Joel Hunter, found his telephone number, and dialed it. When Hunter didn't answer, he left a voicemail and a callback number.

He uncapped a pen and scribbled beneath Natalie Carlisle's body: HER EARS.

When he'd decided to call it quits, he got dressed, shrugged on his jacket, called a cab, and walked out of the hotel.

Chapter 37

It was dark. The pale moonlight trickled through the window, offering little light to the space, aside from pinning his shadow on the floor.

Rooker had spent the silent hour and a half back to Hemet listening to the drone of the yellow Crown Victoria and the sickly phlegm cough of the driver, with his head down and his eyes either closed or staring blurredly at his phone's display.

Hunter hadn't called him back. But it was late. Most people would be asleep by now. When the cab dropped him off at the curb half a block down the street, Rooker tipped well and asked the man to wait for him. Forty-five minutes at most, and he could keep the meter running. Then Rooker got out and hurried through the yards of his former neighbors.

He'd painted the room he was sitting in twice. Once when Laura was pregnant. He'd done it blue after she'd told him they were having a boy. The second time was when Britton turned six and wanted to change it to a dark gray to resemble the solar system. Laura protested and said it would be too dark. But Rooker painted it anyhow and stuck lights up on the ceiling that looked just like the constellations and spiraling galaxies that fascinated his son.

Laura said that one day he'd outgrow it all. She was probably right. And that was fine by Rooker, who would paint it over again, as many times as it took, whatever color his son wanted.

Suddenly he thought about how he sometimes stumbled over his words in front of his son, thinking he needed to hand-pluck the perfect ones to say. But his son wasn't a print editor or some newspaper subscriber. Being there to say something—anything—was better than what he ever had. There were no valuable lessons to be learned from his father, unless you count that a straight punch travels fastest or that a solid hook to the temple or the solar plexus was good night for any man. If Britton ever asked about his grandfather, the only bedtime stories he could tell him were more like nightmare fuel. *Your grandfather made me kill someone when I was just a few years older than you. He clocked me good one time—well, many times—but this one time, he left me there in the fetal position on the basement floor.* He'd always changed the subject.

He spent years trying to perfect the speech he'd one day need to give, about who his grandfather was and what happened to him. And why some people would tease him without ever getting to know him. There was no hiding it. Or hiding him from what was on the internet.

He listened to the front door unlock and open. Then the flick of the switch as light seeped in through the bedroom door that he'd opened a crack. The door creaked open.

"You really ought to move that key," he said.

So far, he'd done a good job of keeping the bottle at bay. It was propped up on the bed the way a fancy restaurant server presents one tableside.

"Jesus!" He heard her let out a short breath. Had he been any closer to her, he was sure he'd be able to hear her heart thundering in her chest. She held a palm there over her blue scrubs. "I thought you were in LA?"

"I took a cab. Why are you getting home so late?"

"I picked up a shift," she said. "The hospital's been crazy lately. You scared the hell out of me."

"I'm sorry."

"Maybe one day we can have a conversation where you don't say that. How did you get past them?"

Laura's hand, fingers still clutched on to the key fob for dear life, pointed outside where Rooker knew the black FBI surveillance van was parked.

He shrugged. "I know every inch of this neighborhood, remember? They probably didn't see me. I'll make sure to get another set of eyes on the house. Just to be safe." Before she could protest, he added: "It doesn't smell like him anymore . . . the room. What happened to his clothes?"

Her eyes shut, and she raked her fingernails along her forehead. "I hung on to them for a while . . . But the thera—" She stopped herself. "I was told it wasn't healthy. Sitting in here. Sobbing into his T-shirts. For a while it was just about every night. Then less and less. I donated everything about a year ago."

He didn't know how to feel about that. For the last five years, he'd held on to the hopeless thought that some piece of his son still existed within these walls. That his clothes would be folded in the drawers. The telescope would still be positioned by the window, pointed at the moon. He was mistaken. In almost every way he could see it, his son was gone. But not just gone—removed.

He forced away the selfish thought. *Britton may have been taken from me. But I'm the one who left.*

"Who are the flowers from?"

She laughed. "Just a guy I've been seeing. You might like him; he's a writer. If you want, we can do dinner and—"

He held up both hands. "I'd rather you shot me."

A smile lined her face.

"I loved him, Laur . . . more than anything. You and him . . ." He stopped. He tried to swallow hard, to send the aching burn down deep into his belly so that he could at least speak. It was no use.

He pulled the chip from his pocket. Twirled it between his fingers and tossed it to Laura, who caught it like she was cradling a death-stiffened bird. "Six months," he said. "Twenty-eight weeks. What do I have to show for it? That chip . . . that keeps reminding me how bad I want to drink. Because look at how evil this world is. How the hell can you not want a drink. A different mass shooting every day. Serial killers leave messages for you by name. A head in a box and a note on top of it that says *my* name. *Mine.*

"And you know what? Step one is admission. At these meetings . . . they want me to say that I'm powerless against alcohol. I can't even do *that.* Because I don't believe it in here . . ." He jabbed a finger hard into his chest. "I'm one stubborn bastard." He paused. "You were married to me; you know that better than anyone. I'm not willing to say that I'm powerless to anyone or anything . . . *except now.* Except for evil. And when it just keeps knocking at your door . . ." He breathed out a shaky breath and cleared the rasp that felt like a rake climbing his throat. The tears that were building but not falling. "*Knocking and knocking . . .* How am I supposed to just sit by and do *nothing?*"

For a long moment they stared at each other. And then Laura's eyes glossed over. She wiped away a tear as it dripped down her cheek. And then she trudged somberly toward him. "Your gift, dear . . . you see it as a curse. And that stubbornness inside you always will. But you're too good in there"—she pressed her palm over his heart—"and too smart here"—she tapped his temple—"to believe that what you're doing is *nothing.*"

Her voice soothed him. He pictured her fingers running through his hair, his feet kicked up on the arm of the couch and his head in her lap, that voice just a whisper so she wouldn't wake Britton. "More people would be dead if it weren't for you."

That last part could be argued, he thought. Strangely, he heard Hartley Caldwell's voice suddenly. *"You think it's all about you."*

That's right. It's because of me that you and Sadler came out of hiding.

She hugged him and his shoulders slumped, and the thought of Gunner's fingerprint, along with the Peekaboo Killer's voice, faded away. His forty-five minutes were almost up. He pressed his face into the small of her inner shoulder. His hands clutched on to her shirt, not ready to let go just yet. "I really am sorry."

Chapter 38

December 24, 2021

The Madman set a fresh roll of duct tape, the knife, and a ball-peen hammer down in her lap. He'd driven five hours—most of which in the far-right lane only a few miles above the speed limit—to the hum of his blood. The fizzle of wind rushing through his window cracked open. The jagged pulse of the diesel motor.

He hadn't run any red, or even yellow, lights. He was a careful person.

But now the van was hidden in the brush outside, where he'd let it coast after he shut off the engine. He sat in the center of the sofa, the mask hot over his face, staring at the two whimpering bodies tied up in side-by-side leather armchairs. Their pleas caught beneath the silver tape.

The husband had been gone for only half an hour, and now the gravel driveway hissed and popped under the tires. The Madman pictured him parking outside the raised wraparound deck that reminded him of a clown on stilts and walking through the dark house, not knowing it would be his final moments.

◆ ◆ ◆

"I'm back," the voice hollered. "A hand with the groceries would be nice." He swung the door shut with his heel.

In both hands, fingers burning, he lugged the plastic bags into the kitchen and used his leg to leverage them up onto the kitchen counter. *Why is it so dark in here?* He walked back out into the living room, where he found his wife and son tied up.

The last things he heard were the shuffled steps behind him, the heightened groans in the two chairs where his family was tied up, and the eerily calm voice before the hammer came barreling down.

"Hello, Warden."

Chapter 39

It was Christmas Day. In his mind, a 70-degree California evening didn't particularly scream festive, with heat shimmer glistening over the streets of Los Angeles. Waves of haze slithered over the holiday lights, making them appear as though they were burning.

Rooker wondered if he'd ever truly liked it here in the City of Angels, or if his oldest memories had been ravaged by tragedy.

As a child, Rooker never really cared for Christmas. His mother would sneak him gifts behind Gunner's back, and he'd been too afraid to open them if his father was around. But as a father, he'd come to love the magic of Britton diving beneath the tree and pulling out all the presents he thought were from Santa. He loved watching Laura smile as she opened the few presents that he'd wrapped horribly for her.

Now the day only reminded him of everything he'd lost.

Rooker stepped into the conference room where Jack Hall and Deion Quincy sat. "Where's Eckhart?"

"My guess"—Hall crossed his arms and sighed—"at the bottom of a bottle. He's not answering his phone."

At the third bar he tried, Rooker found Scott Eckhart with an exhausted, stubble-ridden face and an empty glass and a fresh one with ice in front of him. The low lights made his irises look black. He twirled the full glass slowly in his hand, watching the dark liquid circle until he brought it up to his lips.

Most of the seats at the bar were taken. Luckily the one he needed wasn't. Rooker plopped down onto the stool beside him, the cracked leather sagging beneath his weight. "Bourbon?"

Eckhart didn't lift his eyes. He spoke into the glass. "Jameson."

"What are you doing here, Eckhart?"

"What's it look like?"

Rooker peered around the dive bar, appraising the paint and wallpaper peeling behind a group of twentysomethings at a rickety table wearing unbent-brimmed Angels and Lakers caps. Ever since he'd realized that the Los Angeles Angels in Spanish translated to "the angels' angels," he could never take the team seriously again. The man to Eckhart's left had a salt-and-pepper beard and wore his gray hair in a ponytail. Leaning forward with his forehead in his right hand, behind red, spectacled eyes, he struggled to read his cell phone, which he held too close to his face. The woman to Rooker's right reeked of cigarette smoke and asked too loudly what time the Lakers game was starting. On the television, the Boston Celtics were down against the Milwaukee Bucks in the fourth quarter.

At the back of the bar, an ATM flickered red and green from the neon signs hanging above.

Eckhart's phone lit up on the wooden bar top. He had more missed calls and text messages than Rooker could keep track of. "I think your family is looking for you."

"Yeah? What about Lewis? He was like family. What about his family?"

"Barry Lewis understood the risks of the job—"

"Bullshit, Lindström. You think anyone gets into this thinking they're going to hunt a serial killer?"

Before Rooker could reply, the bartender, a heavyset man with white hair and dark, bushy eyebrows, appeared. He nodded at Rooker. "What can I get you?"

"I'm good," he said.

"Nonsense." Eckhart tilted his drink and polished off the rest of it. "You know who this guy is, don't you?"

The bartender surveyed Rooker. "You do look familiar—"

"That's Rooker Lindström," Eckhart slurred. "The celebrity. The Man in the Lake and the Peekaboo Killer." He shook his head. He slammed his glass down hard, and it broke in his hand. "They were no match for the prodigal son. They say he's so good because he's got his daddy's brain . . . he can think just like him. A monster hunting monsters, imagine that?"

Sensing trouble brewing, the bartender pressed two meaty hands palms-down against the bar top, spiderlike curls of hair growing out of his knuckles. "I won't have any issues in my place, you hear me?"

Rooker waved him off with a gesture of his hand. He took out his wallet. "I'll pay for the glass." He turned to the lead investigator beside him, who was losing it. "Look, Eckhart. I came here to bring you back."

"And I want to bring Lewis back."

"I wish it worked that way. It doesn't. If you want to make it up to him, you catch the guy who's still out there."

Last night, he'd turned down Laura's offer to stay the night and instead caught a fitful hour of sleep in the back seat of the cab. His head had bobbed and snapped upright. In the wakeful moments, he stared through the plastic partition that separated the front and rear seats at the neon brake lights all set ablaze, thinking about the odd feeling of being in his ex-wife's arms. Even after all this time, their love floated electrically between them, a warm, tingling sensation covering his skin, but neither of them spoke of it.

The thought of Laura's roses on the table by the front door kept him up till 4:00 a.m. He wasn't interested in meeting the writer dating his ex-wife, but it didn't keep the image of a faceless man standing in his house from lodging in his mind.

Rooker had managed nearly two hours of sleep in the hotel room when he woke to a call from Joel Hunter early that morning. Hunter claimed that Natalie Carlisle's ears had been pierced within twelve hours of her death, and he took that as the killer must've pierced them himself. He had thanked Hunter, not sure what that information meant yet, and hung up.

By the time he and Tess reached the field office, Eckhart had sobered up, showered, and shaved. He was dressed in a pale-blue dress shirt, tie, and dark slacks. But the dark circles beneath his eyes lingered.

All their leads in the investigation were pinned to the wall or displayed on a projector screen. Rooker was drinking black coffee from a Styrofoam cup when Jack Hall jogged through the doors with a worried expression on his face. First, he whispered to Eckhart, who in turn side-eyed Rooker and murmured something back.

"Listen up," Eckhart commanded. "We may have something. Place called Brentmoor."

Rooker shut his eyes. *It can't be.*

Hall held up what looked like an invitation card, sealed in an evidence slip. Rooker stared at the message on the envelope: To ROOKER AND FRIENDS.

The invitation was typed out in black cursive font, and the address looked like an old headline cut out of a newspaper:

You are cordially invited to:

Brentmoor

"What's Brentmoor?" Tess asked.

No. Please no. His palm covered the tightness in his chest. A sharp pain overcame him—a sickness spreading within, building from the pit of his belly, climbing up his throat—with the very mention of the name Brentmoor. He'd been there only once, but he'd never forget all the empty sets of eyes on him, vacant and dark as dead ones. Or the day she came home, and the way she stared vacantly at the songbirds while he brushed the tangles from her hair in long strokes. A hideous amount of hair webbed in the bristled teeth, as if he were grooming a shedding dog. "A psychiatric center," Rooker answered.

Hall scoffed. "*A psych ward?* No, no, no. It's far from a mental institution. It was an insane asylum."

Tess's eyes narrowed. "I don't get it. Why would the killer send you—"

"Because he's playing games," Rooker shot back.

"No," Hall said. "I already checked it out. It's because your mother was sent away there. Here—" Hall dumped a file into Tess's hands. "There was a report that she tried to kill herself in front of her sixteen-year-old son."

Rooker's fist clenched. "She never tried . . . She was sick. You try marrying a psychopath and see how you manage. How did you even get that?"

"Is it still there?" Tess asked.

"Brentmoor Psychiatric Center closed down twenty years ago because of some unlawful"—Hall gestured air quotes with his fingers—"experiments on patients. It's just an abandoned building now. The dare-seeker types sneak in at night from time to time because they say it's haunted. Really, I think it's just some adrenaline junkies who use it as foreplay."

"Let's pack it up," Eckhart ordered. "Vests on. The van leaves in five. Sounds like someone's left us something to find."

Without turning to face her, Rooker stared straight ahead and said, "She never tried to kill herself."

"I'm sorry," said Tess.

"She's the only person who ever had my back. Her and Millie."

"What about me?"

Still not looking at her, he said, "You pick and choose, when it's convenient. Like most people."

"Ouch."

Two foggy white lights splashed holes into the darkness until they were a block away from the facility. "Lights off, Jack." The rest of the way they drove cloaked in the shadows. Rooker listened to the hum of the motor and the thumping in his skull. The van crept to a halt at the curb. Hall killed the engine.

"All right, we're here. Let's go."

The van doors unlatched, and they filed out into the night.

Rooker imagined it thirty years ago, with beautiful red brick and perfectly manicured grounds. Orderlies and nurses out for an afternoon stroll. But now as he stood in a sea of wild grass that twisted around his shins, he stared up at the four-story-high building where tall shrubs consumed the low border of gray concrete and dark roping vines crawled up the sides and snaked through broken windows. Beyond the building, dead trees swayed catatonically with the wind. The edge of the roof appeared charred, and shingles and exposed wood suspended toward the ground. He suddenly pictured his mother loopy and drugged in a flowy hospital gown, staggering in shuffled steps down a hallway not far off from the one at Pelican Bay, a shell of the woman he remembered.

"Fuuuuuck this, boss. Can't we come back in the morning?"

"Don't be a pussy, Quincy."

"Man, it's always the Black guy who gets it in places like this."

Hall snickered.

"It's going to be dark inside. You'll be the hardest to find. Let's go." Eckhart slapped Quincy hard on the back of his vest, the Velcro crackling, and led the way.

Eckhart pulled out a flashlight with his left hand and flipped it on. With his thumb pressed against the tailcap switch, he crossed his wrists right over left, the Glock 17 held firmly. He nodded at Hall, who gave the entrance door—marked with a black spray-painted arrow that pointed inside—a good push.

The door creaked open, and Eckhart's team moved inside.

The air turned stale. In the flashlight's beam, Rooker eyed the peeling mint-green walls. Pieces of the ceiling had crumbled to the cold concrete floor, which was smattered with the foul-smelling droppings of whatever critters were hiding within. Rooker imagined a bomb going off in the room, or a flesh-eating virus that had somehow spread to the walls.

"Quincy, on me. Hall—" He nodded at Rooker and Tess, then in the direction of the right side of the room.

Hall nodded. He held a flashlight high above his shoulder in his left hand, with his arm in an L shape. The light sprayed in front of him, and he moved with his eyes just above his pistol's sights.

Rooker peeked into the first room on his right. Layered in thick, sandy grime, it reminded him of the powdery snowfall he'd watch coat the lake behind Lindström Manor. Mounted to the wall was a white sink with black mold growing from the exposed valves and porcelain smeared in red that could only be blood. One end had been smashed to pieces. On the ground beside it were wooden crutches splintered where they'd been busted in half. Three old folding wheelchairs—ruined leather and bent spokes—were positioned ominously in the center of the room, as if three people Rooker couldn't see were sitting in them, talking to each other. There was a thin wooden chair there with a padded back, and straps and buckles intended to keep a person's head and body motionless.

Rooker pictured pure chaos unfolding here. Maniacal laughter. Ear-rupturing screams. Bite-proof masks that made patients look more like supervillains than people. If places like this still existed, he could picture Tate Meachum buckled down to a table and some evil doctor cutting open his head.

From a shattered windowpane a foot above a sealed-off fireplace, the wind breathed cool air down his neck and spine. He fought the urge to shiver and moved back out into the corridor. The team was scattered in the depths of the hall. The only sign of them was the faint glow coming from one of the many open rooms.

Rooker moved hurriedly toward one of the lights until the room opened up to a wide staircase. The balusters resembled a set of broken teeth, and the railing itself was warped and rotted. Where the starting step was rounded and missing planks of wood, Rooker stepped over.

"Hey," Tess whispered behind him. "What're you doing?"

Rooker shrugged. "You coming or what?"

She shook her head and took the pistol out of the back of her jeans. At the landing, the stairway ended at a large set of murky windows—one arched and one rectangular on either side—overlooking the courtyard. From there, two other sets of stairs continued up to the third floor. He took the stairs to the left in cautious steps. Tess moved ahead of him with her pistol up and her flashlight crossed over it. The heavy air freed a drop of sweat from his forehead.

The third-level corridor was empty. On the floor, sheets of paper were scattered along with trash and large pieces of ceiling that had come down. There were ten rooms. But one, with white pillars that bordered the entrance to a larger room encased in glass, had its door propped open.

The first room they entered had been trashed. An old mahogany table was flipped upside down. The radiator beneath the window— where vines had slithered inside to the wet floor—had been smashed.

Rooker stayed close behind Tess as she cleared room after room.

When they'd made their way inside the largest room on the floor, there had to be twenty beds spaced out. Black-rusted metal bed frames and thin, stained mattresses that reeked of decay.

They made their way up to the fourth level. At the top of the stairs, Rooker saw the black arrows spray-painted on the floor leading to the faint light at the left end of the hall at ground level, and a shadow moved.

"Tess." He nodded his head in that direction.

She raised the SIG Sauer and aimed down her sights, glancing fast at the ground and back up, stepping carefully to avoid the debris. She cornered the eastern wall and moved.

Snap.

The noise made them both duck low and spin around, Tess with the pistol ready. But they saw the large figure standing there, peering down at the broken glass beneath his boot, and knew it was only Jack Hall. Tess nodded her head in the direction of the light, and they moved together.

They cleared the other rooms quickly. They moved toward the last doorway, until a rat—fat and reddish brown—scurried out beneath their feet. Followed by another. Rooker imagined that whatever the killer had left them to find, it had brought the rodents out to feast.

In the last room was where they found it.

Filthy seafoam-green tiles ran halfway up the wall, and a panel of opaque windows looked out over the courtyard, vines growing through two that had been busted open. Crinkled leaves skated across the floor. Despite having the look of a torture chamber, the room had served as a doctor's office. There was a shelf of broken drawers where instruments once had been stored and a large light mounted above a medical chair. On the chair was a body dressed in a gown, its hands and feet strapped down. One of the fingernails on the right hand was black. The left hand was wrapped delicately in bandages. The flesh at the feet had been picked at, and Rooker pictured the rats tearing away with their little teeth.

The face was covered by a photograph that took up an entire sheet of paper and had been duct-taped around the neck and head.

A frigid shiver cut through him. Her face was how he tried his best not to remember her. It was from when she had been admitted to Brentmoor. Distant, unblinking eyes. Dark patches around them as though her face had sunken in.

It was his mother.

"Christ," Eckhart said behind them. He and Quincy came into the room.

With a gloved hand, Eckhart wedged his pocketknife beneath the edge of silver tape and cut it. Then he gently unwrapped it from the face. The photograph careened to the floor.

Rooker's mouth opened. He took a step back.

The dark face was ruined. Several fractures and bone breaks were hidden beneath the bubbled skin. Contusions unlike anything he'd seen. The nose had been smashed. The dark ring around the left eye closed shut. The victim's mouth drooped open, dripping blood.

It looked as though someone had slowly driven their tires over the skull, until all the bone and tissue and brain had popped. But he knew someone had done this with repeated strikes to the head.

"Shit," Rooker hissed. His legs buckled, and he covered his mouth with his hands.

"Who is it?" Quincy asked.

"Is that—" Tess stopped.

His wife's and son's names were carved into the concrete of Meachum's cell. Just as Rooker's was. "It's Lamonte Hastings. The warden at Pelican Bay."

Chapter 40

ERT took over at Brentmoor. Work lights powered by generators had been stationed everywhere since electricity to the building had been shut off decades ago.

Hall ran his fingernails through his stubble. "How could he have found him—Hastings?"

"Yeah," Eckhart said. "I thought you said he was long gone."

"I thought he was," Rooker told them. "I don't have a clue where he went. But the killer clearly found him. What worries me now is his wife and son. Jada and Terrence. Their names were carved into Meachum's cell too."

"I'll get a search out for the wife and son."

"Why in the world would he kill the warden?" Quincy asked.

They stuck around to watch a man in a long-sleeved navy-blue ERT shirt snap on a pair of purple gloves. To Rooker, the careful unwrapping of the bandages reminded him of a mummy being unraveled, or a cocoon ready to hatch something beautiful. The white cloth unwound farther and farther until finally, the last piece of it uncovered nothing beautiful at all. It was a hand . . . but no ordinary hand.

Definitely not Lamonte Hastings's hand.

It was a skeleton. Filthy, dark bone. An odor of putrid earth and decay radiated off it. Pins at the wrist had secured the skeleton to the edge of flesh where Hastings's hand had been cut off.

Rooker's body went cold.

Jack Hall gasped. His mouth fell half open. *"Holy shit . . ."*

"Holy shit is right," Eckhart said.

"San Jacinto Valley Cemetery." Rooker scratched the skin just above his eyes. "I'd bet all my money there's a grave that's been robbed."

Hall turned his head to the sheet of paper with the face on it. "You mean—"

"Yeah," Rooker interrupted. "I think it's my mother's hand."

Hall pulled up something on his phone. "Boss. Hastings doesn't have any other properties in his name. But there's one in his mother's name . . . a home listed out in Oregon. Thirty-three Marina Lane, Gleneden Beach."

That had to be it. Rooker could picture Hastings scaring his wife and son in the middle of the night, telling them to pack what they could and get in the car.

"That's a five-hour drive from the prison," Eckhart said. "I'll make a call and get some people in the house."

Eckhart made two calls. The first one was to the Lincoln County Sheriff's Office in Oregon. It hadn't taken long before the local police found Jada and Terrence Hastings bound to chairs side by side. They were alive, but far from okay. Judging by the blood pool in the room, they'd watched the warden die right in front of them.

The second call was to the cemetery where Amanda Lindström was buried. Sure enough, the staff found a grave plot dug up. The casket had been smashed open. Whoever had done it had stolen the left hand, closed the casket, and scattered the loose soil back over the top.

The left hand . . . if there was some sick meaning to it, he had a feeling he knew what it was. It's the hand you wear your wedding ring on. A sickening feeling in his gut told him it meant *till death do us part*, and by *us*, it meant him and the killer.

He imagined his mother being reburied with her hand missing and hoped that the cemetery could hold off until after the bone had been examined so she could be put back together.

Rooker understood that death was the only constant in this life. Watching a loved one pass away from old age in a bed was sad. But witnessing someone brutally murdered before your eyes . . . or finding your son's body mutilated . . . that was far different. That was something you could never unsee.

Rooker spent all night typing up an article with a sour taste in his mouth. In the wordless gaps in his typing, he'd pressed his elbows into the desk and massaged the dull throbbing behind his eyes, dropped to the ground and performed straining amounts of push-ups, or sipped the bitter caffeine that had lost its warmth.

He replayed Deion Quincy's words over and over. *"Why in the world would he kill the warden?"*

Rooker didn't have an answer.

And now it felt like another name that Rooker could add to his own list of people dead because of him. If he could drink a toast to Hastings now, he would.

Just after three in the morning, Rooker sighed and fired the email off to Dezzy King's inbox. A jet landing soon at LAX hissed overhead. Snores boomed through the thin wall behind him. Letting out one long, convulsive stretch, he sat up and wondered what he'd just done. Had he just kicked the hornet's nest? With one glance at the bed, he decided it was no use and headed for the door. Breakfast wouldn't be served for hours. Still, there was a coffee machine.

Yet as he strolled down the hall, he found a foggy-eyed Tess Harlow pouring herself a cup.

"What're you doing awake?"

She rolled her eyes. "I don't sleep much anymore."

"You sound like me."

"Lately, more than you know. How are you doing?"

"I don't know. I never expected him to go after Hastings. Lamonte . . . he was one of the good guys. Hated when I called, sure. Didn't want to get mixed up in my bullshit, but he always answered the phone. He always helped. I didn't know him *that* well, but for some reason I can't shake something that he said to me years ago. It was when Meachum got to Pelican Bay . . . He told me that the devil was behind bars, and it was time to go back to living."

"Is that why you're up?"

"I just sent an article to the *Times*. After it's edited, it'll probably hit the website next week."

She shook her head. "Why can't you stay out of trouble?"

His eyes lifted. He shrugged. "It's information the public should have. Nothing that interferes with the investigation. And something that won't make our killer happy. I gave him a new name."

"*Why?* Eckhart is going to want your head on a platter."

"Well, I wish him luck with that. I've been thinking . . ."

"About?"

"What Tate said. 'One old and one new.' Instead of focusing on missing persons, I think we need to look back at old murder cases."

She crossed her arms and snickered. "We wouldn't even know where to start."

"Hear me out. We look at unsolved cases. We search for anything and everything where someone's been bludgeoned to death. Beaten with a blunt instrument. Anything that remotely could be related.

"And what about suspicious deaths? What if he made it look like an accident? Or suicide? Or let someone else take the fall? Look at Meachum. He's not innocent, but Esparza was right. We don't know who he killed, or *if* he killed *anybody*. He could've just been an accomplice. Help or don't. I'll check it out alone if I have to."

"Hey, don't do that," Tess said. "I'm not saying I won't help. I'm saying that what you're talking about doing is going to take some time. *A lot of time.*"

"We can't predict who he's going to go after next. The best we can do is try to throw him off—that's the point of the article. To get in his head . . . while we do the important work and dig up whoever it is—the victim—that Meachum thinks we'll never find. The killer is linked to that person in some way. I'd bet my life on it."

"That's nothing new. You've been risking that ever since I met you."

Rooker smiled. "So you'll help me?"

"Yeah. I just think it may take more than just the two of us."

"Well, then, tell me what you have in mind."

Chapter 41

December 26, 2021

The sun was radiating off the parked cars and glass buildings but not shining through the dusty blinds drawn tight at Isabel Esparza's apartment. The shades and curtains all looked as if they'd been shut for weeks. Grime coated each slat. Beyond them was darkness. Too dark to see anything.

Her unit was on the second level of what looked like a massive home with a square bite taken out of the center. Two large palm trees reached out of the earth. In the gap was a concrete path to the other units, a patch of grass, and a smaller tree. A staircase climbed up each side and connected at the back. Up the stairs and at the first door on the left was where they stopped.

Tess banged the edge of her fist against the white security door once. Twice. Three times. "Esparza! It's Tess Harlow."

They waited. There was no response. She knocked again.

This time, the blinds rattled. One lifted and snapped back into place. Behind the screen in the door, just a shadow.

"Yeah?"

"Esparza? It's Tess and Rooker."

The door opened.

In the shadows, Tess caught the bruising that hadn't yet fully healed around her eye. The last time she'd seen her, the eye had looked sewn shut, but now it was mostly open. Her right hand was wrapped. White bandages wrapped around two of her fingers—there were multiple fractures. She wore a long, loose-fitting shirt and no pants. "Come in," she said distantly. "Hope you don't mind; it still hurts to wear clothes."

Tess nodded.

Inside, it was cold. The AC unit in the wall blasted on the highest setting. Tess imagined the walls of the seven-hundred-square-foot space shivering. "Sorry. Doctors said I'm not supposed to sweat. What can I do for you?"

Tess appraised the darkness. Bottles and bottles of pills were lined up like soldiers and ran nearly the entire length of the small kitchen counter. She imagined most of it was for anti-infection and the pain.

Esparza sat down slowly on the edge of the chaise portion of a gray sectional couch.

"We're hoping you could help us," said Tess.

"If you couldn't tell"—she waved her white bandaged hand—"I'm on paid leave. I've gone into the office once since everything happened. Sat down with the higher-ups. Since then, I've been here."

"You can help from here," Rooker said. "That part was Tess's idea."

"Help with what?"

Rooker and Tess exchanged glances. He was the one who spoke. "We're going to start looking into unsolved murder cases that date back thirty years."

Esparza laughed. "What now?"

"I don't know if you've been brought up to date on the case," said Tess, "but Meachum said something cryptic the last time he spoke with Rooker. He told us there are two victims we haven't found yet. 'One old and one new.'"

"So why not start with the 'new' one? Someone would have reported them missing. Wouldn't that be the one that's easier to find?"

"Maybe," Rooker said. "I hate to say it, but the problem with that is it doesn't lead us to the killer. Now the older victim . . . we have a feeling that one does. We think he killed someone he knew."

"How exactly am I supposed to help?"

"We need to look into unsolved murder cases," Tess said. "If something looks suspicious, we pull the file. We're thinking that we should narrow down the results to victims who have been severely beaten. Also, see if there's anyone with a blackened fingernail."

"Beaten? That because of Miggs? Sounds to me like you're on a wild-goose chase."

"You have a better idea?" asked Rooker. "And there's another victim as of last night—Warden Lamonte Hastings from Pelican Bay. He was beaten beyond recognition, right in front of his wife and kid."

Tess could see that had gotten Esparza's attention. She no longer looked vacant and stared at Tess intensely for a few seconds.

"Does Eckhart know about this?" Esparza asked.

Tess said, "No. He's stretched thin as it is. We can do it, but not on our own. If you haven't noticed, Rooker and I don't trust many people."

"And why me? Because I'm a woman?"

Tess wanted to reply, *No. Because you're the only one smart enough to see right through the two killers in front of you.* But she sighed wearily instead, and Esparza made a "forget about it" gesture.

"I still think you're looking for a needle in a haystack," Esparza said. "The parameters of your search need to be smaller."

"We're listening," said Rooker.

"Where was Hastings killed?" she asked.

"Oregon. Little beach town called Gleneden," Tess said.

"Okay. So with the exception of driving to Oregon to kill Hastings, every murder has been here in California. I think the search should be California only. If we don't find anything that fits, we can widen the search. And I think each of us should be responsible for a time period. If you're looking at the last thirty years, one of us should take 2010 to 2020, one takes 2000 to 2009, one takes 1990 to 1999. Maybe even stretch it to thirty-five or forty years to be safe. Keywords will help us: strangulation, bludgeoning, repeated strikes, hammer, et cetera. But narrow it down too much, we risk something slipping through the cracks."

"Good," Rooker said. "You're hired."

She leaned forward, wincing. "I trust my team, you know."

"I did too," Tess said flatly. "You remember how that went. Gregory Sadler posed as Elias Cole for years, sitting a few desks away from me every day. I'm not saying someone on your team is the Madman. But I want to play this close to the vest. All I'm asking is that you help us rule out one haystack."

"Fine," Esparza shot back. "When do we start?"

"Now."

Chapter 42

Prior to their visit with Esparza, Rooker had spent the morning tracking down Diego Rollins, the son of Julieta Rollins, who was the last suspected murder victim of the original Madman.

"Again, what are we doing here?" Tess stared at the beige ranch home where the white garage door was stuck a quarter of the way down on a slant.

He replied, "I figured we'd start with the epitome of a wild-goose chase. Come on." He stepped out of the car, and Tess followed him to the door. He was following a hunch. There was something odd about Natalie Carlisle that had embedded bug-like in his brain. Hunter had said Carlisle's ears were very recently pierced prior to her death. It was very likely that the killer had done it himself. But what Rooker didn't understand was: Why?

Rooker rang the doorbell and the chime brought an older woman to the door. She had dark curls of hair and time-ravaged tan skin and was wearing a pair of reading glasses. She peered down over them.

"You who I think you are?"

Just past her was a mantel with picture frames as close together as bowling pins. He made out Julieta Rollins in quite a few of them. In one she wore a hospital gown and held her son, Diego, in her arms, probably for the very first time. Rooker had a photo of Laura and Britton just like that, somewhere. In another photo, Julieta had her hair tied in a ponytail, bangs all over the place, while holding on to the back of a bicycle that a small Diego was sitting on wearing a helmet far too big for his head. There was one of Diego in a cap and gown—middle-school graduation, he assumed—standing in front of the school steps beside his grandmother. His mother was already gone by then.

"I'm afraid so. I was hoping I could speak to Diego, ma'am. Only for a few minutes."

"Mm-hmm," she muttered. "Diego," she called out.

A moment later, Rooker was staring at a boy he hadn't seen in some time. He'd sprouted quite a bit, shoulders broader and muscles beginning to fill out, though his face remained remarkably similar.

"Mr. Lindström, right?"

"That's right. You remember me?"

"It's okay, *abuela*." The boy opened the door and stepped outside. "Yeah, you look better now. Hard to forget. Drunk, asking questions about Mom. If I remembered anything about the night she was killed."

"Do you?"

"Nah, man. I was a little kid. Sleeping. Never heard anything. You came back, though, after you caught the guy. I think you wanted me to know I was safe."

The memory of him visiting Diego Rollins the second time had escaped him, probably due to the state of inebriation he'd been in. After you catch the person responsible for destroying the most important part of your life, what else is left to do but get shit-faced?

Rooker had checked up on the boy over the years—really, just Google searches—to see what popped up. Nothing ever did. He imagined that was a good thing.

"You got big. You staying out of trouble?"

"Yeah, taking care of my gramma. All A's and B's. Working part-time after school to help her out. I seen you on the news. You really think the guy is still out there? The one who killed my mom?"

It was not that Rooker didn't have it in him to lie. If he put himself in the boy's shoes, he wouldn't want to be lied to. He'd want the truth. Rooker smiled weakly, his eyes distant and unable to match his mouth's grin. "I think so. I'm sorry . . ." His voice trailed. "I thought I had him. Turns out I only solved half the puzzle. I'm going to have some police looking after you and your grandma, just to be safe."

"Okay."

"Do you mind looking at a couple of things for me? I have some photos here. If you don't recognize anything, it's no big deal."

"Go for it."

Rooker plucked the first photograph from a manila folder. Handed it to the teenage boy. "Recognize it?"

In the photograph was the face in the rocks, the graffitied concrete, and the barred tunnel.

"Devil's Gate dam, right?" He handed it back to Rooker.

"You ever go down there?"

"A couple times with friends."

"Never with your mother?"

"No, not that I remember. Why?"

"No reason."

He tried another one. But the boy reached out and snagged the stack of photographs from him.

"Wait," Rooker told him. "There's some in there you shouldn't see."

The boy shook his head. He riffled through them one at a time until he landed on one of his mother's face after she was found dead.

"That's what I didn't want you to see." Rooker held his hand out to take them back. But Diego stared long at the photograph.

"I don't think she owned earrings like that." He handed the photo back to Rooker.

Rooker's pulse quickened. "Why not?"

"She was allergic to gold."

Chapter 43

On their way back to the hotel, Rooker got a call from Joel Hunter, saying he could come in and see what he had on Lamonte Hastings's autopsy report.

Natalie Carlisle's ears had just been pierced prior to her death. What Diego had said about the earrings couldn't be a coincidence. His mother's ears were already pierced, but she would never have worn gold. Rooker couldn't be sure yet, but he had a feeling the killer had taken her earrings and replaced them with someone else's. Maybe even the victim prior to Rollins.

He and Tess took a detour to Boyle Heights, where Hunter worked out of the Los Angeles County Department of Medical Examiner-Coroner building. The facade was old, beige, and red brick. Outside the building above a tall wrought-iron fence was an LED sign that read: LAW AND SCIENCE SERVING THE COMMUNITY. Rooker and Tess strutted up a long, wide set of stairs that led between two square columns and into the main entrance.

Inside the autopsy room, they found Lucian Hurst in a white coat with his back turned to them, scrubbing his hands beneath a chrome faucet. On the table was a body covered in a white sheet.

He turned over his shoulder and started drying his hands with a towel. "Rooker, Tess. How's the investigation going?"

"Just great," Rooker answered sarcastically. He tried his best not to inhale too deeply; the room carried a strongly astringent odor, along with the smell of death. "There's a family out there that will forever associate Christmas with watching this man being beaten to death."

"I'm sorry, I didn't mean to . . ."

"It's okay," Tess answered.

"I get it," Hurst responded. "Everything seems so personal. To dress him up as your mother . . . to rob her grave. It's sickening."

Hurst usually stood back quiet and perceptive, and even though he was just being kind, Rooker wasn't in the mood to discuss his mother or the case. Not with a man he knew next to nothing about.

Luckily Joel Hunter walked into the room then, in a pair of blue gloves and bifocals strapped at the base of his prickly-stubbled head. "Shall we?"

He motioned them over to the table, and Hurst put gloves on and pulled the sheet down just above Hastings's hips. His face was unrecognizable. Hunter said, "The facial contusions on your victim have caused an epidural hematoma here where the skull fractured, meaning there is bleeding between his skull and the outermost layer of the brain, the dura mater. It would have been life-threatening untreated, and there are patients who die without immediate treatment. This beating that he underwent is what killed him. But the reason I've called you here is the hand. Whoever did this has medical knowledge."

Tess said, "What makes you say that?"

"There are killers who dismember their victims, sure. Gunner Lindström beheaded his victims. Maybe twenty years ago there was someone in Turkey known as the Severed Leg Killer who murdered victims throughout Istanbul and left severed legs to be found. It isn't exactly a rarity when it comes to serial killers; there are a lot of cases. What I do think is rare is when you see the amputation site so clean. It resembles an operation a surgeon would perform to prevent the spread of disease.

"Here at the base of the cut, you can see that part of the bone has been filed down and ice has been used on it prior to the pins being inserted and the skeleton added."

"So you're saying he's not new to this," Tess replied.

"I wouldn't think so," Hunter said. "By the way, I didn't really know how else to say this, but your mother's hand has been returned to her grave."

Rooker nodded.

"But my point: experts seem to believe there's often a correlation between dismemberment and occupation. There's a good chance his job has something to do with a medical, if not surgical, practice."

Rooker sighed. "I don't mean any disrespect, Hunter. If you had said that five, six years ago . . . I would have agreed with you. But right now, he's ahead of us. He has photographs of us along with the entire FBI task force hunting him. He's picked two victims connected to Tate Meachum that we would've never guessed he'd go after; how he even found Hastings is a mystery. Gregory Sadler had a brutality about him, but this guy seems to be even worse . . . like he's able to switch it on and off. I mean, he beat Hastings and Miggs to a pulp. The rest were killed methodically. He seems to have planned all this well ahead—he knew about Brentmoor, for Christ's sake. He got the best of Eddie Arroyave and used his family to turn him into a pawn. Caldwell was dormant for more than fifteen years before he killed Malin Jakobsson, and eight years after—and somehow, I get this gut feeling that this guy is even more patient . . . like he doesn't have the same need to kill. Who knows if he ever would've resurfaced had it not been for Natalie Carlisle finding him."

Lucian Hurst looked from him to Tess. "Don't you think you're giving him too much credit?"

Rooker replied, "Maybe not enough." His head throbbed behind his skull, and suddenly he felt sick looking at what was left of Hastings's inflated face.

Just as he was about to say something else, Tess interrupted him. "Thank you again." She looked at Hurst and then Hunter. "We'll get going."

They walked back the way they came, and the moment they were outside, Tess spoke. "You can't start doing that again."

"Doing what?"

"Acting like the world and everyone in it is out to get you. Because then you take it out on anyone near you."

He smirked. "That sounded like Millie."

"Well, she would've been right."

"She usually was." He paused. "When I was investigating this after . . . let's just say I had the same thought as Hunter right now. I thought the time of death on the fingernail meant something . . . that I was looking for someone with a medical background. Whether it was someone who performed surgeries or worked as a mortician or had been operated on in some capacity. But then I found Meachum. And now I don't know what to think. Because I feel as though I can't trust my own thoughts . . . like everything I'm thinking is what he wants me to think."

PART III

Three weeks later

Chapter 44

January 16, 2022

Rooker sipped bitter black coffee from a paper cup. It tasted like charcoal. He'd done his best to eat the powdery scrambled eggs and a bland bagel from the hotel's breakfast selection.

After he'd finished, he wiped egg from the corner of his mouth and the crumbs from his shirt, crumpled the paper cup in his hand, and threw everything away.

His head throbbed as it typically did from a lack of sleep. The bright-white ceiling lights—especially the one flickering in his peripheral view—didn't help. He was thinking about Julieta Rollins and what her son had said about her being allergic to gold. His mind went to Natalie Carlisle, but then his attention was snatched away. He got a call, his phone buzzing on the table. It was Dezzy King. "Yeah," he answered.

"Rooker, it's Dezzy. I want to get another story out. That op-ed piece was a hit. Everyone loved it, and I'd like to strike while the iron's hot. Can you get me something similar?"

"What do you mean it was a hit?"

"Web traffic, views, new subscribers—everything is going up since your article. The people want more. I was thinking add another story about your past and sprinkle in some updates on the investigation. Which reminds me: I've got my own mystery to sort out."

Rooker knew that what was selling was less about his writing and more about him. He would never escape the legacy of his father, his child's death. They would always be what defined him. At least as far as the public was concerned. This new case was just a distraction.

"I've got an obits guy—Michael Boyd—missing." Dezzy continued. "Hasn't phoned in or emailed. I'll have to get someone else to write the damn things."

Funny, Rooker thought. He remembered some of the old-timers at the newspaper. Guys with scissors and glue, cutting up pieces of articles and carefully laying them out in new ways. The obit desk was no exception. Where better to get material than from your old files?

"It's always in the files," Rooker muttered to himself. "Dezzy, I'm going out on a limb here, but there's something stuck in the back of my head. The killer is a writer." *Not unlike me,* he thought. "He is used to writing newspaper style. He's making handmade newspapers. He writes the articles himself. When did your guy go missing?"

"Around the time all this crazy business started. But Rooker, this is a stretch. You've been working on this too long. You are seeing connections where there are only a few lines of text. I'm sure the guy will turn up soon. I'll take that article as soon as you can get it to me. These people will eat it up."

But something in this moment felt right. Rooker ended the call and did a quick Google search of Boyd, which turned up only obituaries he'd written. *Trust your gut.* That's what had led him to Meachum. But Michael Boyd had no other articles and zero images. He was a ghost.

Chapter 45

"Esparza." She banged her fist on the screen door a second time. "It's Tess."

As the locks unlatched and the inside door cracked open, a bleary-eyed Isabel Esparza stood in the shadows. "What's going on?"

"I wanted to ask you for something."

"You already have, remember? You want me to dig up old homicide cases dating back thirty years and for me to not tell my team about it."

"Look . . . Can I come in?"

Esparza hesitated, then opened the screen door.

"How are you feeling?"

"Like I look," Esparza replied. "Can we cut the small talk?"

"I wanted to see if you've gotten anywhere. Any names, leads, something we can check out."

"I've been up all night looking. I told you, I'll let you know when I find something. Now if you don't mind, I'm in a shitload of pain. And I need to get some sleep."

Tess didn't have time for sleep. This wasn't the kind of case you could sleep on.

"There's one more thing . . . I want you to leave Rooker alone." Tess knew she shouldn't say it, but she couldn't help herself. Rooker wasn't the villain here. He had secrets—didn't they all—but the key was something else.

Esparza snickered. "Well, there it is. That why you're here?"

"No. I think there's something in the homicide records. That's why I'm here."

"*Bullshit.* You know what I think? You killed Jan Cullen and Clyde Miller. And he killed the girl they found beneath that cottage. So now maybe you feel guilty if he takes the fall for it, and maybe if he does, he drags you through the mud with him."

Tess could feel her cheeks flush as the blood rushed through her body. Esparza wasn't wrong. But then she thought about Millie and how she'd ended up here on this case . . . about second chances.

"Look, you've got your mind made up about him, and about me. I'm here to find the Madman. Don't forget it was me and Rooker who found you hobbling out of that tunnel half-dead—" Esparza's eyes widened, and Tess took a breath. They'd all been spinning their wheels for weeks, but that was no excuse to taunt Esparza over getting injured, especially in the line of duty. "You want justice for something right now . . . for the shitload of pain you're in? Help me find the homicide case that's connected. *Please.*"

"Fine. I'll drop it . . . for now."

Chapter 46

When Rooker arrived in the field office, his phone buzzed, and he walked out of earshot. "Yeah," he answered.

"Rooker, it's Dezzy again. Sorry to call twice in one day—"

"I haven't been able to start that assignment—"

"No, that's not why I'm calling. That guy that I told you about, Michael Boyd, I got ahold of his editor. Anyway, he tried to run down Boyd's address, and it came back to an apartment in Los Angeles. But the name on the apartment is Todd Evans. When the editor called, Evans said he has a roommate that hasn't been back since late November. The guy's name is Reed Thompson."

Rooker's blood froze. "Thanks, Dezzy. I've gotta go."

He was in a daze. His aching skull went numb. Rooker hurried into the room and said, "Pull up everything you can find on a Reed Thompson."

Tess wore a look of concern. "What's going on, Rooker? Who is that?"

"Reed Thompson writes obituaries for the *LA Times*. My editor there said they've been trying to find him—he's been missing almost two months."

Jack Hall crossed his arms. "So?"

Rooker marched to Hall's laptop, which was hooked up to the projector, and started typing a name into a search bar. He hit enter and they all gazed up at the screen—at a page full of blue links. He clicked on one.

Her face was beautiful yet pale. He remembered her from the boxed files that were tucked away in Peter Sundgren's attic.

"Oh my God." Tess covered her mouth.

"Who is that?" Hall asked.

"That is Astrid Thompson. Reed's dead sister. Reed believes my father killed her."

During the Gregory Sadler case, Astrid Thompson's file was the only one missing from Gunner's records in the basement level of the Itasca County Sheriff's Office.

Rooker thought of Peter Sundgren. Sundgren had told him that while investigating the murders Gunner committed, Astrid Thompson was the victim he'd thought of for years. He said that unlike the others, who were all single women, she had a long-standing relationship. The cut across her neck was far more jagged—imprecise—than the other victims'. Sundgren wondered if Gunner was in a hurry or if for some reason he'd begun to lose his strength.

Rooker had finally put Sundgren's mind at ease; Astrid Thompson was killed by none other than the teenage Gregory Sadler, a disciple of Gunner Lindström. That explained why her file was missing. Sadler took it out because she didn't belong to Rooker's father.

There was no telling whether Reed Thompson had just climbed to the top of the suspect list or if he himself was a victim of the Madman. But if he was the killer, and if Gregory Sadler and Reed Thompson had ever been in contact, Sadler never told him he killed Reed's sister.

Chapter 47

Rooker dialed back Dezzy King. When he answered, Rooker spoke fast. "Dezzy, I need you to go through his desk."

"Whose desk?"

"Michael's desk. Or whatever the fuck his name is."

"Rooker, is it really that important? I'm sure the drawers are locked. The guy doesn't want people rifling through his shit when he's not here."

Rooker was losing patience. "Look, I know this seems like a stretch. But I'm not going to leave this alone until we are sure. Get the key. Open the desk. If it's just gym shoes and a rotting lunch bag, you can rub my nose in it."

Dezzy paused. "Give me a couple of minutes."

Rooker waited on the line, listening to the chatter and background noise that came over the phone. He heard the clatter of keys, and Rooker listened as the drawers opened one by one.

"All these drawers are empty."

"Keep trying them."

"Wait . . . I've got something. There's an obituary here without a date . . ."

"Is it Natalie Carlisle's?"

"No, Rooker. It's yours."

Shit.

"One more thing," Dezzy said. "Lindsay Morris sits across from him. She said she overheard him talking to his girlfriend, maybe wife."

Horror shot through him in the form of a thought that made him feel sick.

He remembered Laura's voice when he'd asked about the flowers.

"Just a guy I've been seeing. You might like him; he's a writer."

Not only had Reed Thompson disappeared around the same time Natalie Carlisle was murdered, he wrote for the damn *LA Times*, and he was dating someone. In his churning gut, Rooker knew.

Chapter 48

Laura had spent her morning exercising at a Pilates studio, where an instructor kicked her ass in a dark monochromatic room with blue neon lights and shiny cement floors.

With the night off, she set up a date and went home.

Once inside, she set off to the bathroom and started the shower. For a long time after Britton died, it was a place she went to cry. Before Rooker left, she had walked around like a zombie, and between her sister Cora and her mom and dad, she was treated like she was on suicide watch. For weeks she would start the shower and sob as quietly as she could.

But now she got out of her sweaty sports bra and leggings and kicked them to the rug, then hopped in and smiled at the thought of her date.

After she dried off, she rubbed lotion over her bare skin, wrapped the towel around her wet hair, and dressed in a cream-colored ribbed top, black lace panties, and a black skirt.

In the kitchen she gave the homemade Bolognese a stir. She'd made the tagliatelle pasta from scratch—on a cutting board she'd made a volcano out of flour, cracked and dumped eggs into the center, and beat them, gradually mixing in the flour. Eventually it formed a ball of dough, which she rolled out, cut, and twirled into the right shape.

It'd been quite some time since she'd done so much for a date, and for some reason, and she hated herself for thinking of him, it reminded her of Rooker.

When she heard the car pull into the driveway and the door shut, she set a pot of water on the stove and turned it to the highest setting, salted it, washed her hands, and poured two stem glasses half-full with a primitivo red.

She did one last tussle-fix of her hair.

"You're early." She smiled as he walked through the entry with a red bouquet. He wore a white dress shirt unbuttoned at the top, blue plaid pants, and tan dress shoes that buckled closed. He looked handsome. She kissed him and took the flowers out of his hands.

"I couldn't wait to see you," he said and sat at the kitchen island, where he stared at her with playful eyes, tapping his fingernail impulsively. "It smells incredible in here."

She smiled. "I did everything from scratch," she said.

"What can't you do?" he asked.

"I'll let you know when I find something." She laughed and handed him one of the glasses.

When the bubbles and steam rose from the pot, she dumped the pasta in and asked him about work. He tapped his fingers again and told her that the writing he did wasn't exactly invigorating, but someone had to do it. After a few minutes, she turned off the burner and forked a piece of pasta on a dish, with a small spoonful of sauce. "Taste test?"

He grinned. "I'd like more than a taste."

"Smooth. Maybe if you're lucky," she said, and in her peripheral she noticed her phone had lit up. It was Rooker. Her hand closed over the phone quickly, and with a finger held up, she pulled it to her ear.

◆ ◆ ◆

"Hey," she answered skeptically.

"Where are you right now?"

Rooker couldn't hear much in the background. Maybe a metallic sound, one like a fork scraping a plate. "I'm having dinner. Can it wait?"

"I need his name."

"What?"

"Is it Reed? Reed Thompson?"

"How could you—"

In the most urgent tone, he said, "Listen to me. You need to get out of there right now. He just became a suspect in our case."

"I can't do that right now. I told you, I'm about to sit down and have dinner at the house."

"I'm sending police there now."

"Okay, great. I can look at his chart when I come in tomorrow."

"If he comes near you, you grab a knife from the kitchen. Otherwise, lock yourself in a room. Get outside and run. Whatever you do, stay away from him."

Laura ended the call.

◆ ◆ ◆

"Is everything okay?"

She smiled at him. "Yeah, everything's fine. Just work calling me on a day off. I was hoping to get a night where I'm not bothered."

He sat there as though he was waiting for her to sit down. She didn't.

He folded his napkin, tossed it on the table, and stiffened. "Laura?"

"Yeah?"

"Who was that, really?"

Her pulse was out of control. Reed was tall and lean. There was no way she could overpower him or sprint out the front door. She'd have to get out one of the bedroom windows or lock herself in a room and hope the police made it to her in time.

With a hand pressed against the counter, he tapped slowly and pushed off to stand. "Why do you keep looking at the door? Is something the matter?"

She shook her head nervously. "It's nothing, I promise. Work has just been more stressful than usual the past few nights."

"Laura . . . why are you lying?"

Her eyes narrowed. "I'm not."

He took a slow step toward her. Then another. She took a step backward and he stopped. His dress shoe fell perfectly centered in a piece of white tile. His finger brushed over the counter and tapped. "I saw your phone. Why is Rooker calling you?"

"What . . ."

"Laura, I thought we were just going to have a nice dinner."

"That's what we're doing. I . . . I'm sorry. I think I've just been doing too much today. I can feel a migraine coming on. I'm just going to get some aspirin. I'll be right back."

Laura sauntered slowly from the room and could feel his eyes on her. Before she'd answered the phone, Reed's eyes had seemed calm, maybe lustful, but now they seemed predatorial. Whether she was imagining it or not, she trusted Rooker more than anyone when it came to her safety. He was a man who would die for her, and she felt in her heart that he still would.

When she was out of Reed's view, she hurried into her bedroom and locked herself in. She backed away to the far wall and crouched down. From the afternoon light that came in through the windows and from out in the hall, she saw his shadow and his shoes. She hadn't even heard him move.

The door handle clicked. She heard a thud, then his muffled voice as though he'd pressed his face against the door.

"Laura." Rhythmic ticks reverberated through the door. Then a slow carving sound scratched up and down. "Why don't you just open the door and let me taste you again." She heard a dark laugh that was foreign to her. "I don't want to kill you, Laura. I really don't."

Thwack.

The door vibrated, and she now saw the point of a blade from her kitchen drawer wedged through to her side of it.

She felt herself shaking. Fast, he struck the door over and over until finally it broke off the hinges and blasted open. She screamed. That's when she heard the front door open and boots thudding into the house, voices screaming at the man who stood almost perfectly still, attempting to pull the knife from the door. Then there was a quick electric snap, and she watched Reed Thompson's smile fade as he convulsed to the ground.

Chapter 49

Since Reed Thompson was the prime suspect in Natalie Carlisle's murder and the investigation was a federal one, Eckhart got him transported the same night to Los Angeles. Sitting with his arms manacled in front of him, Thompson wore a look of fatigue. His head drooped. The white dress shirt he wore had crinkled, and his pants were ripped at the knee. They'd taken his shoes.

"I've arranged for you to speak to him," Eckhart said. "If he's going to talk to anyone . . ."

Rooker nodded. "Thanks."

"Same thing goes. You don't touch him. You can give him this"—Eckhart put a folder in Rooker's hands—"but that's all."

Rooker walked to the door, opened the file to see what was inside, and closed it. The door opened for him.

He sauntered to the table and took a seat across from the man. There were three uniformed officers in the room. One by the door behind Rooker, and two standing with their backs to the wall over Thompson's shoulders.

Rooker imagined he had just enough time to cradle his hand behind Reed's neck, bash his face into the table, and get one more shot in before he was pulled away.

Without looking up, Reed muttered, "I haven't done anything. I'd like to see my lawyer."

Rooker said nothing. He just stared coldly, waiting to lock eyes with the man who slept with his ex-wife.

Reed looked up and seemed unsettled. "Did you hear me? I'd like my lawyer."

Rooker's lips tightened, and he nodded slowly, dangerously.

"And I'd also like—"

He didn't so much as blink. "Do you think I care what you'd *like*? Do I look like I'm here to help you?"

Reed shrunk backward in his seat.

"You know who I am?"

The man snickered. "Everyone knows who you are."

"And who are you? The real Madman?"

Reed Thompson said nothing. His eyes flicked down to the table.

"Look at me, Reed."

Reed didn't look up.

Not until Rooker slammed the edge of his fist hard on the table. The officers flinched and inched a step forward. Reed's eyes went wide, the whites in them flickering. "Do I have your attention now?"

Reed stared at Rooker with a look that he knew all too well. It was fear. He'd grown up in a home wearing that expression. Worry lines formed in his face, and his pupils shrunk to black pinpricks. "I would start talking if I were you. Because right now you're the only suspect in the death of Natalie Carlisle. Do you have amnesia? Any kind of dementia? Alzheimer's?"

"What?"

"I'm asking because I can see that you suffer from obsessive-compulsive disorder, the need to tap your finger. Is there a reason why you do it five times?"

"When I was a kid, I was told that if—*after*—I counted to five, I could do anything."

"Who told you that, Reed?"

Thompson's face blanched, and his jaw constricted as if it'd wired shut. *"My sister."*

"Your sister, Astrid."

"Don't you *dare* say her name!"

The scream reverberated off the walls. Rooker shook his head. "What a fool you are."

Thompson's face began to flush.

"I'll tell you what, Reed. You are no 'madman.' You're far from it." Rooker tapped the file in his hands and slid it across the table. "Gunner never killed your sister. Gregory Sadler did. And I know that for a fact, because he told me to my face. Do you want to take the fall for killing the people in that file?"

"I didn't do it."

"After what you did to Laura, I don't give a shit what you did. The FBI has one suspect. That's you. But I'll tell you what I think. I think you're that same *scared* little boy who had a thing for his sister."

"Stop it—"

Rooker leaned forward. "What a disappointment—Tate Meachum makes you look like a coward. I don't think you've killed anyone. But I'll tell you who else doesn't give a shit. The *real* killer.

"The one who let Tate Meachum take the fall for years before he resurfaced. The one who let you think Gunner Lindström killed your sister . . . just so he could manipulate you into doing anything he said. He framed you better than he did Tate. I mean, to date my ex-wife . . . He'll let you take the fall now."

Reed began tapping faster, harder on the table. He said, "I think I want my lawyer."

"That's fine, Reed. Your lawyer will come in here, and they'll tell you not to say another word. At that point, I can no longer help you."

"You don't want to help me."

"You're right. I already told you. I'm not here to help you. So it's up to you, really. Help yourself, or lawyer up and I walk away. You can take the fall just like Meachum did."

"I'm not a killer."

"Good. Then let's get started, shall we? Who is he?"

"Oh, come on. I have no clue."

"Where does he live?"

"He didn't send me a postcard."

"He must contact you, right?"

"He uses prepaid phones. I get a few text messages from a different phone number, and then he won't use that number again."

"I need everything that you know about him. You must have something."

"He said: *'We're the same.'* That was one of the first messages he ever sent me."

Chapter 50

The Madman was skimming over the article in the *LA Times* with his back pressed against the countertop when his wife strolled too noisily into the kitchen and planted an obnoxious kiss on his cheek. He didn't look up. Her hair was damp from her shower, and it felt like a cold web on his face, and he pulled away.

"What's that?" she asked.

He shook his head. "Nothing really." He turned his phone to her. "They think that killer is on the loose still."

"You mean that guy they called the Madman?"

"Uh-huh." The Madman squeezed the phone too tight. When he noticed his white-knuckled hand, he fought hard to open it. "Now they're calling him something else, though: the Headline Hunter."

"Not sure I like that."

He didn't either. He did like the article about the death of Joey Miggs. But not this one.

His wife rummaged through the tidy cabinet for her lucky mug. "I thought they caught him years ago. Tate Meachum?" Glasses clinked and clanged toward the back, until the Madman had enough.

"I guess it wasn't him." He hurried over to her and snatched the white mug from where he knew it would be.

"Thank you, dear. Why are they calling him that?"

"Because he taunts the FBI with his own newspapers . . . he writes stories on his victims and leaves them for the police to find."

"Jesus," she hissed low. She pressed a button on the black coffee machine, and it gurgled loudly, bubbling like blood and air in a dying throat.

Chapter 51

The room was pitch-black when he woke up to the violent buzz. At first he'd thought it was a wasp that'd gotten through the AC unit. Or maybe he'd been dreaming it. But when he squinted at the bright display of his phone vibrating on the nightstand, the hairs on the nape of his neck bristled at the menacing large numbers that read: 11:37 p.m.

He snatched the phone. With his index finger he punched the green button and listened to the low hum of silence. He switched on the light next to him. "Hello?" he said hoarsely.

"My, oh my. Rooker Lindström."

An ice-cold chill ran down his spine. His pulse began to race, hammering in a way that terrified him.

He threw the covers off and sat over the edge of the bed. Most of his clothing from the day prior—a black long-sleeve shirt, heather-blue chino pants, and brown leather boots—was in a heap at his feet. He scratched at his scarred shoulder. "The one and only."

"Right. You're famous now," the voice said. It sounded robotic. *Voice changer,* he remembered Eckhart saying. "Thanks to me. This is our first chat, isn't it?"

"I believe it is. One time it was Sadler who called me. The rest were your pal Tate."

"I don't know that I'd call us pals."

"What would you call him?"

"A fan."

Rooker thought about that. A fan? "You're more careful than Meachum. Is that why I caught him instead of you?"

"You caught him because I wanted you to catch him. I led you right to him."

"Did you kill my son?"

A snicker. "Ah, the million-dollar question. Let me ask you something: How do you kill what's ready for death?"

"I never really liked riddles."

"You give it a reason to live. I've done that for you."

"Oh, thank you," he replied sarcastically. "So what's the endgame?"

"Isn't it obvious, Rooker? I gave you a purpose. Now I'm going to take away everything you have left, just like—" Just then, Rooker heard the whoosh of a car passing. Weak yellow headlights headed down the road outside. But that sound . . . it came over the phone. Didn't it?

He stood and hurried to the large window. Inched back one of the corner blinds as gently, as little, as he could. He peered out and saw the figure standing on the curb across the street. It was dark. The streetlamp closest to the curb was out. But he could tell that whoever was out there was staring right back at him. "It was nice chatting, Rooker."

A truck came down the road then, the piercing lights slashing two specter-like clouds between them. When it passed the spot, the shape was gone. Rooker slipped his pants and shirt on quickly. He ran from his room and to Tess's door. He knocked hard. "I need you. Now."

He heard her footsteps moving fast on the carpet. The door unlatched and opened. "What?" She sounded annoyed. With one hand she tucked a couple of loose strands of hair back over her ear and fixed her ponytail.

In that split second he noticed the empty beer bottles on her nightstand and the open notebook lying face down on the blanket, along with her white shirt and pajama shorts.

"Grab your gun. Let's go."

Her other hand came from behind her back and into view. She already had the SIG Sauer in her hand.

On the way into the lobby and to the doors, he filled her in on the phone call and the person watching him. Rooker bolted outside barefoot alongside Tess. She sprinted to the spot he'd said with the pistol in both hands. Rooker showered the area with a mist of white from his phone's flashlight. Beyond the sidewalk was a main road and a narrow bike path, with train tracks on the opposite side. Past the tracks, tall oak trees swayed mechanically above a ground that resembled a dark, floating abyss.

Rooker's brain throbbed spastically in his skull. The sudden rush from sleep to alertness left his muscles exhausted.

"Let's go," he said.

"Rooker!"

But it was too late. He'd already shot off into the darkness.

Chapter 52

January 17–January 18, 2022

She lost him.

Somewhere in the darkness that hovered over the ground in the form of black fog.

She moved fast. The hair in her ponytail whipped back and forth. Traffic in the distance hissed steadily, and headlights bounced off the buildings surrounding her.

She stopped between a square stucco furniture shop on the corner—a floral cushionless sofa outside it and an AC unit barely hanging on inside the window—and an apartment complex that climbed three stories.

That's when she thought she saw someone in the alley.

Walking fast.

She turned right and picked up the pace. She ran as hard as she could. Past graffiti-tagged trash bins and parked cars, security storm doors and locked garages. The night air stinging in her lungs. Legs burning hot.

She crossed a street and kept after the figure in the alley that was too far ahead of her still. Despite the pain in her chest, she felt she was gaining on him, sprinting past rosebushes that climbed over a concrete wall and the body of an old muscle car hidden beneath a gray tarp. When the alley turned into a street again she nearly collided with a moving

SUV, the horn's blare scaring her stiff, and she took off to the left, and then turned right, where the blue street sign read **EXPOSITION**. She saw him. Sprinting hard on the sidewalk. She picked up her pace again and heard a whistled squeal somewhere in the distance. *A train. The son of a bitch is headed for the train.* She could see the tracks, the white letters that read KEEP CLEAR. There were only a couple of people waiting, backpacks slung on their shoulders, spaced out around the Metro sign and the signs for the E Line and Westwood/Rancho Park station. She wasn't far behind him now. "Freeze!" she screamed. His square back was to her. Even through the light-blue jacket, she could see he was powerfully built, and she knew she shouldn't get too close. His didn't move. It was as though he weren't even breathing.

The tracks hummed with electricity. The smells of coffee and cigarettes and oil and hot metal.

Standing before her was a man around six feet, two inches. Though she couldn't see his face, it was the Madman. She was sure of it.

She heard the squeal as the train approached the station and slowed. He turned the slightest bit, his face concealed beneath the brim of his cap. The edge of a smile. Tess inched closer.

Suddenly she saw Jan Cullen's leather-jacketed back—the exit hole of where she'd shot him through the chest—before her. She blinked the vision away, and a wisp of hair and drop of sweat fell in front of her face. "On your knees, hands behind your back!"

The onlookers waiting for the next train slowly backed away. They looked afraid.

"Can I see some identification," he said.

"Fuck you, asshole."

"Please," he pleaded. "Someone help me!"

"You're under arrest—"

"She isn't a cop! Someone please—"

Just then, she caught Rooker sprinting toward her in her peripheral. The figure in front of her shifted to her left and she fired. But she missed. The blast echoed and someone screamed. She swung her arms to follow him and fire again, but he was fast. The shot went off, and he didn't even flinch when it tore into his shoulder. He spun and knocked the pistol out of her hands, then spun again and hit her hard above the eye with an elbow. She fell back onto one knee. Her ears rang painfully. Her eyes blurred.

She lurched for the gun.

Just as her fingers wrapped around the grip, she took aim and watched the train doors start to close. His head was down. Another second or two and he'd be out of view. She fired and watched the back of his arm jerk forward. Then once the doors closed, he turned around. She thought she could see him smiling.

"Tess!" She felt Rooker's arm under her. She pushed off the ground and stood. "Are you okay?" he asked.

She felt the numb spot and the warm sting of blood on her head. Dark circles and bright stars flashed in her line of vision. Waves swirled in the corners of her eyes.

◆ ◆ ◆

Rooker took the gun from her, put an arm under her back, and felt most of her weight against him as they walked.

"We have to call the police," she muttered. She staggered then, and he pulled her closer.

"I'll get Eckhart to put police on all the next stops the train makes. But if they get here and find out you fired a gun, we're in deep shit."

"There are cameras," she started.

"I know. That's why—"

"I don't mean for me. I meant that he's on them."

Rooker didn't tell her that the man he saw had his head down and that any overhead cameras surely hadn't seen his face. Instead, he called Eckhart and told him the killer was on the train.

When they returned to the hotel, Eckhart was standing out front with his arms folded across his chest. Jack Hall and Deion Quincy were beside him. At least they could cross off members of Eckhart's team from the suspect list; they now all had alibis on account that no one was bleeding heavily from the shoulder.

"You two look like shit," Hall said.

It was true. They were covered in grime and sweat. Dark circles stained the underarms of Rooker's shirt. Windblown strands of hair stood up. Tess looked the worse of the two. She had a small gash above her left eyebrow and pricker thorns embedded in her left leg, and her white T-shirt was now dirt-pocked and blotched with her own blood.

Eckhart had deep rings beneath his eyes and an expression that was a mixture of worry, anger, and exhaustion. "The hell happened?"

While Rooker explained the phone call and the chase, sweat beaded cold down the nape of his neck.

Eckhart sighed. "You should've come and got me. I made a call. It's late, but I've got as many bodies as possible on every exit off that train. We'll have the camera footage soon. Both of you go and get cleaned up."

Chapter 53

1996

He was just a boy when his mother was taken from him. An eleven-year-old with the muscle tone of someone out of prepubescence.

On a Saturday evening, his mother was applying blush and mascara for a date. Her silky blonde hair ran in shiny waves down to her collarbone. She wore a beige dress with a floral print that flowed down to her shins—a string-tied bow in the chest—and the dainty gold earrings he'd gotten her for Christmas. They were honeybees. He'd mown the neighbor's lawn for months and months just to save up for them. When she'd opened them on Christmas morning, she cried and squeezed him tight.

His father was gone from the picture. She was seeing someone new that he hadn't met. But he could tell she liked him. Since his father left, he'd become the man of the house. He didn't want a new one stepping in to take his place.

Before she'd gone out, she kissed him on the forehead, wiped the red lipstick smudge with her fingertip, and said she'd be back in time for a late supper.

It was nearly midnight when he phoned his grandparents—11:37 p.m. to be exact. And it was a day and a half later that they'd flown to Minnesota and pulled up in a taxi at the curb. Another twenty seconds for them to rap their knuckles on the door.

His grandfather had wanted to keep him a secret from the world. Should anything ever happen, he was told to call him rather than the police. His grandfather was the one who alerted the authorities of his missing daughter.

Only they never found her. And she never came back.

He was forced to pack his things and stay with his grandparents. They lived in a one-story ranch in the desert. Palm Springs. All around was nothing but yellow grass and sand and rock and palm trees. Coyotes howling in the dead of night. The cries of prey falling victim to a predator.

There was nothing to do. One day, his grandfather found a mouse skeleton not far from the yard. A few days later, there were two more. One afternoon, he caught the boy hiding, sawing away with a pocket-knife. Taking the rodent down to the bone.

"*Goddammit*, boy!" His grandfather yanked him up by the collar and dragged him past the carport into the garage. There was a workspace there. A long oil-stained table with a wood top. "Give me your hand!" When he tried to pull away, the old man snatched his hand and slammed it palm-down against the wood. "*Look at that. Freak, just like your daddy was.* You ever hear of a game called Bishop?" His grandfather spaced out his fingers so much that it hurt. "Pinfinger? Five Finger Filet? Usually you play it with a knife. How about we start with this." The old hand pulled a hammer down off the wall. A wood handle and a silver ball opposite the face. He held it firm in the air. "Don't you ever—*ever*—let me catch you doing something like that again. You hear me?"

The boy didn't answer.

That was when the hammer swung down between his thumb and index finger. Then between the index and middle. Hurling down against the nailless bed of skin of his ring finger, the bone crushed. When the boy went to yank his hand away, his grandfather pressed down harder, swinging even harder between the fingers. Until again he caught the boy high on the knuckle of his thumb and it snapped.

The boy's eyes went wide. He glared up at the man. Throat burning. He breathed angrily. Fighting off tears.

"Go get some ice. Tell your grandmother what happened and I'll give you the whooping you deserve."

It was months before the boy tried anything again. But this time, it was the day that marked one year since his mother left and never came back. He trapped a rattlesnake. Brought it into the house and let it into his grandfather's bedroom. He wanted it to kill the old bastard. Bite him. Strangle the life from him. He didn't care. Just kill him.

But when the boy set the trap on the end of the bed, the snake hissed low and loud. Loud enough to stir the old man from his sleep and fling the blanket off him, the snake soaring to the linoleum floor. He watched his grandfather grab a gun from behind the dresser and shoot the snake in the head. His grandmother screaming and crying in the bed.

Standing in the doorway, the old man locked eyes with the boy. "Get your backpack."

The old man dressed. Stained jeans and a lightweight flannel shirt. Stomped his bare feet into a pair of old work boots. He rushed into the boy's room and grabbed all his things and threw them into the kid's backpack. "Put it on and wait here."

Through the wall he heard his grandparents.

His grandmother whispered, "He's just a boy, hon."

"That ain't no boy," his grandfather argued loudly. "We gave him food and a home. We ain't his mother, sure. But the bastard just tried to kill us. Was ready to stand and watch. Ain't no boy, Marie. That's a demon if I ever seen one."

His grandfather rushed out of the room and slammed the door behind him. Pulling him by the backpack, he got him into the passenger seat of the truck and slammed the door shut. The old engine ticked. His grandfather pulled a T-shirt out of the pack on his back and tore it in half. Then he tied it over the boy's face. In a cold, calm voice, he told the boy a story he'd never heard.

"Your mother was sick as a dog, boy—when she had you. *Out of wedlock.* And when you came out, you was dead. Dead for ten whole minutes. No heartbeat. They nearly stopped trying to save you. Your mother begged them to keep trying. And eventually, bam! Your heart started going. Fast too. That's what they said. The pregnancy and the birth nearly killed your mama. That's why she loved you so much. Because you lived even though you weren't meant to. God didn't have plans for you. And now that I see you for what you are, I know it for certain. It wasn't no wet nurse or doctor that brought you back to life. Wasn't no God. It was death himself. Damn grim reaper has a hold on you."

After that, the old man didn't speak. The boy reached out and wrenched the steering wheel. The truck swerved. But the old man managed to right the wheel in time. Stopped. And then with a closed fist, he cracked the boy in the jaw. Beneath the blindfold his cheek split. Everything went numb and dark until he came to. Blood ran warm down his face. For hours they drove. And drove. Silence. Just the roar of the engine clocking somewhere above eighty. The wind rattling the windows. Until eventually the vehicle skidded to a gravel-crunching stop. The old man reached across him and pushed open his door. "Get out. I ever see you again, I'll shoot you dead. Send you back to the reaper."

That was the last time he heard his grandfather's voice. And once he stepped foot on the ground and shut the door, his grandfather made a hard turn and drove back the way they came.

Years later he found his mother. In a photograph. A series, really. Crime scene photographs taken at Lindström Manor. A padlock on the wood floor. An evidence marker beside it. A drop-in ice chest. White. Large enough to fit a body or two. It was open. Filled at least halfway with cubes and unbroken blocks of ice. Little droplets of red splashed a few of them. And severed heads spaced out. They didn't look real. More like mannequins with wigs fitted on them. Only they were real. He knew because of one photograph he'd found. He had to zoom in to make sure. But there they were. Just as he remembered. Her hair was blonde.

Her face was like a bad plaster mold of how he remembered her. In her ears . . . fourteen-carat yellow gold. The earrings he'd picked out, bought, wrapped in paper illustrated with reindeer, mistletoe, mittens, and a present-filled sleigh, and handed her on Christmas morning. The honeybees.

Chapter 54

Rooker appraised the bandaged gash and the colorful lump over her eye. "How do you feel?"

"Like I got elbowed in the face."

Rooker smiled. "Well I'm glad you're okay. If something happened to you—"

"I know." Tess winced and lightly prodded at the lump with the tip of her finger. "I'm fine."

"On the phone . . . He called Meachum a 'fan.'"

"You think it's true?"

What reason did the killer have to lie? "I don't know. He said that I found Meachum because *he* led me to him. I don't think the two of them ever met. Meachum might've just been obsessive—*a follower*—of the real killer. I think somehow, he was able to make contact."

"You want me to believe Meachum found out who the real killer was?"

He shrugged.

"And then he was perfectly okay with taking the fall? Why would he do that?"

Rooker shook his head. "Because he's insane," he said defensively. "I don't know what I think anymore."

"Even if you were right, I think we've gotten about all we're going to get out of Tate Meachum. He's been locked up for six years. If he hasn't given the killer up by now, he never will, or he doesn't know who he is. And by the sound of it, the Gavel's got a pretty good chance of getting him out."

"You're probably right." Meachum on the outside of a prison's four walls was something he'd never thought could happen. He didn't want to think about it now. "There's one more thing."

"What?"

"On the phone . . . he said he was going to take everything from me. And then he said 'just like' before I heard the car in the background and realized he was outside the hotel." He did his best to remember exactly what was said.

"I'm going to take away everything you have left, just like—"

Just like what? Just like everything had been taken away from him?

Rooker nodded his head in the direction of the little black book on the bed. "What's the journal?"

She shook her head. "It's crazy."

"Look around," Rooker said.

It forced a weak smile from her cheeks. "I write their names."

"Whose?"

"Everyone. Nora Vandenberg. John Riggs. My dad. Millie. All the people that are gone . . . that I couldn't save."

"Ah. Let me guess. You aren't writing these names so that you won't forget them. You write them to remind yourself . . . to blame yourself."

Her eyebrows raised in a way that told him he was right.

"So you're just going to beat yourself up over it the rest of your life?"

"Isn't that what you do?"

He smiled sadly at the empty bottles of alcohol on her night table. "It seems like you're taking too many pages out of my book."

"It worked out fine for you."

"My life isn't one you want to copy and paste. Trust me. Want to hear something *truly* crazy? I stood in front of the bathroom mirror a few nights ago . . . Millie was standing behind me."

"That doesn't sound so bad."

"No? She looked like she'd climbed out of her grave. Cadaver white. Dirt and bugs falling off her. Dead hair falling out of her scalp. It was like she wanted to say something to me, but her mouth was filled with rocks. I have to take these damn pills in the hope that it keeps me from seeing things like that. Is that what you want staring back at you in the mirror?"

For a long moment she didn't answer. Then she said, "Maybe it's what I deserve to see. She hated me before she died."

"Millie never hated—"

"I never gave her a shot. And then I acted like *such* an idiot. I just wish I could tell her I'm sorry." Tess's voice wavered. He'd seen that look of despair many times in the mirror. Whether the Madman got to her or not, he could see he was losing Tess. Enough.

He hadn't told a soul the story he was about to tell. He hadn't even told Laura. He imagined the tale died when his father took one last breath . . . *but if there was one person who needed to hear it . . .*

"I was fourteen years old. Olivia Campbell," he said, watching the shock grow in her gold-flecked eyes. "She's the one Peter Sundgren was searching for." Peter Sundgren was the lead detective tasked with finding a serial killer who decapitated his victims and left behind a trail of missing women. He was the one who caught Rooker's father. "For decades Sundgren failed to locate a missing girl that he was sure Gunner killed. She fit the profile. When I went to him during the Sadler case, he handed me her file. I could tell that her disappearance ate away at him for years. This is the truth I couldn't tell Peter.

"I was in the woods that evening. Anytime my father forced me to go along with him to the cottage, I stayed out there in the woods as long as I could. I'd do anything to stay as far away from him as possible. But that night the sky fell fast. And all I heard were the howls—coyotes were always moving in packs through the trees—and they were close by. I ran as fast as I could, all the way back to the house.

"When I got home, Gunner was waiting for me. And this girl with long hair and eyes sparkling with fear—Olivia Campbell—was bound by her wrists and feet. My father told me that if I didn't kill her, he'd kill us both. So I grabbed a pillow . . ." He paused. "To this day, I believe he would have killed both of us. Without even flinching. So the bones . . . the girl you found under the cottage—"

"Olivia Campbell."

Rooker felt nausea rising and ran to the bathroom. Once he caught his breath, he splashed some cold water on his face. Then he held a clean hand towel beneath the spigot until it was damp. Then he walked back and handed it to Tess for the cut on her head that had begun to blotch red through the bandaging. "Are you going to arrest me?"

"Even if I had a badge still . . . you were just a kid. It's not going to bring her back. But . . . I have to tell you something too."

"You don't have to say it—"

"It's not about Cullen and Miller. *Esparza* . . . when I got here, she told me she thought you killed the girl too. She wanted me to help her prove it."

He sighed. "I'd tell her what I just told you. I was a boy. If I hadn't done it, there would've been two bodies beneath the cottage. And we probably never would have been found. Because you would've never met some asshole who would burn the place to the ground one day."

She smiled weakly. "I'm the only one who knows?"

He nodded. "I never told Laura."

"But still," Tess said. "What I did . . . I wasn't a little kid. I wasn't forced to do it. I made that choice."

"It doesn't matter. You'll have to live with it. Just like I have."

For a long moment they sat in a comfortable silence that reminded him of years ago. Tess was someone he'd come to respect and admire. There was a small number of people he'd encountered who ever made that list.

"Want a drink?" she asked. "I need a drink."

"No, thanks. I quit. Six months ago."

"Wow." She stood, wearing a surprised look.

"Yeah," he said. "It was going great until I saw the news . . . the body in the drainpipe. I knew it then. It was happening again. I just want all of this to be over. To run away somewhere no one will find me."

She laughed. "And go where?"

"I don't know. My grandparents lived in Gothenburg, Sweden. I've never been. What about you?"

"My dad had a cabin out on Cavanaugh Lake in Cohasset. It's like a hideaway, tucked back in the trees. No other properties in sight for close to a half mile. That's where I'd go."

Tess sauntered toward the bathroom, where in the doorway she flipped the light switch, removed her shirt, and shut the door behind her.

The water hissed. Shortly after, he listened to the cadence of water-fall change, envisioning her naked body moving beneath the shower-head. He did his best to shake the thought away, but then he could only think about the night he'd slept with her. The two of them were high-strung during the Sadler case. It took a bit of liquid courage and loneliness for them to end up in bed together, and for him to stay the night. He'd never forget the way her lips tasted, stained red with the fruitiness of a bottle of wine they'd passed back and forth.

He went to the door and held his palm to it. His face was pressed so close he imagined he could smell the soapy water. "Why *did* you do it?" he asked.

For a moment there was no answer. The spray of water held the same staticky sound, and he knew her body had stopped moving beneath the rain. Then it stopped, and Tess opened the door with a towel wrapped around her. "After Millie . . . I couldn't breathe. It felt like I was choking. No matter how hard I tried, it was like the oxygen all around me was fighting to stay out. But that night . . . after I left that apartment . . . I felt calm. I could breathe again."

Chapter 55

January 18, 2022

The Madman had made his head-down trek to the farthest train car and exited at the first stop. The longer he waited on the train, the more opportunity it gave the FBI and police to send out as many officers and canines as they had.

Though he was careless and managed to get shot, he had mapped out the train and his escape way ahead of time.

A lot of thoughts came flooding into his mind. He was shot twice by a SIG Sauer P226, which meant the bullets that went through him were most likely 9x19mm Parabellum. A 9mm-diameter bullet would create an entry hole smaller in size because of the way the tissue retracted into the wound. He could feel the two areas burning, leaking, but he ignored it. He reached his arm systematically toward his deltoid and touched the wet blood where the first bullet exited. The other bullet lodged just below his elbow joint, the anconeus muscle, if he had to guess.

The first thing he needed to do was to stanch the bleeding.

Any decent place he could go would have cameras. For that reason, he'd stashed a small backpack at the base of a dumpster one block from where he was now.

He curled his left arm upward against his body and held his wrist with his right hand, making sure that his coat was soaking up the blood and that none of it was dripping to the ground.

Sirens swarmed the train station only minutes after he was gone. A few police vehicles raced past him, their high-pitched wails deafening as they closed in and growing fainter as they passed him.

He hunched down and snagged the strap of the backpack and pulled it from underneath the putrid smell. Unzipping his jacket, he shrugged it off quickly, then removed his shirt and tore it in half. The fabric hissed. Out of his pack, he pulled a small medical kit. He pried it open and pulled out a couple of gauze pads. The first one he pressed to the wound at the back of his shoulder. Exit wounds tended to be larger and bleed more profusely, so he started there and wrapped a piece of cloth around the gauze that bonded to his skin. He placed another gauze pad against the entrance hole in his shoulder—a reddish-brown ring around it—and held a piece of cloth against it. Then just below his elbow, he held another pad there tightly and used a fair bit of medical tape from his pack to keep it in place.

There was a change of clothes inside the bag along with a handgun, knife, and mask.

The Madman opted for the jacket, zipped it up over his bare skin, grabbed his pack, and walked for a while before he hailed a cab.

Chapter 56

"Found something."

It was Esparza. Tess put her on speakerphone and said, "Go ahead."

"There was a murder-suicide out in Palm Springs some years ago. Old man by the name of Johan Helmer. He was bludgeoned to death with something small. Looks like his wife, Mariam, killed herself. Slit her own throat. I'm sending photos now. In the report, the police said it looked like some tools were taken from the garage."

"Wait," Tess said. "You're saying the wife killed him, then killed herself?"

"No, actually. It looks like they didn't know what to make of her death. But the report says that she wasn't home when the husband was killed. She had an alibi. She was working part-time as a travel nurse. She had patients that she'd check in with at their homes. She was working the day she died until five o'clock."

"Okay," Tess said. "So she came home, saw her husband dead. And she killed herself?"

"No," Rooker said. "Whoever did it could've still been there."

"You think they killed her?" Esparza said. "Made it look like suicide?"

"I think they *told* her to kill herself." Rooker suddenly had a thought. "Did they have kids?"

"A daughter, Annika."

Rooker's blood froze. Esparza continued. "Now, get this: she lived in—"

"Minnesota."

Tess looked peculiarly at him.

Esparza said, "Yeah . . . how did you—"

"Annika Helmer . . ." He shook his head. "She had a home on Cass Lake. It's about fifty miles west of Deer Lake. Only an hour drive. My father killed her."

"Wait . . . ," Esparza said.

Tess looked at him in disbelief. *"You're sure?"*

He nodded. "I'm sure. She . . . her *head* was identified." Rooker opened his laptop. Pulled up the file labeled GUNNER and scrolled through a folder of images. He stopped on the porcelain-white faces lined up side by side in the ice. Turned the screen to Tess. "This one"— he pointed to the frozen expression in the middle right—"is Annika Helmer."

"So Gunner—"

"No," Rooker said. "Gunner didn't kill Johan and Mariam. I don't understand . . . but somehow Annika Helmer would explain the 'one old' when Meachum talked about the two victims we missed. But there's something we aren't seeing."

Tess said, "Johan's murder and Mariam Helmer's suicide were five years later. You think it's connected?"

"I don't know," he said and looked at Tess. "Want to take a drive in the morning?"

Chapter 57

The 105 miles to Palm Springs took over three hours with traffic, accidents, and roadwork interspersed on the I-10. Rooker and Tess left before the hotel had started its overpriced breakfast service. Even though there was still a purple-black knot and small cut above her eye, she didn't mind driving, which Rooker was glad for—though based on the beer bottles in her room, maybe he should have been behind the wheel.

They needed to understand what had happened to Johan and Mariam Helmer. Esparza had been able to access the testimonies of the neighbors, and one of them was still alive and local. Fredrick Barton. The man was eighty-three years old now. He still lived in the house across the street from the Helmers. Barton could be their stroke of luck—if he could remember anything important.

As the landscape changed from city to rolling hills to desert, Rooker racked his brain over the skin taken from Carlisle and Esparza and the fact that Natalie Carlisle's killer had pierced her ears.

What does it all mean?

Why skin them now?

C'mon, Mill. I could really use your help right now.

But she didn't come.

Hell, he would've taken the Millie that climbed out of her grave, covered in bugs and dirt, rocks spilling out of her mouth. As much as it hurt to see her like that, he needed some damn help.

Think, Rooker. Something is staring you in the face.

He flipped through the case file and crime scene photos and saw his own scribbled note beneath the photograph of Natalie Carlisle's body. HER EARS.

He shuffled through the photos from Gunner's victims again until he found a close-up of Annika Helmer's head. She was wearing gold earrings. Honeybees.

Bees are arthropods. They shed their exoskeletons to grow. The Madman skinned Natalie Carlisle and Isabel Esparza. Was that his way of shedding their skin? Did he skin them because of Annika Helmer's earrings? Why now? And why the newspapers? To make Reed Thompson seem like the perfect suspect?

Fredrick Barton's home had butterscotch-yellow vinyl siding that needed replacing, along with small square windows that looked as old as Rooker. Rocks, overgrown hedges, and every shape and size cactus bordered the home. Rooker and Tess walked to the old concrete tile around the front door where his knuckles clanged against a metal screen door, the hollow beat carrying through the inside of the house.

A minute later the inside door swung open. In the dim light, Rooker made out a crooked figure with wild white hair, a flat nose, and thin lips. "Help you?" His voice was hoarse. A smoker, Rooker imagined. The smell of cigarettes clung to the old man's skin and clothes.

Rooker nodded. "Mr. Barton?"

"That's right."

Tess cleared her throat. "We're working with the FBI. Tess Harlow, this is Rooker Lindström. We have reason to believe that our case is connected to what happened to the Helmers."

Fredrick Barton shook his head. "Sad story, that one. Helmers were good people."

"What can you tell us about them?"

"I've lived in this house all my life, believe it or not. They were private people, but I'm sure I could tell you a lot. Care to come in?"

"Please," Tess answered.

Fredrick Barton unlatched the screen door, and when it opened, Rooker noticed how badly his body warped to the left, with a large bulge in his abdomen from what he guessed was a hernia. Barton led them past the kitchen, which had an old coat of white paint and appliances just as ancient.

In the corner of the living room, a rusted radiator pumped warm air through shivering webs. Barton plopped down into a rocking recliner. Rooker and Tess sat side by side on a threadbare sofa.

"What would you like to know?"

Tess shifted forward uncomfortably on her cushion. "You said the Helmers' story was a sad one. Why don't we start there."

"It's no secret around here. That poor girl . . ."

"Annika."

"Mm-hmm," he muttered. "Murdered by that Lindström."

Rooker felt Tess's glance in his peripheral but said nothing.

"It was only five years later, Johan and Mariam. Gone too."

Tess asked, "Did you ever see anyone come around the Helmer house?"

"Anyone that looked to do them harm? They were simple people. They didn't leave home often. They were religious, went to church every Sunday. The kind of people who read the Bible before bed."

Rooker asked, "What about Annika? Was she like that too?"

Barton shook his head and snickered. "Wouldn't say so."

"Why's that?"

"She didn't come here often. But then . . . ah, I don't know . . ."

"What is it?" asked Tess. "Any detail can help, even if it seems insignificant."

"Before my wife passed . . . she was sick for a while. Had a hospice nurse come a couple of days a week to look after her. Anyway, I remember thinking it was the nurse coming, but the car turned in to the Helmers' driveway. After the daughter flew the coop, she didn't come home much. But it was her. Stomach looked bigger than mine."

Tess looked at Rooker and back to Barton. "Annika Helmer was pregnant?"

"Sure as shit. Had the baby at home a few months later too. Saw the midwife myself."

Rooker leaned forward. "You're positive?"

"Yep. I know what I saw. I don't think she was married, which couldn't have made her parents happy. Seemed like they were trying to hide it, pulled the blinds closed right away. Got something better than that too."

"Let's hear it."

"When Annika went missing, it was on the news. Wasn't that long after that a boy was staying with the Helmers. Have a picture of him here somewhere, next to his grandfather. He lasted maybe around a year. And then I never saw him again."

"We're going to need that photo. What was the boy's name?"

"Matthias."

Chapter 58

January 19, 2022

As Tess pulled onto the highway to head back toward LA, Rooker called Esparza and brought her up to speed.

"See what you can find on Matthias Helmer. We'll have to find a photo of him and get someone to run an age progression, see what he might look like now."

"Wait . . . Hold on," she said, and they heard her typing fast. "I think I found him. There's a Matthias Helmer listed . . ."

Tess voiced the exact thought running through his mind. "It can't be that easy."

"I'm staring at it right now," Esparza said. "There's not even a birth record. There was never a missing person's report. For years there's no sign of him at all. He's a ghost until the age of eighteen, which is when he surfaces and gets his GED. Then he served four years in the Marines and disappeared again. Until he showed up more than twenty years later at Summit Senior Living and Care Center with an old ID on him and he was confused why he was there."

"It could explain the study," Tess said. "The one Natalie Carlisle was working on. He had his DNA sent in to test for predisposition to Alzheimer's."

"There's more," Esparza replied. "He suffers from paranoid psychosis. You're talking psychotic episodes: hallucinations, delusions, disturbing thoughts. Looks like he's been in a residential-care facility for years."

"Then he can't be our guy," said Tess.

Rooker sighed. "We won't know until we talk to him. Where are we headed, Iz?"

◆ ◆ ◆

Rooker waited for the slow automatic doors to open and stepped in beside Tess. An older man with a walking cane and a pair of soiled, lumpy adult diapers flipped them off before he was led away by a nurse.

"If Helmer is here . . . he can't really be our killer," Tess muttered.

Behind a long laminate desk, a Black woman with short, curly hair and a gold name badge on her navy-blue scrubs shook her head at the patient. "Hi there. Visiting?"

"Yes," Tess said. "We're here to see Matthias Helmer."

"Mr. Helmer," she repeated with shock. "I've been here four years now, and I've never seen Mr. Helmer with a visitor. Are you family?"

Tess smiled. "Not really."

"Well, Mr. Helmer is one of our easier patients. And I'm sure he'll be happy to see you. If you would just sign in here." Brenda—that was the name on the right side of her chest—tapped a clipboard with freshly painted blue nails where handwritten names, dates, and check-in and check-out times were scribbled.

Rooker watched over Tess's shoulder as she wrote her name so illegibly that he couldn't make it out.

"How long has Matthias been here?" he asked the attendant.

"Actually . . . hold on one moment. Julie," she called out.

A large woman upward of fifty with frizzy blonde hair in a scrunchie ponytail walked over in deep-green scrubs. She rested her palm on the table and breathed a heavy sigh.

"Hey, Julie. They were asking to see Mr. Helmer."

Her eyes narrowed. She adjusted the stethoscope around her thick neck. "Mr. Helmer?"

"That's right," Tess said.

"How exactly do you know him?"

Tess cleared her throat. "We're working on a case with the FBI. I'm former detective Tess Harlow, this is my colleague in the investigation, Rooker Lindström. Matthias Helmer's name came up. It's important that we speak with him."

"I was here the day Mr. Helmer was admitted. He walked in those doors right there and stared right through me. He showed up out of the blue with a whole list of notes sent over by the hospital. Paranoid psychosis. Alzheimer's disease. Mute.

"He didn't know who he was. And we couldn't verify his identity either. All his fingertips have been burned off. Mr. Helmer thought that a group of people was following him, so he permanently destroyed the layers of skin to the point that the ridges of his fingerprints wouldn't regenerate. Luckily, he had his state ID on him, and this—" Julie bent down and unlocked a drawer. She handed two small pieces of metal to Rooker. "I tried to put them up in his room, but he had an episode."

Rooker looked down at the silver set of dog tags. They read:

HELMER.

MATTHIAS A.

The rest of what was engraved below had been hammered flat, now illegible.

"An episode?"

"He forced himself to stop breathing. Then he started convulsing. We had to sedate him." She removed her palm from the table, and Rooker appraised the partial smudge of her sweaty handprint. "Does he need a lawyer present?"

"No," Tess said. "We only wish to speak to him."

"I'll take them," she told Brenda. "Follow me, please."

Julie came around the desk. Then she walked them down a long corridor where the fluorescent lights hummed menacingly overhead.

Rooker smiled feebly whenever he made eye contact with one of the residents, most of whom seemed nearly motionless. A woman with an egg-size bald spot in the center of her curls beamed at him. She wore a heavy perfumed scent that made Rooker hold his breath as he passed.

Julie led them into the second-to-last door on the left. She rapped her knuckles delicately on the doorjamb.

"Mr. Helmer, you have visitors."

The room was basic. There were no flowers or cards or framed art. One wall, the only one with a window, was covered in old white wallpaper with a pattern of thin flowers. A black-and-white analog clock ticked neither forward nor back.

Beyond the bed, a light-brown door was open, most likely a handicap-accessible bathroom. In the areas that weren't wallpapered, the walls were a smooth dull beige. An outlet over his bed where the corded white landline telephone and the motorized bed plugged in. On a tiny nightstand beside the phone was a little brass lamp switched off and a pile of notebooks.

At least eight of them. The kind that children write in. Spiral notebooks with superhero characters on them. Little composition notepads that Rooker remembered his son had taken home from school. And then there was one on the bottom, leather-bound and secured shut with a thin brown leather strap. For some reason, even though it was at the bottom, it struck Rooker as being more valuable than the others.

Lying in the bed was a large man with disheveled spiky blond hair and a sunken face, wearing a sterile-white sweater. His feet poked out from the blanket. His toes were bone thin, pointing talon-like at an empty space where black antennae cables reached out and a small television had once been fixed to the wall.

"What happened there?" Rooker asked.

"Mr. Helmer normally enjoys his TV. But the recent murders . . . he's been a bit on edge lately seeing it on the news. We had to take it for now."

Rooker nodded. He caught the markings that resembled dirt smudges—reddish brown—all around the sole of his left foot. They were from old injection sites. Heroin, if he had to guess. People chose their feet because the veins there are easy to find, and it's easy to hide them from people who know where to look. Little did most people know, those veins are also incredibly thin and tend to burst.

Rooker turned and whispered into Tess's ear, "It isn't him. It can't be."

He sauntered to the left side of the room and surveyed the mangled face and throat.

He appraised the worn face and gray eyes that sunk into the sockets. "Who are you?"

"I'm sorry, sir. But Mr. Helmer hasn't spoken in more than ten years. He likes to write."

He likes to write. He likes to write what? Rooker suddenly envisioned the man handwriting the stories and the newspapers they'd found on the victims. *Impossible.*

When the man tried unclenching his fist, Rooker saw it. It wasn't the same as the others. One of his fingernails . . . it was gone.

Was he a victim and somehow lived? He pictured the time of death carved into it. But maybe this man had survived, and the nail died and never grew back.

But when the rest of his hand opened, Rooker saw that all the fingernails on his left hand were gone. The tips of his fingers were bent. Someone had crushed each one of them.

For the first time since entering the room, the pair of vacant gray eyes locked onto him.

Rooker spoke to Julie without turning from the man. "I'm sorry, but I need to ask him some questions."

"That's fine, if he doesn't get agitated."

"May I?" Rooker pointed at the perfectly straight stack of note-books climbing a foot high.

"Mr. Helmer doesn't like it when people touch his things. You'd better let me." Julie walked over to the stack and spoke loudly. "Mr. Helmer, I'm going to give you one of your notebooks and a pencil. Okay?"

The man didn't move.

Julie pulled the top notebook slowly, carefully, as if the creature in the bed were going to strike if she moved too suddenly. She placed it gently in his lap, then put a pencil in his right hand.

"I asked you a question. Who are you?"

He didn't blink.

"Is your mother's name Annika Helmer? Did she go missing in 1996?"

Again, he didn't respond.

Rooker began to wonder if he even could. He couldn't shake the feeling, the one that broke out in a bubble of cold sweat in the pit of his back, that something here was very wrong. His shirt began to stick to him. The air felt as though it were being sucked out of the room. It was getting harder to breathe. He pried at the collar of his shirt and tried again.

"Are you related to Johan and Mariam Helmer? Johan Helmer was killed five years after 'you' were sent to live with him."

A drop of drool slung from the man's open mouth. And then his fingers fell into place over the pencil. He wrote:

He said that one day you would come.

Rooker froze. "What? Who did?" He snatched a handful of the man's sweater and tugged. "Who!"

"Rooker!" Tess said and reached for his arm.

"That's enough, sir." Julie moved into Rooker's field of vision. "You need to leave."

"Did you just see what he wrote—"

The man was swirling the pencil around now. The woman came around him on his right side. "There are no words there. Sometimes he just scribbles. Likes to feel the pencil in his hand, that's all."

Staring at Tess, he pleaded, "Come on. You saw that, right?"

"We'd better be going. Thank you, Julie."

Rooker grabbed Tess gently on her wrist. "I need you to get Julie out of here," he whispered.

She sighed. *"Jesus."*

"Please."

"Julie, do you mind if I ask you a couple of questions?" Tess's head tilted toward the hall.

Julie hesitated. "Sure."

They didn't go far. But it was enough to see Julie's back to the room. Rooker pulled out his phone and unlocked it. Went to the camera and started recording. From the stack of notebooks, he pulled the leather-bound one and set it on top.

A rage screamed in the eyes of the silent man, where the ash color glared two burning holes through Rooker. He started breathing rapidly. Then stopped breathing altogether. His throat constricted.

Rooker hurried. He riffled through the notebook from start to finish, holding the phone's camera above it. Then he did the same with the notepad the man had just written in. He tore out the paper the man had scribbled on and stuffed it into his pocket.

He ended the recording and set the books back in order. "I don't know who you are, but you aren't Matthias Helmer," Rooker said. Long, skinny veins popped out of the man's neck. His face was losing color. "By the looks of it, he did this to you. And you're scared to death of him."

Rooker started out of the room, and Julie noticed the shuddering face of her patient.

"What did you do? Brenda!"

Rooker did not answer. He and Tess hurried out past the unmanned desk and headed to the car.

Chapter 59

Rooker was in deep thought, just as he had been the entire drive back to the field office. He had squinted against the harsh sunlight that sprayed across the passenger seat, with too much time to think and only enough energy to muster half-attentive answers to Tess's questions before the car fell silent. On their return, they filled in Eckhart and his team.

Eckhart shook his head. "From what you just told me, the man has a whole bunch of shit wrong with him. Including Alzheimer's. How can you be sure it isn't Matthias Helmer in that bed?"

"Because his fingernails are all gone. All the fingers on his left hand looked as though they'd been broken. Someone tortured him. If that weren't enough, his fingerprints are gone too. Think about it. You want people to believe someone else is you, how simple is it to just put an old ID on their body and destroy one of the only ways to see if the person is who they say they are."

"Did you ever think that the man in the residential-care facility *could* be Helmer, and the killer is someone else?"

"I doubt myself all the time. But I watched him write, 'He said that one day you would come.'"

Eckhart sighed. "So our killer lets Meachum—apprentice, accomplice, copycat, who knows—take the fall. Now we think we've found out who he really is, and we find a mute Alzheimer's patient in his place." Two of his fingers traced the wrinkle that furrowed from his forehead down between his eyes, then they ran down to his cheekbone. "If Helmer knows we've found the facility, he'll be sure we know who he really is. He'll go into hiding."

"Not necessarily," Rooker said. "Not if he's living under a different name."

"Which he has to be," Tess said.

"There's no photograph in his military service records," Eckhart said. "We need a more recent photo of him than this." He slapped the old photograph Fredrick Barton had provided of Matthias Helmer as a boy onto the table. "In the meantime, Quincy is running the age progression. We'll get the photographs out ASAP."

"What're you looking at?" Tess asked.

"Just doing some light reading." Rooker snickered and turned the laptop screen for her. He'd uploaded the recording of the notebooks, scrolling through the frames so that he could read page by page.

"Anything?"

"Take a look for yourself." He froze on a page where the only lines written fell as:

The bugs are in my head.
The bugs are in my head again.
The bugs. They listen.

"A lot of gibberish so far . . . Wait," he said. "Look at this." He pointed at the line and read it aloud as she hovered over his shoulder.

"'Dr. Death has the coldest hands.'"

"Am I meant to understand this?" Tess asked.

"When I investigated the original case, I was trying to find someone with a medical background. Or someone who worked in funeral services. A gravedigger. I was looking at everything. But who at a crime scene notes the time of death?"

"The medical examiner."

"Right. I thought that whoever I was looking for profited off death. But then I found Meachum."

"Maybe that's what he wants you to think."

"That's what I thought. But maybe it's what he *needs* me to think. Maybe he led me to Meachum because I was getting close. Come on, Tess. Our guy carves the time of death into the fingernail. He has cold hands. He wears gloves. A morgue is cold. Dr. Death . . . I mean . . . it's connected."

"Need I remind you about Walter Erickson?" Walter Erickson was the medical examiner on the Gregory Sadler case. His father had worked as a medical examiner during the murders committed by Gunner. Rooker thought it was all connected and that Erickson was the killer, until they broke into his home and found him dead, hanging by a rope in his study. Sadler killed him and staged it to look like a suicide. "You thought he was our guy, and he wasn't. What happens when you start pointing the finger at Joel Hunter and he ends up dead too?"

Rooker couldn't argue with that, but "Dr. Death" was the only thing in the notebooks that made any sense. He kept scrolling, with Tess leaning over his shoulder, reading line after line that made him feel as crazy as the man who had scribbled them.

Chapter 60

January 19, 2022

This box would be his coffin.

He'd given up screaming for help a long time ago. Sound didn't travel into this room, or out. There had been times his mind had invented noise—sirens, someone coming to save him—but they were as much a ruse as his eyes spotting a pinprick of sunlight. As much a trick as his eyes still able to see his "missing" poster taped up to the wall. Or the crime scene photographs of his ex's head in a freezer box and her parents dead in their Palm Springs home. Though he couldn't see the images, he could feel them all around him.

He'd gone almost fully blind. Since he couldn't see, he stopped moving.

The air was still and rotten. But really, that putrid, awful smell was him. On the ice-cold concrete where the soiled mattress lay inside a steel cage, his body—covered in prickling sores and scabs and burns—was decaying. His breath came out in shallow wheezes. With most of his fingers broken, his hands frozen stiff, there were no more push-ups or crunches. No more attempts to weaken a part of his cage and break free. Gone was the thought that he could overpower his captor one day. He'd been given just enough food and water to live. But he was going to die in this room.

One day a year, the man in the mask would play a sick game. He'd tell him the date and offer him two items to choose from: a ball-peen hammer or a chef's knife. It was a lifeline out of this hell, only he'd been too much of a coward to end it all. It was easier to say that one would rather die than experience something like this. It was a different thing entirely to be the one to have to do it.

The sickest part, though, was that he now knew who was doing this to him.

Today, the door swung open and the light switched on and the rubber-tread footfalls landed softly and their sound died as quick as the snap of a finger. He peered through the milky eye that still held a fraction of vision. He tried to focus as best he could on the date, and the two weapons held out.

"You don't have to do this," he sobbed.

His captor had chosen the date of the first and only time he'd laid eyes on his child—the day his son was born was the day he left. Now he knew that the man standing in front of him was his son.

Chapter 61

Eckhart hung up the phone. "I just got a call from the LAPD. They just found a body off an anonymous tip. The MO doesn't match our guy at all . . . but they found something on him we need to see."

Outside the abandoned Hawthorne Plaza Shopping Center, there was a line of black-and-white LAPD patrol vehicles parked at the curb. Their lights flickered red and blue off the gray concrete building.

Renovations for an outlet mall were meant to be underway years ago, but the building had been cordoned off with yellow caution tape that mostly had been stolen or carried away by the wind. Now the mall looked like a desolate wasteland out of a postapocalyptic film. Trees branched out of the concrete, sprouting up as high as the multilevel parking garage climbed. Tall weeds and dead grass and bushes seeped from the cracks that edged the building.

Inside, dirt and rock and broken glass and wrappers for you-name-it littered the ground. Heaps of yellow caution tape had been tossed to the floor beside the graffitied walls. Rooker read one with black swirling letters: DEATH TO THE WORLD.

That's nice, he thought.

Through two large holes in a portion of the western wall, light seeped down in a pair of dim white circles. Yellow ducts and thin piping ran the length of what looked like a warehouse ceiling. A set of rust-orange stairs zigzagged without a railing up to the next level. Exposed cement footings and metal rods were in place for structures that had been planned to be built. Spray-painted numbers that must've been some kind of building code. Dark pooling stains on the concrete.

"Watch your step," a voice echoed in the stale air.

Rooker saw why. There were no glass barriers around the escalators or on any of the areas that overlooked a lower level.

The narrow escalator steps were dark but specked white. All that remained were the stairs and balustrades, where large black bolts that reminded him of Frankenstein's neck popped out of the ground. There were no handrails, and the bottom landing dropped off to a steep step down. At the bottom the temperature dropped.

He followed behind Eckhart. A thick white grime seemed to cover everything. Rooker figured was best not to be inhaling it, so he took shallow breaths and kept moving.

Down another set of escalators into the lowest level of the mall, spots were pitch-black. Had it not been for the police officers waving around flashlights and the floodlights set up in the distance, the entire level would've plunged into complete darkness. In the misty white and yellow beams, what was left was merely exposed steel beams and concrete flooring.

They'd followed the floodlights and had been walking for a while before they came to a wooden door fashioned out of old plywood. There was a stench coming from behind the wood walls. The door had already been pried open. The edge near the handle had splintered, and thin pieces of wood had broken off to the cold gray floor.

Once he was close enough, the smell . . . the corpse surely had rotted. It reminded him of the smell when he and Millie found Aurora Hedstrom's husband, Don, dead in the bathtub years after she'd shot him. This odor was even worse.

Rooker peeked between the gaps of limbs and bodies blocking his view. When he bumped into a shoulder and patted blindly at it in apology, he stood in the doorway. It wasn't at all what he'd expected.

Layers of gray foam ran down the perimeter of what looked to be an eight-by-ten box. It even covered the ceiling. Someone had not only created a makeshift room out of wood and nails, but they'd sound-proofed every square inch. Crime scene photographs were taped up to the walls—ones of Annika Helmer, and Johan and Mariam Helmer—along with a "missing" poster for a man named Jesse Nelson, who had disappeared five years ago. And within the room was a cage large enough to fit a taller dog breed.

In two areas, the black bars had been scratched at and either punched or kicked. But the steel was far too strong.

Beside the cage knelt a balding man with shoe covers, a white coat, and a mask. Rooker didn't know how such little hair could look unkempt, but the stuck-up silver strands did. His dark eyes looked far more serious than the first time Rooker had seen the coroner, Joel Hunter.

"Agent Eckhart." Hunter sounded muffled behind what looked like a painter's mask over his mouth. His eyes drifted to Rooker standing in the open doorway.

"Dr. Hunter," Eckhart said beside Rooker. "Thanks for coming on short notice. What can you tell us?"

Hunter let out a heavy breath that rattled with the horror before him. "He's only been dead less than a day."

In Rooker's eyes and mind, that couldn't at all be possible. Inside was a male's emaciated naked body that must have been dead at least a week.

"What? How—"

"It's too soon to be exact, but judging by your victim's skin . . . his eyes . . . he's been subjected to long periods of complete darkness. He's blind in his left eye and nearly blind in his right. Some of the injuries are postmortem. I'd say he's been locked here in this cage—*in this room*—for at least four, maybe five years."

"My God," Quincy said through his fingers.

"You're telling me he's been held captive in this room all that time?" Rooker asked.

"That's exactly what I'm telling you. His body, if I had to guess, has only been given enough nutrients to sustain him."

"In other words, they barely fed him, gave him just enough water to keep him alive."

"Correct. He has sores covering most of his skin. Do you see these markings here? That's from a cattle prod. Some dish out up to six thousand volts of electricity."

Jack Hall cleared his throat. "This one looks a hell of a lot more personal."

Eckhart said, "We were told there was something found on the body?"

Rooker noticed the shine beside a yellow evidence marker inside the cage. There was a chef's knife covered in blood. "It seems he was given the knife; the blood spatter on the floor and the incision in his wrist would suggest that he did it himself."

Hall looked closer. "What's going on with his hands?"

Rooker knew that Hall wasn't referring to the fingers that all seemed to be broken. Hunter nodded. "This man has anonychia congenita. It's a condition that affects the nails. In some cases, not all of the nails are affected, or only parts of the nail may be missing. Unlike your other victims, the killer didn't do this. I believe that since birth, this man's fingernails were missing. But that's only part of why I called you. Take a look at this."

Chapter 62

Beneath the soiled bed inside the cage were two messages carved into the concrete with a piece of bedspring:

Dr. Death has the coldest hands.

My son, Matthias.

"Jesus Christ," Eckhart said.

Quincy added, "Jesse Nelson . . . this guy—he did this to his father?"

Eckhart's brow furrowed, and he shook his head angrily. "Five years he's been missing. How the hell does no one find him down here?"

"Look at how long it took us to get down here," Tess answered. "No one was ever going to find him. Not unless someone was going to revive the building or demolish it."

Outside, Rooker leaned back against the door of the car waiting for Eckhart and the rest of them to file out into the sunlight. With his face turned up to the sky, the warmth invaded his skin. His head pulsated. The image inside that room was one he'd never forget, one that already felt tethered to his soul, and suddenly he heard Caroline's voice in his mind. *"Make it back in however many pieces you can, and I'll put the rest back together."*

For a large part of his life he had been mad at the world, and too angry and stubborn to want to be rescued. But right now, there was nothing he wanted more.

When he peered down and his blank stare fell over the mess of broken boards on the ground outside the front doors, he pondered the words written in the notebook. Dr. Death . . . did it mean something? Or were they just the words of two people who'd lost their minds?

Whatever it meant, he couldn't help but think they were wasting time.

Matthias Helmer was out there. Living as someone else. Natalie Carlisle managed to find him. Then he'd tracked down Miggs and Hastings. Hunted them like prey. He'd tortured Esparza. Killed Lewis. And the man dead on the ground in there, if he was right, was Helmer's father.

The first thought he had was that the killer may have inherited his father's condition—anonychia congenita. The newsstand owner described the man as wearing cotton gloves. If he were out there wearing cotton gloves in the summertime, he was hiding some visible identifier. Unless again, he wanted Rooker and the FBI to think that.

Maybe once they found the real Madman, all of this would be over. Or would there always be someone out to get him?

He checked his watch. It was Saturday. He thought back to his favorite thing about Saturday mornings, the day of the week he would sleep in until Laura or Britton would wake him. Then he'd make breakfast and watch whatever cartoon was on in the morning with his son.

The last place he wanted to visit was another morgue.

Chapter 63

Rooker wanted only peace and quiet. Maybe some time to close his eyes and listen to the hum of the engine. He'd called for a cab to take him to the Los Angeles County Department of Medical Examiner-Coroner, where he wanted to meet Joel Hunter as he took a better look at the body. Really, he needed to run some thoughts by him, and Hunter would be there shortly.

While the yellow cab droned on the I-105 E, he was drifting in and out of a light sleep, which ended when the driver merged onto the 710 Freeway and into traffic. It was for the best, anyhow. All he kept seeing was the dead man they suspected to be Jesse Nelson.

Dr. Death has the coldest hands . . . What the hell does that mean? Dr. Death?

Rooker had hit a dead end.

Few people had encountered the Madman and lived to tell about it. The man who had gone insane, occupying a bed in the assisted-living facility. Isabel Esparza, who remembered next to nothing aside from the fact that her captor wore a mask and gloves and knew his way around firearms. Now that his old friend had been released from police custody, Rooker decided to call Eddie.

When the answering machine played, he felt like a complete idiot. He pressed the red button and looked out the window at the palm trees and an overcast sky. In the sequence of turns after getting off the exit, his phone rang. It was Arroyave.

"Eddie? It's Rooker."

Silence. "Hey, man. Look . . . I'm sorry—"

"Don't be." He hesitated. "I don't blame you. Not anymore. You may have fed me some bullshit, but I'm the one who wrote the article. And in the hotel . . . You were protecting your family. I probably would have done the same thing. Listen, I wanted to ask you about that night."

Eddie sighed. "There's not much to tell, Rook. He caught me slipping. I got my ass whooped."

"You were a detective, Eddie. Your brain is hardwired to pick up on the smallest clues. The only two other people who came up against this guy and lived, one went insane, the other is an FBI agent, and she couldn't give anything useful in her testimony."

"You must be desperate," he said.

"As all hell," Rooker replied.

"I told you. I found the alleyway—"

"Start from the beginning. You got the text message."

"Yeah. I was at Ralphs picking up milk. I thought I remembered a vehicle, but that whole night is like a bad dream . . ."

"What did it look like?"

"Hear me out, man. I can't remember what was real and what wasn't."

"Eddie—" The cab stopped out front of the building. Rooker paid cash, got out, and headed for the doors.

"Black. A black Econoline. It had a decal . . . looked like there was a clock . . . It was raining hard, though. I was soaked by the time I got into the building. Then the next thing I know I'm being dragged down the stairs like a rag doll. He had gloves on, but they were freezing. The guy was strong, man."

Rooker opened the door, and his footfalls were a quick pitter-patter slapping and echoing down the stairwell. "Do you remember anything about him?"

"I was out of it . . . but I swear there was something . . ."

"Anything helps, Eddie."

At the bottom level, he swung the door open and saw Lucian Hurst behind the glass blowing onto his gloves.

His hands . . .

"There was something swinging . . . in front of my face."

Something swinging . . . And then he saw it in his mind. *The ring. He wears it around his neck.* "Holy shit."

"One more thing . . . it was raining, but the clock . . . I thought the hands of the clock looked frozen."

Rooker produced a smile, but his insides felt as though they'd frozen over. "I gotta go."

He ended the call.

In his mind, Rooker replayed a memory of the time he'd stepped into Hemet Valley Mortuary, and he suddenly thought he'd solved most of the puzzle. Lucian Hurst wore his wedding ring around his neck. The time Hurst identified the twenty-two-carat earrings Natalie Carlisle had on, and then made the extra effort to seem like he knew nothing about jewelry. He was the one who pierced her ears. But what about the black van Ernestina Zepeda—Joey Miggs's neighbor—had seen?

It all had something to do with Annika Helmer's earrings.

And Rooker's suspicion that Jesse Nelson passed on his condition to his son . . . Come to think of it, he'd never seen Hurst without gloves on. Except for the one time where he was washing his hands . . . and then they were hidden beneath the towel.

The hands. Whether it was the medical examiner or the clock hands, he knew. Lucian Hurst . . .

Helmer . . . Lucian Hurst is the Madman.

Chapter 64

January 21, 2022

"Rooker, it's good to see you again," Hurst spoke.

"Yeah," Rooker tried. "You too. Is . . . is Hunter here yet?"

"No, he isn't. Can I help you with something?"

"No," Rooker said too fast. "I mean, it's just the body we found. I thought I'd see what Hunter had to say when he took a better look."

"You're more than welcome to wait."

"It's okay. The scene there made me feel a little sick. I may just get going—"

"Nonsense," Hurst said. "I think you should wait." Hurst began to slowly pull off his glove, and Rooker's eyes lingered there too long. When he looked up, Hurst was eyeing him like a predator.

"I really should get going, sorry."

Rooker turned out of the room and sauntered to the stairs. Once he was out of view, he bolted up the steps two at a time. He moved as fast as his body would allow. At the top, he ran out of the building and called Tess. She answered fast.

"I need you," he panted. "It's Hurst. I need you to pick me up. No sirens."

"Rooker—"

"*Please!* Please listen."

◆ ◆ ◆

Rooker had walked a half mile before he stopped at the gas station where Tess, Eckhart, and Hall had shown up.

"He knows" was the first thing out of Rooker's mouth.

"He knows what?" Tess asked.

"He knows *that I know.*"

"What are you saying?" Hall asked.

"He started taking his gloves off. He caught me staring. It's like he knew . . . I'm telling you, it's him. I called Arroyave. He said that whoever dragged him down those stairs, there was something dangling from his neck. That's where Hurst wears his ring. He said he remembered the guy wearing gloves and that his hands were ice cold. When I just saw Hurst, he was blowing onto his gloves. And Eddie said he remembered a black Econoline van, but it had a decal on the side. He thought it looked like a watch face, and the second and minute hands looked frozen."

"The guy works in the morgue," Hall said. "Of course his hands are cold."

Quincy crossed his arms. "Do we think the van is stolen?"

"A similar vehicle was described by Miggs's neighbors," Rooker said. "The time frame between when he went after Miggs and then Arroyave was more than a week apart. If the vehicle was stolen, he probably would've dumped it at some point. I think he owns it."

Eckhart's face wrinkled with thought. "Maybe our guy repairs watches. If Arroyave was right about the van . . . If Helmer pierced Natalie Carlisle's ears like Rooker said, that could be the connection to Annika Helmer's earrings. He could have a small repair shop or work at a jewelry store. But slow down," Eckhart said. "Lucian Hurst?"

"It's him," Rooker said. "I know it is."

◆ ◆ ◆

Lucian Hurst was gone.

When Joel Hunter arrived with the body, there was no sign of him.

Back in the field office, Eckhart had everyone looking for a jewelry store with a logo like the one Arroyave had given Rooker.

"Annika Helmer never married," Rooker said. "The father must've run away. So years after the mother disappears, maybe the son puts two and two together: his mother vanished, and not only did she fit the profile, but she was only an hour away from an active serial killer. So maybe he finds the crime scene photographs . . . he finds his mother's head in an ice chest. An assistant medical examiner would have access to all of it. And so he tracks down the father, maybe he blames him for his mother's death because he wasn't there. And he holds him prisoner. It's Hurst."

Eckhart shook his head. "It's too flimsy, Rooker. We still have no proof it's him."

"I've always thought it was someone close to the case. I mean, look at how close he is. Helmer reinvents himself as Hurst, and he assists Joel Hunter, the man who performed the autopsies on his victims."

"If it's true . . . it's kind of brilliant," Hall blurted.

"I think I've got it," Tess said. "Til Death Jewelers."

Chapter 65

"How does that book end?"

"Hmm?"

"*The Black Echo.*"

Spoiler alert: an ambush, Rooker thought. *People die.* He appraised the serious expressions of the team adjusting their tactical gear and checking their firearms. "They get the bad guy. And then everything was better, at least for a little while."

Tess picked at the white skin where her scar embedded deep into her fingertip. "Doesn't sound like our story, does it?"

"Not really."

She strapped on the Velcro of her bulletproof vest and asked, "How do I look?"

"Like you belong."

She smiled. "I'll see you in a few."

"Good luck."

She inserted a full magazine into her P226, racked the slide, and held it with the barrel pointed to the floor and her trigger finger extended along the frame. She stood beside Scott Eckhart, who had a Heckler & Koch MP5 submachine gun in his grasp. "Ready when you are."

"I already told you. You're a civilian, Harlow—"

"A civilian who's caught two serial killers. As I see it, you're down two bodies—Esparza and Lewis. You're the one who flew me out here, put me in."

He shook his head and sighed. "The exits are covered. Plus I've got extra guys already—"

"I want to go in," she replied.

"You have a death wish?"

"I didn't come all the way here to sit and watch."

"Hall," he called out. "You're on me."

Hall nodded. "Got it, boss."

"Quincy, you and Harlow."

Quincy touched knuckles with her.

"Presidents," Eckhart said to the man and woman standing side by side, "thanks again for the assist." Tess had learned that their surnames were Tyler and Ford, and they were SWAT operators pulled from the FBI Special Weapons and Tactics Team in the Los Angeles field office. "You two are on the back hallway; our blueprints have a staircase there that goes down to the basement. Me and Hall have the front door. Quincy and Harlow, side entrance.

"Need I remind you—our guy is a former Marine. You know what they say: 'Once a Marine, always a Marine.' We go in fast. If he's unarmed, we take him alive. If he's armed, shoot to kill. I don't want to have to talk to another family. I want this son of a bitch, for Esparza and Lewis. Everyone in position. On my go."

The seconds ticked with terror far slower than her pulse. Sweat and goose bumps broke out over her skin. She tugged at her vest that suddenly felt too tight, making the pounding in her chest even stronger. Once Eckhart gave the go-ahead, Tess moved fast beside Deion Quincy. The two skulked through the side entrance and silently down a dark hallway, lurking into position like shadows through the night.

◆ ◆ ◆

Ray Tyler and Valeria Ford rushed the narrow hallway behind the store. The walls were gray cement, the floor streaked with shades of gray and black with wear. Overhead, fluorescent lights flickered beside ducts, and a red exit sign glowed above the gunmetal door at the end.

But the door they took was the one in the center of the hall on the right.

Ford cornered the door. Sweat flattened her hair beneath the helmet, but she and Ray had done this more times than she could count.

Ray turned the knob and swung the door open. Valeria went first. Aiming down the concrete steps, she flipped the light switch and the basement floor came to life.

She moved down the steps, swinging the barrel of her MP5 at the spaces where she would think to hide. At the bottom, Valeria turned left and felt a breeze when Ray turned right with the shotgun.

The walls down here were lined with empty shelves. An old cash register covered in cobwebs sat high on one of them.

At first glance, the basement didn't appear to be some kind of killing floor. It seemed to be used for storage when needed.

But when Valeria Ford caught movement in her peripheral, it was already too late. Her ear exploded. She fell to the ground. Ray Tyler whipped around at the man and managed to fire two shotgun blasts as pistol rounds turned his cheek to a burning numb that slowly faded away.

Tess heard the shots from below and burst through the door. In the middle of the hall, the door was open. Quincy passed her and moved down the stairs. She followed close behind.

"Jesus Christ," Quincy said.

The presidents were dead. Tess turned to the ruined face of the third body on the ground. She moved toward it, kicked the pistol away even though there was no need. She knelt and lifted the long-sleeve shirt and found the two spots where she was positive the shots she'd fired at the man on the train had hit. They were bandaged. He was definitely shot. She stood and backed away from the blackened hole with brains and strings of hair pooled beneath the head that was once both Matthias Helmer and Lucian Hurst.

Chapter 66

It was over. After a sequence of gunshots rang out, Rooker watched nervously as Eckhart, Hall, and Quincy filed out of the building. He inched forward. *Where is she?* Then behind Quincy's large frame, he surveyed Tess Harlow's saunter, the wisps of sweaty hair, adrenaline painting her somber face red.

"Where are the presidents?"

She shook her head.

"Helmer?"

"He's dead too."

"You're sure?"

She nodded.

He closed his eyes and took a deep breath. "I'm glad you're okay," he replied. "What the hell happened?"

"Helmer was waiting for them in the basement. He killed Tyler and Ford. By the time I got down there, they were dead, and Helmer's face had been ripped apart. I checked his arm and shoulder; the two places where I shot him in the train station, the wounds were there. The files and computer missing from Natalie Carlisle's home are down there too. It's him."

"*Jesus.* Are you all right?"

"I'm okay."

"You know, I think you should stay with them."

"Oh yeah?" She laughed. "Just join the FBI?"

"You're as good as any one of them. They could use you. Some advice: throw away that book. The names you write down in it didn't die for you, and they aren't dead because of you. Most of them, anyway."

"What if I don't want to do this anymore?"

"You'd be lying to yourself."

Rooker watched Scott Eckhart unstrap the submachine gun from his chest and remove his vest before he came over. "Tess, Rooker," he said. "I have to say, I wasn't on board with you two coming on, but you've been a great help to my team. Thank you."

Eckhart shook their hands.

"Lindström, I hope I don't ever need you again . . . but if I do—"

"Let's just hope you don't."

While the sirens closed in on them, Rooker thought about Caroline and Red and Geralt. It was time to go home.

Chapter 67

January 24, 2022

Rooker tossed his bag into the overhead compartment and plopped down into his aisle seat. He let out a long sigh. The FBI had been kind enough to put him in business class. The seat next to his was empty.

He couldn't wait to be back. The longer the plane was on the ground, the longer this air felt like it infected him.

He pulled the seat-belt strap across his lap and latched the buckle.

The engines seemed to ignite then. As his seat rumbled beneath him, he wondered if he could hate this place any more than he already did. He was sure this time that he would never come back. Not for anything or anyone.

The pilot's monotone came over the PA, letting the passengers know about the skies and the flight time and to fasten seat belts.

Once they were airborne, Rooker shifted in his seat and, with his elbow against the arm of the chair and his head in his hand, shut his eyes.

The plane hissed loudly as the wheels touched down, and he thought about Caroline. If she didn't have to work, she would have been there to pick him up in Minneapolis. Drive him the three hours home.

Much like him, she specialized in the darkness. Talking about the evils in the world and the gruesome homicide cases that happen every day. She had one of the most watched segments played on FOX News. It partly had to do with him, but he never mentioned it.

Tonight on *Late Night News with Caroline Lind*, she would recap the Madman murders and reveal the identity of the serial killer shot and killed by the police, Matthias Helmer. She was a numbers girl. Ratings and viewers. And this evening she'd have the world in the palm of her hand.

He dozed fitfully in the back of the taxi. The driver was sixty-five, maybe seventy, with white hair slicked back, crow's-feet that reached all the way to his sideburns, and an old zippered jacket over a button-down shirt. The man was ready to talk his ear off had he not made it a point to shut his eyes in sight of the rearview mirror.

The driver went silent.

Rooker's eyelids fluttered. Nearly each time he lost consciousness, his body jolted awake.

When he'd given up, he opened his phone and searched for the FOX News segment. Nearly midnight now, the segment would've hit the web. He pulled the video up on YouTube and turned his phone screen, watching it with the volume lowered, but not low enough for the cabdriver to miss.

"That the news lady? Caroline Lind?"

Rooker nodded. "Yeah."

"She's a looker, ain't she?"

He smiled. "Yeah, she is."

Rooker unlocked the front door and stepped inside. The ground floor was bathed in black. A spotted head perked up and slowly got to its four-legged feet. "Hi, Red." He dropped his bag to the floor, knelt, and entertained the licks as long as they lasted, petting the old dog under his chin. Balled up on a blanket on the sofa was Geralt, purring while Rooker went to him and patted his white fur.

Caroline lay there completely still beneath a black silk robe. "Hey." He nudged her arm lightly. "I'm home."

She unfurled an eye and smiled. "How was your flight?"

"Good. I watched part of the show in the cab. The driver said you're a looker."

"I hope you tipped him well."

He smiled.

Caroline got up and wrapped her arms around him. Her fingers fell into the pitted muscles in his back. Then she swept his face up in the sea of her dainty hands and kissed him hard on the lips.

"Are you okay?" she asked.

"Physically? Yeah. Mentally . . . wounded, but alive."

"Don't leave me again."

"I don't plan on it. I'm going to take a quick shower. Go get in bed."

Rooker locked the front door and went upstairs.

He undressed and turned the water on. For the first few minutes, he stood perfectly still beneath the hard rain. Then he washed himself quickly, and just as he finished, he heard a crash from somewhere in the house. He turned the water off and listened. Aside from the buzzing silence, the only thing he could hear was his blood pumping as though it were filling his ears. "Caroline?"

He snatched a towel from the rack, ran it through his hair, and wrapped it around his waist. His hand hovered over the door handle. Then he stood off to the side, pulled the door open, and peeked into the hallway.

It was dark. The radiator clicked and he nearly jumped. He couldn't hear Caroline.

Moving quietly, he stopped at the doorway and inspected the dark bedroom. Caroline wasn't in bed. He went to the nightstand, slid the drawer out slowly, and grabbed the pistol he kept there. He released the magazine, saw that it was loaded, and shoved it back in.

He walked back into the hallway and noticed the prints of his wet feet. He checked the spare bedroom. The closet door was open a crack. The room was empty. When he went back to the hallway, at the bottom of the stairs he saw the figure move.

But it was only Caroline.

"I just needed a glass of water . . . ," she said.

"I'm sorry," he said. He put the pistol behind his back.

She climbed the stairs. The moonlight bouncing off her petite thighs. "It's over, Rooker. No one else is out to get you."

He wasn't sure he'd ever believe the latter. It seemed that there would always be someone who wanted him dead. But he wasn't stubborn enough to argue with her tonight.

"I lied," she said as she passed him in the hallway and sauntered into the bedroom.

"About what?"

"I didn't need a glass of water." Caroline untied the robe, and it fell weightlessly to the floor. He stared at her perfect shape, the round bottom in a strawberry-red lingerie set. All that obstructed his view was a tiny sheer triangle of floral-embroidered fabric. When she turned around, she watched his eyes like gnats take in every inch of her. His eyes stopped at her breasts, where her pale nipples were visible behind the see-through mesh.

"Wow," he said.

She smiled. "Happy New Year."

Despite his pulse climbing and his fast breaths, he felt like he was floating toward her. And when he got close enough, she pulled the loose knot on his towel and watched his member spring into her hand as the white cloth fell.

"You wanna put that away?" She nodded at the dark handgun still in his hand.

"Mm-hmm," he muttered.

"Need a hand?"

"Mm-hmm."

She walked him by his stiff member until he opened the drawer beside the bed, placed the handgun inside, and shut it.

Caroline pushed him onto the bed and took off her bra.

The two of them typically had leg-weakening, chest-heaving sex. But tonight they made love gently and fell asleep with their warm limbs intertwined.

Chapter 68

January 24, 2022

In the lower level of the Los Angeles County Department of Medical Examiner-Coroner building, Scott Eckhart and Jack Hall stood beneath harsh fluorescent lights that detailed every inch of their exhausted white-specked faces. There were multiple bodies beneath sheets now. Joel Hunter had been working overtime.

"His wife is here, boss," Hall said to Eckhart.

He blew out a stifled breath. "Christ," he muttered, massaging the painful migraine behind his forehead. "Tell me you've got aspirin."

Hall shook his head. "Sorry."

Everything in the last twenty-four hours had gone completely off the rails. And now they had him—Matthias Helmer. The Madman.

It was a strange set of events that had come full circle. They'd come to the mortuary after the first victim, Natalie Carlisle, had been killed. Standing there the entire time was Matthias Helmer, the Madman killer, under the alias Lucian Hurst. They'd found over one hundred textbooks in the "jeweler's" study and in a storage attic of the home all dedicated to forensic pathology, forensic science, even mortuary science.

What remained of Helmer's body was pale beneath a white sheet. The two older gunshot wounds—one to the shoulder and one to the arm—were there. That was where the footage from Los Angeles Metro

Rail security cameras and bystanders' cell phones confirmed Tess Harlow had shot Helmer the night at the train station.

Although the nickel-size 9mm bullets had not been fatal, the shotgun blast to the face had done the trick. Ray Tyler had gotten two shots off with the Benelli M4 Tactical Shotgun before he caught one to the neck and collapsed. He was found with his hand clutched to his throat, but he had choked on his blood well before backup arrived. A mist of blood sprayed out between his fingers to a speckled stain on his clothes and the floor beneath him. One of the shotgun spreads ravaged the wallpaper behind Helmer's left side. The other plugged craterlike holes through his face. That's what a 12-gauge can do.

Hunter was expected to identify the body on the table in a short amount of time. But much like the man Rooker Lindström mentioned in the senior-care facility, this male had no fingerprints. And dental records wouldn't work, with most of the teeth having been obliterated in the firefight.

It was a tough call, but one that Eckhart was willing to make.

Suddenly he thought back to what felt like a year ago, when he'd first met Rooker in the airport, and he told him he was the one in charge. He reheard his words. *"I'm sorry to hear that."*

The death toll had been high. He'd lost a close friend. Rooker was right.

He wondered now, staring at the faceless body, what he would have done differently.

That was when the pitter-patter of footfalls echoed outside the door. It brought him back. He cleared his throat.

The doors opened. In walked a woman beside Jack Hall. Her face was sad. Worry lined her forehead. Her dark eyes were reddened and heavy. The white shirt she wore had wrinkled, the neck creased as though she'd used it to wipe her face.

"Mrs. Hurst, FBI Special Agent Scott Eckhart. This is Dr. Joel Hunter. I'm very sorry to bring you down here so late. It pains me to have to do so, I want you to know that."

Vivian Hurst hadn't even known her husband was working for the Los Angeles County coroner's office.

Her head turned away from the body and her eyes closed. She sniveled hard. "Can we just get this over with?"

"Yes, ma'am. If you'll please take a look at the body . . . we're hoping you can identify this man for us."

"You want me to tell you that man under the cloth is my husband. The psycho you've been looking for."

"We need you to confirm that it's him. I'm sorry—"

"You think I don't want to? I woke up in the middle of the night to my husband shoveling in the backyard. He said he was burying a possum that got caught in one of our traps. A few nights ago, he came home late with bandages on, and during the night he's bleeding from his arm. I see the shooting on the news, and I didn't even piece it together. Now you tell me you found a woman's skin in my backyard, and my husband was a Marine who lived a whole different life every time I thought he was going to his jewelry store. I still have no idea what to tell my daughter. So if you think that I don't want to do this . . . Anyway, it should be easy."

"Why is that?"

"Flip him over."

Eckhart and Hunter exchanged looks. Then with gloved hands, Hunter manipulated the body so that she could look at his back.

Her face grew angry. "Is this some kind of joke?"

"No, ma'am—"

"I get a phone call that my husband is dead!"

Eckhart put a palm up. "I don't underst—"

"My husband has a tattoo across his upper back. It says 'FEAR.' That's not him."

Chapter 69

Rooker was in a deep sleep when the phone buzzed violently on the nightstand. He had a missed call from Scott Eckhart. The blinding display couldn't be right. He checked his watch on the nightstand. But the hands of his Bremont matched the time—3:15 a.m.

"Yeah," he mumbled. He unfurled his other eye to the white snow falling heavily out of a raven-black sky. The wind breathed hard enough to rattle the windows. A snowplow droned somewhere in the distance.

"He's alive, Rooker. Helmer's alive. The body at the morgue isn't him."

The haunting whir of the wind outside froze him, dread seeping ice cold in his bloodstream. He sat up. "What?"

"*Helmer is alive.* He staged it. I was sure it was him . . . he had the two GSWs where Harlow shot him. But the wife said he has a tattoo on his back. Our body in the morgue doesn't. I've got an alert out; he'll be on the FBI's Most Wanted."

"*Shit.* I have to go. Let Harlow know."

"I tried, but I couldn't get through to her—"

"I will." He ended the call.

How . . . how is that possible? The body Tess found in the jewelry store basement had been shot exactly where she'd hit Helmer in the train station. The wounds were old. *If it isn't Helmer, who is it?* Helmer had always been one step ahead. He'd framed Meachum and used Reed Thompson. *Did Helmer shoot someone in the same places he was shot and plant them there?*

He shook Caroline awake.

"What is it? What's wrong?"

Rooker leaped from the bed and yanked the blinds shut. "We need to go." He pulled on a pair of underwear and pants and rolled a shirt fast down his torso.

Caroline shivered and covered her bare chest with the blanket. "What?"

He didn't answer. Instead he moved to the bedside drawer, pulled it open, and snatched the Glock 17. He checked the magazine and fed a bullet into the chamber.

She propped herself up, the tiredness in her face substituted with fear. "What's going on?"

"He's alive, Caroline. Matthias Helmer."

"What about the body . . . the police—"

"It isn't him. We can't stay here. There's no time."

"Can't I pack a bag?"

"I said there's no time."

"Rooker, wait—"

"He's here. In Minnesota." Rooker could feel his presence in his bones and the danger vibrating in the air. Whether Helmer had managed to board a plane or drive the thirty hours to Minnesota, Rooker knew that the threat was more than real, and he was up against a monster that would do anything to kill him now. "This man has been trained. Do you understand? He's not Caldwell—if he gets to you, there's no telling what he'll do. Pack fast. We get Red and Geralt in the car and we go." He held up two fingers. "Two minutes."

"Go where?"

Rooker didn't answer. Because he didn't know. Not yet. But once they were in the car and driving, he'd figure it out. And he'd feel a hell of a lot safer than he did here.

Caroline got the message. Inside of her allotted two minutes, she'd dressed and thrown a bag together with everything she could think of: toothbrush, toothpaste, soap, shampoo, changes of clothes, and a heavy quilted jacket.

Downstairs, Rooker snatched the car keys off the hook and went to the window. He manipulated the edge of the curtain and peeked out at the car. The driveway and the top of Caroline's SUV were covered in at least four inches of powder. The vehicles parked at the curb and in the driveways across the street were too. Chimney smoke vanished in the dark sky. He stomped his feet into his pair of boots that sat on the edge of the rug by the front door.

Maybe they could just wait for the police to arrive. Eckhart must've sent them right after he'd called. The clock was ticking. He decided. "Ready?"

She nodded and patted Red nervously with the leash in her other hand.

"Wait here," he said. He pulled the door open and moved fast. The howling dark wind unnerved him. The swift cold plunged deep in his skin, but he was running on a high of adrenaline. He ducked low. Stared into the emptiness beneath the vehicle. Nothing but weather-bleached black pavement and a tiny faint circle of oil from the car. He got up quickly and dusted the powder from the glass and aimed the barrel of the gun through the windows of the car. He checked the front and rear seats. He opened and scanned the trunk. Even swung the rear passenger door open and flipped up the cargo space hidden in the floor behind the seats.

Nothing.

"Come on," he said to her. "Geralt," he hollered. "Geralt, come here, boy."

The cat often took his sweet time outside, even on the cold nights when he wanted to come inside. *Come on, you damn cat.*

Caroline moved too quickly. Her sneakers slipped in the wet snow. She caught herself with a fistful of it, pushed herself off the ground, and threw herself into the passenger seat, brushing the snow from her knee and hand.

They didn't have time to wait for the damn cat. Luckily, the white furball rounded the corner of the house. Once Geralt came pawing effortlessly through the snow toward him, creating little quarter-size divots in the snow, Rooker cut off the distance between them and snatched Geralt up in his arms.

Caroline had already managed to help Red's old bones, lifting his back legs into the back seat, where she'd also thrown her bag. Rooker handed Geralt off to Caroline, shut her door, and ran around to the front of the car, swiped his sleeve across the windshield, and hurried to the driver side.

Panting, he flung the door open, slid into the seat, and shut the door. With imprecise ticks, his shaky hand jabbed at the ignition until it caught. His pink fingers went numb. "Come on," he muttered. The engine squealed in the blustery quiet, and he shot out of the driveway onto the road.

"How sure are you about this?" Caroline asked.

Fear had pried sweat from the pores in his scalp and middle back.

"Sure enough." Luckily the roads had been plowed recently, so he drove faster than the speed limit. The snowfall fell fast in chunky white spheres. The wipers groaned trying to keep up with it.

He dialed Tess Harlow. It went to voicemail. "Helmer's alive. You need to go somewhere safe. Call me when you get this."

"Jesus, Rooker. Why would he come all the way out here? Surely he could have killed you in LA. If he disappeared once, what makes you think he's not already somewhere far away with a new identity?"

"Because he wants to watch me lose everything—everything I care about. He wants to be the one to take it all from me."

Once they hit the on-ramp Rooker gunned the accelerator. The car shot up to seventy-five miles per hour. The highway flickered with a wet sheen, but the conditions were okay. The shoulder and silver guardrail were coated in snow. Every few seconds his eyes darted to the rearview mirror to see if anyone was following them. As far as he could tell, no one was.

"Do you know where we're going yet?"

He peered into the mirror again. "To find Tess."

Chapter 70

January 25, 2022

Tess was dreaming again.

Her mother was in the kitchen at the counter baking brownies. She had been smoothing out the top of them with a silicone spatula. The room smelled like milk chocolate and electric heat. The oven clicked, then beeped when it reached the right temperature. "Mom?" Tess called out.

But her words didn't leave her lips. Her mouth moved, but there was no sound. Just a hollowness in her head. Janice Harlow stood there in her soiled pajamas that made her gag. An ugly plaid pattern that had darkened with her sweat and filth. The bananas on the counter turned black as the swarm of flies hummed territorially around them. Her mother opened the oven door, slid the metal pan onto the top rack, and shut it.

Tess stepped closer. Slapping away at the bugs that formed a nasty cloud before her face. She tried again, only louder. "Mom!"

Janice Harlow stood perfectly upright then, like the bones in her back infused with liquid nitrogen.

"What have you done?" she whispered. *"WHAT HAVE YOU DONE? WHAT HAVE YOU DONE!"*

She jolted awake.

Her hand was in a world of pain. Groggily, she looked down at her index finger, where her bone had been snapped at a near ninety-degree angle to the right. Her fingernail throbbed excruciatingly. It had turned black.

"Bad dream?" the voice asked.

She breathed hard and tried her best to move. But she couldn't.

Every muscle in her neck seemed to ache.

The last thing she could remember was the blinding white light emitted from her phone and Scott Eckhart's name as the caller, before the screen went black. A voicemail and text message came through at the exact same time. The text message had read: Helmer is alive. I'm sending agents to you.

She remembered being in the car. Driving home from the airport. It was late and the roads were quiet. Then there were white headlights blinding her. She had squinted and looked to the side of the road. But then she was hit. And she lost control of the car.

She realized now that she was hit in the back bumper and that the lights had bounced off her rearview and side mirrors.

The car had flipped over the guardrail. The violent screech of metal scraping and sparking. Then everything became fuzzy. Her mind had recorded blurry memories . . . Being tied up. Dragged away to a vehicle. The trunk closing. Everything around her dark.

Rope had been cinched tight around each of her wrists and ankles. She was bound to a dusty old wooden chair. Her head bobbed like she was trying to tread whitecapped water. The floorboards beneath her were chalky, and the room had a musty odor that mixed with the smell of blood dripping from her nose.

"I can see why you picked this place." He stared out the windows at the snowcapped trees and the snowfall that blanketed the acres of surrounding land. "And why Joe Harlow would buy it. It's beautiful here. No one around to bother you. And if anyone came looking, you'd see them well before they saw you."

"Tell that to the FBI when they get here."

He smiled.

"No one's coming. You must know that, just like you know we're alike. Two men ruined your life. You killed them. I could have killed you in the train station. I could have killed you the night you left the hotel and pulled a gun on those men. But I didn't. I don't particularly enjoy killing."

"*Bullshit.* Am I supposed to thank you?"

He smiled again.

"Do you know why I didn't kill you? Because there's still time for you."

"Time for what?"

"For you to become like me. To see the world for what it is. The news portrays a tragedy every day—they profit off it like Rooker's new whore—and a different person, a different group, dies. Every. Single. Day. But no one cares anymore. Because it happens every day, and it didn't happen to *them.* It didn't happen in *their* backyard. But guess what: it happened to me. It happened in *my* backyard. And no one gave a damn. Not until she was identified as one of Gunner's victims. Some people are handed the shit end of the stick and expected to shovel it their entire life. I wasn't going to do that. That's what my life would've been had I not left *Johan* and *Mariam.* Some people—like them—don't deserve the physical shell they're living in. And how easy it would be to just"—he snapped his finger—"remove it."

"What's your plan now?" Tess asked. "The world will know Lucian Hurst and Matthias Helmer are one and the same. Your photo will be everywhere. You won't be able to hide anymore."

"I'm not finished yet. There's a difference between hiding and waiting. I've stood by . . . I've been patient. I've watched Rooker for many, many years. Without him ever knowing. I've walked past him on the street. I've watched him go mad—*deteriorate*—trying to find his son's killer. I've watched you. And do you know what I see?"

"What's that?"

"In you, I see a piece of art that is unfinished."

Chapter 71

It wasn't difficult to track her down. Rooker remembered the story of her father's cabin in the woods. There were no other cabins for a half mile.

If that weren't enough help, he spotted a tarp-covered vehicle outside the cabin tucked away by a few trees.

He dialed Scott Eckhart, who answered after only one ring.

"Eckhart, it's me. I need you to track my phone. I think I found them."

"Rooker, don't do anything—"

"Stupid? Yeah, I have to. It's a cabin that was in Joe Harlow's name. If you send in the cavalry, he'll see them coming and she's dead."

"I'm getting units mobilized as we speak, but I'm all ears."

"Snipers. The best you've got. Make sure they don't shoot me."

He ended the call.

He told himself that if he didn't move, she was dead. He'd been through too much with Tess to let her die. And he'd already lost too much of his life to Matthias Helmer.

Rooker stayed low and ran back to the car, where Caroline sat in the passenger seat. "I have to go," he said to her.

"No, you don't," she said angrily. "You found her. Let the FBI go in."

"The longer I wait, the less time she's got. He'll kill her, Caroline."

He patted Geralt and Red on their heads and kissed her on the lips. "Get in the driver's seat and wait here. If you hear gunshots, you drive. Get far away from here."

Rooker took out the pistol and ran off into the trees.

The cold tore through his shirt. His chest raced. Rooker made a beeline for the side of the house, hoping that Helmer would mostly be checking the back, or the front where the long tire-packed path stretched nearly one hundred yards to the front steps. He dashed low to the ground, snow climbing over the lips of his boots, the cold crawling down around his skin. The ground was uneven. His knee buckled where it dropped off, but he caught himself and kept going.

He told himself that Tess would do the same for him. He knew he was right.

The problem: Helmer wasn't like the others. He was a trained soldier, and more intelligent than Sadler and Caldwell. He'd manipulated Astrid Thompson's brother into helping him. Rooker's only chance at saving Tess and getting out alive was to kill Helmer immediately.

He stopped at the base of a tree and pressed his back to it, catching his breath. Listening to the sharp whistle of wind through the trees, ice-cold air stung his throat and invaded his lungs. The smell of winter and pine burned the hair in his nostrils. Looking back the way he came, he saw the heavy snowfall spit down, making his footprints disappear. In the distance a branch cracked, and the snow from it thudded near silently to the ground.

He turned around and pressed his face close to the tree, noticed his breath clouding and held it, then stayed still with just a few inches of his face exposed so an eye could catch sight of the cottage.

In the dark, aside from gray rock fireplace and the layer of white coating the roof, the cabin exterior seemed as though it'd been covered in oil. In the daytime it was probably charming, but at night it had the feel of a horror-flick destination where everyone went to die.

He saw the reflection of bare trees quivering on the surface of two tall windows that resembled eyes. There was a thin glare from the faint light of the snow. A set of steps, the first few hidden beneath snow, led up from ground level to an old wooden deck wrapped around all four sides of the cabin. A wooden bench and chairs were covered.

Rooker moved again, trying to stick to the shadows.

It was too dark from a distance to see inside the cabin. But he moved fast and unpredictably, low to the ground in case Helmer was able to see him. The smaller he made himself, the better he felt as a moving target. Though no part of him felt good.

Running face-first into the cold wind sucked the breath right out of him. He stopped once more at the base of a dead tree, breathed hard, blew warmth into the raw pink of his hands, and sprinted the last stretch to the bottom steps. He dove into the snow, hidden by the edge of the deck. He kicked his boots off, pushed off the ground, and crept up silently onto the deck. He made out a dim light inside and skulked out of view of any windows. Tiptoeing in socks through the wet slush, his feet submerged toward the front door. He hadn't entirely thought out a plan, but now as he closed in, he intended to swing the door wide open and go in guns blazing. But once he made his final step, the floorboard creaked beneath his weight.

Gunshots rang out. Rooker fell to the ground beside the door, unsure if he could return fire. He didn't know where Tess was and couldn't risk shooting her.

He clawed through the snow to the side of the cabin, shot three times at the window, knocked out the broken pieces of glass, and climbed inside.

The lights went out.

Glass crackled beneath him. Numb from the cold, he didn't feel the blood that leaked out from his right foot, merging with dripping water. He reached an arm out until it grazed the wall. He stayed there for a moment.

"Toss the gun, or she dies right now."

Rooker tried to calm himself down, but his brain, his heart, the pulse in his neck and his wrist—everything was thumping too fast.

"Toss it, Rooker."

His eyes started to adjust to the darkness. Ravaged sheet-covered furniture filled the room, layered with a smell of what could only be dust and time. "If I do, I'm dead. And so is she."

"How about this: if you toss it, I'll let her live. But *you*? You know that can't happen."

Rooker closed his eyes in desperation. "Why did you feed Reed Thompson to the FBI? He was more like you than anyone. Yet you threw him to the wolves."

"Are you jealous that he fucked Laura?"

"The man we found in the abandoned mall . . . that was your father, right?"

"He was no father to me."

"You made him kill himself, though."

"I didn't make him do anything. I simply gave him a way out."

"Like your grandmother?"

"You are clever, Rooker. I'll give you that."

Clever might not save him this time. He thought maybe he could get Helmer talking long enough for a sniper to take him out. But with it pitch-black inside the cabin, the only option would be for them to use night sights, and then there would be no way to positively identify the target. "Was your grandfather the first person you killed?"

"You know what that old man said to me? He said I was delivered by death himself. That the damn grim reaper has a hold on me. Funny—I've never been afraid to die. Never been afraid of pain. Maybe he was right. But killing him didn't feel good or bad. There was no right or wrong."

Rooker shifted the slightest bit to his right, then left. Staring down his sights into the small gap.

"Last chance. Toss the gun. Or she dies."

He winced. "Fine. But you need to tell me. Who killed my son? You? Or Meachum?"

"Just to be clear, who dies is irrelevant. A child wouldn't be an issue . . . but Tate was obsessed. After your little article about me, he would've done anything I said. So I told him exactly what to do. To my surprise, he did well."

Rooker's jaw clenched. Boxing was like a chess match, a series of thought-out moves and countermoves. But in a situation like this . . . it was strike first or die first. He just needed to avoid hitting Tess in the cross fire. He swung the pistol around the corner.

What felt like an ice-cold flame burst through his left rib cage and he squeezed the trigger. The excruciating pain flared when the knife pulled an inch outward, and the man in front of him barely flinched from the bullet that ripped through his upper chest.

In the next second, he'd forgotten where he was and snapped out of it, just in time to pull his head back fast, but Helmer's elbow caught the end of his jaw. The pistol rattled to the floor and slipped into the shadows.

Rooker fought the urge to curl forward and stood rigidly. Warm blood trickled from the hole in his side. He flicked out a measuring jab, which bounced off the edge of Helmer's skull just as a heavy kick thrust into Rooker's leg. He staggered back.

Helmer charged in low and Rooker caught him with a straight right, his legs buckling only for a moment before all his weight slammed Rooker into the wall. Rooker felt it give way as though he'd sunken into an old chair. A hard knee exploded into his midsection. Rooker coughed and threw Helmer off. He hobbled away and circled toward the center of the room. The gun was somewhere in the pitch-black by the corner of the wall.

He couldn't see it.

Rooker threw a quick one-two; Helmer took it well and connected a sharp fist just below the knife wound.

Black circles of pain flashed behind his eyes.

He couldn't fight Helmer off. He was slammed to the ground. Punches coming at him from left and right. Until Rooker wrapped his legs in a triangle around Helmer's neck and squeezed with everything he had. But he was lifted off the ground and slammed back down with such tremendous force that his head snapped forward. His back seized up and he lost his breath. He coughed again and could taste his own blood.

Helmer spat blood to the wood floor. Panting, he looked at Tess. "You get to watch him die."

Move, he told himself. *Come on. Move.*

He couldn't. His body was giving out. He didn't have the strength left in him. But when Helmer stalked toward him, his brain and muscles reconnected, and Rooker drove his foot as hard as he could into Helmer's shin.

It didn't do much. He crawled away as fast as he could. Pulling himself with his fingertips. And just as his hand closed, he felt the sharp pain of the boot stomp down on his calf. He was dragged back into what little light seemed to seep up through the floorboards.

So much for Eckhart's snipers.

Rooker turned over and squeezed the trigger three times. Helmer's eye, throat, and chest exploded. The body thudded to the ground.

He couldn't move. He didn't fight to move either. The pistol fell from his hand. He could hear Tess muttering. But he couldn't go to her. The last thought he had was of his son, Britton, of finally getting to see him after so much time, of maybe getting to see Evelyn and Millie and a chance to tell them he was sorry, before a tear ticked cold down his cheek and a warm, painless current washed him away.

Chapter 72

February 2, 2022

The small procession of hazard-lit cars moved rockily over the uneven ground. On either side of the wet concrete path, snow seemed to have grown out of the ground and over the headstones. Between them, a bumpy blanket of white covered the earth floor as far as she could see.

Tess Harlow dumped three Tylenol into her good hand and took them with the water that had partially thawed out from the heat whirring on the farthest red notch.

It would be another three weeks before the black splint would come off and she would start rehabilitation. A few weeks after that she could fire a gun.

Beneath the cold gray sky, the snowfall had stopped for now, and the shivering trees looked black beneath the fresh powder.

She got out and stood with her back against a tree, watching the small cluster of people gather around the casket. Many of them trembled beneath black clothes, including Eddie Arroyave and his family, and Rooker's ex-wife, Laura.

Her head hung down, but Tess thought she saw it shaking, and tears falling to the snow beneath her.

Footfalls crunched in the hard snow beside her that'd frozen beneath the tree. She didn't need to look over to know who it was. "I'm sorry for your loss," he said. For a moment she closed her eyes and pictured Rooker standing there. But when she opened them and saw the casket being lowered into the frozen ground, she turned her head and saw Scott Eckhart. "I'll have an office waiting for you with your name on it. Whenever you're ready."

She nodded.

Just as he'd turned, she stopped him. "Can you send this for me?"

Eckhart looked down at the postcard that read:

MINNESOTA
LAND OF 10,000 LAKES

He smiled and walked away and stood beside Deion Quincy, Jack Hall, and Isabel Esparza.

Tess's boots squelched in the wet snow back toward the car. She opened the door, sank into the driver's seat, and let out a cold breath. Rubbing her hands together, she breathed into them and stared at Laura in the rearview mirror. She was dabbing her cheek, which had darkened with running mascara. She sighed. She keyed the ignition and the engine rumbled low. A moment later there was a tap on the glass.

She turned to find Laura standing there in a black dress and wool jacket with her arms wrapped around herself.

Tess rolled the window down.

"Detective Harlow." Laura wiped her pinkened nose with her hand. "I just wanted to say thank you. For all you did for him."

Tess smiled weakly. "I'm very sorry, Laura. He saved my life . . ."

"It's not your fault. He was the most stubborn person I've ever met . . . he was always going to go down swinging." Laura tried to force a smile then and began to walk away.

"Laura," Tess called out. "He talked about you guys all the time. He loved you and Britton more than anything. He was sorry he left."

Laura cried and nodded. Then she was gone.

A teardrop ticked down her face and she wiped it, then rolled the window back up.

On the passenger seat sat a crisply folded blue jacket that she hadn't put on yet. She stared at the three metallic-yellow letters.

And then her phone rang. But not the one in her pocket. She pulled open the glove box and answered. "Manor Investigations."

Epilogue

Gothenburg, Västra Götaland County, Sweden

The six-room fourth-floor apartment at Johannebergsgatan 28 stretched twenty-five hundred square feet—the entire floor—and was listed to Linnea Bundsen. Her documentation—a Swedish passport and driver's license—said the same.

The roads were filled with compact vehicles and scooters, and bicyclists were riding along the cleared walkways or on the street. People were bundled in layers of clothing—insulated jackets, parkas, scarves, and mittens—reminding her how dumb she'd been now that her hands were raw and tingling. She'd passed clothing stores, restaurants, a new tattoo shop and an old barbershop, and a group of students smoking cigarettes and vapes outside the University of Gothenburg grounds.

Feskekôrka—translated to "fish church"—was only a little over a mile from the apartment, and despite the ice-cold air that stole her breath away, at a light jog she made it in fifteen minutes.

The beautiful tan brick, cathedral windows, and pristine white roof resembled a Gothic church, making it one of the most iconic buildings in all of Gothenburg. Sitting on the glimmering water and lit up at night, it might've been one of the prettiest buildings she'd ever seen. But today a layer of ice and snow covered it, along with the seats outside a restaurant where a chalkboard sat with specials that were in Swedish.

Inside the fish market hall, people milled around the entire length of the building, lined with vendors and flake ice and every kind of fish tucked away behind glass partitions. She blew into her hands, pointed out two salmon filets, had them wrapped in butcher paper, paid, and left.

With the hood of her dark jacket pulled up over her black hair, she sauntered against the wind back to the apartment with the bag of fish.

There was a peaceful buzz around the central street.

The lot was full of snow-covered cars. She followed the shoveled path and unlocked the door to her building and stepped inside, where rounded archways and marble stairs led to rustic doorways, a gold bank of mailboxes, and the upper levels. Systematically she'd checked the mail. There never was any. But this time, her eyes went wide at the sight of something. She plucked the white envelope addressed to Linnea Bundsen and tore it open. She pulled out a postcard, turned it over, closed the mailbox, and went up the stairs.

At the apartment door, she jammed the key into the lock, twisted, and pushed hard. The door creaked. A shudder crawled up her spine the moment she stepped inside. It was freezing cold. The large french doors that overlooked the courtyard were open. "Hello?"

She unzipped her jacket and removed her shoes. The herringbone wood floors had a chill that climbed up through her thin wool socks. She called out again when there was no answer, then stepped out onto the balcony. Down below there were three different-size footprints shaped in the snow—likely a mother, father, and small child—and the wind whistled past her into one of the two living rooms. The fluffy white cat chirped from the wooden chair and came inside when she turned around and shut the double doors.

The other two balconies in the apartment looked out over a park called Näckrosdammen.

FOX News and her beloved segment *Late Night News with Caroline Lind* were long gone. She'd come a long way since studying communications and broadcast journalism at the University of Pennsylvania, years of all-nighters cramming for public relations and political science courses. It had taken what seemed an eternity to get a seat in the limelight, to be doted on in hair and makeup, to have a team of sound technicians and writers and producers at her beck and call. She had loved every second of it. But she hadn't resigned or been fired.

The night Rooker left her in that car with the animals was the last time she'd existed as Caroline Lind. FBI Special Agent Scott Eckhart and the Bureau had helped her vanish and become Linnea Bundsen. It had been her idea to run away and their idea to give her the WITSEC treatment. Because there was no shortage of people who wanted Rooker dead, and who knew who might come after her even after he was deceased.

She hadn't yet lived a day when she wanted to go back.

A report that Matthias Helmer abducted Caroline Lind spread like wildfire, and her disappearance and likely death had initiated a media circus. Every major broadcast network, especially FOX News, played snippets of her on the air and showed her headshot. After time went by and they hadn't found her, some of the anchors she'd known started to say they never would.

The next room was lit by the cold gray light coming in through the tall, frost-bordered windows and a small inferno that flickered in the fireplace. She sauntered behind Geralt's wagging tail and stopped in the doorway, watching the man half beneath a blanket with his face buried in a copy of *Fair Warning*.

She shivered, fought the chatter of her teeth, and made it a point to blow out a cloud of her own breath. "It's freezing in here. Why is the balcony door open?"

He set the book aside and reached over to prod at the fire with an ash-tipped poker. He cleared his throat. "Geralt likes to watch the birds."

She smiled. "You mean *stalk* them. One day he's going to fall off the railing . . . or jump."

"He has nine lives."

"Sounds familiar," she mocked. "You've got mail."

Beside him, Red's head perked up and plopped back down.

His rib cage was still covered in white bandages; once healed, it would be another scar she would trace with her fingertips. He set the open book down on his chest, and she kissed his cheek while handing him the postcard.

"Eckhart?" she asked.

He flipped it over.

If you get tired of being dead, I could use a partner.

M.I.

He smiled. *Manor Investigations.* "Harlow."

"She knows?"

She's the best detective I know, he thought. *Of course she knows.* "Tess won't tell anyone."

"So, what now? How long are we staying?"

He sighed. "For as long as you want. No one's coming here to find a dead man."

ACKNOWLEDGMENTS

I would like to thank my incredible agent, Victoria Skurnick, and my tireless editors at Thomas & Mercer, Jessica Tribble Wells and Carissa Bluestone.

Also, thank you to Tom Giustino once again, PhD in neuroscience and semipro sportswriter, for making sure the science inside these pages, and Rooker's mind, is within the realm of possibility.

Thank you to the readers. Words cannot begin to express how incredible it has been to witness the support of these three books and their characters. It truly means the world.

Lastly, I think every author has that book that made them want to read, and that book that made them want to write. Thank you to John Grisham for *The Client*, because before I read that novel, I used SparkNotes for nearly every assigned book until the start of high school.

And thank you to Michael Connelly, whose works have continuously popped up in my novels. If I hadn't been so blown away by *The Poet*, I may have never gone down this crazy path of writing my own story.

To Rooker: thank you for everything.

ABOUT THE AUTHOR

Photo © 2021 Steven Woodfield

Pete Zacharias is the author of the Rooker Lindström Thriller series, which includes *The Man Feared by Darkness*, *The Man Trapped by Shadows*, and *The Man Burned by Winter*. He received a BA in English with a concentration in creative writing. A lover of Nordic noir, dark thrillers, and anything spy, Pete credits Michael Connelly's *The Poet* as the novel that inspired him to become a writer.